RISKY PURSUIT

NANCY G. WEST

"With a multi-generational cast and suspenseful story, RISKY PURSUIT follows Decker Savage into a web of deceit that threatens to derail his life unless he can untangle the heart-stopping events hurtling toward him. This uplifting read shows that courage is achievable, and redemption is possible, no matter one's age."

— LINDA LOVELY, AUTHOR OF THE HOA
MYSTERIES AND RWA GOLDEN HEART AND
SILVER FALCHION AWARDS FINALIST

"Decker Savage sees a scruffy man sitting in a diner with his about-to-be-divorced mother. When the man leaves abruptly, upsetting her, Decker is compelled to follow. His trail leads to a dark house where he overhears an argument and the assault of an elderly man. Compelled to identify the assailant, he is led through a labyrinth of danger that threatens his life and those he loves. In this sensitive and engaging account of Decker's dilemma, we are allowed inside Decker's mind and heart. The tension mounts as he pursues course, courageously defying known danger in his quest to help the victim and ensnaring the reader in concern for a safe outcome. This satisfying story, given the beguiling personality of the main protagonist, could well be the forerunner of a series."

— DIANA HOCKLEY, AUTHOR OF THE SUSAN
PRESCOTT SERIES, REVIEWER FOR KINGS
RIVER LIFE

"Decker Savage's life is in shambles. An accident has taken his younger brother, his parents are splitting up, and his performance on the baseball field is suffering. After overhearing an assault on an elderly gentleman, Decker develops a friendship with the victim, a fellow lover of baseball, and is compelled to pursue his attacker. This compelling, complex, and endearing story of unlikely cross-generational friendship has surprises at every turn as Decker delves deeper into the mysterious attack. The teen detective never imagines how personal his quest will become."

— KATHY SCHLOSBERG, DOCTOR OF
EDUCATION, UCLA

"In this captivating thriller, Decker Savage, in his last high school semester, watches his parents' marriage disintegrate. He accidentally sees his mother with a stranger at a bar and is concerned for her safety. When the man leaves abruptly, Decker is compelled to follow. His investigation leads to fast-paced adventure, rising tension, and hidden truths—a touching story and spellbinding mystery."

— KATHLEEN DANYSH, ARTIST (HUNT
GALLERY) AND TEACHER

ISBN: 979-8-88653-380-4

Fire & Ice Young Adult Books
An Imprint of Melange Books, LLC
White Bear Lake, MN 55110
www.fireandiceya.com

Published in the United States of America.

Cover Design by Caroline Andrus

To my amazing, talented, loving family,
Don, Janie and Alan, Nathan and Kelly
Mason and Mailane, and Connor
Ryan and Joanna, Lily, and Jenna
Carol, Drew and Katie, Jessica
Erin and Scottie and Lucy
Bill, William and Laurie
Marguerite and Michael
John, Wilson and Jenna, Laura and Ken
Elizabeth, Beverly and Bill, Patty
Bobby, Lisa, and Evan
Bryce and Madison, Rhae Chell

And to my friends,
my faithful monthly lunch bunch,
my industrious reading group,
my bridge buddy angels.

YOU BRING JOY TO MY LIFE

CHAPTER ONE

DECKER SAVAGE ENTERED THE DIMLY-LIT BROADWAY CAFÉ AND made his way to the back. His family was disintegrating. Maybe he was disintegrating, too.

He settled in a worn booth, unable to tell where the depressive gray bubble around him ended and the dreary diner began. Christmas lights hung from the muddy-orange ceiling even though it was mid-January. His last high-school semester had begun. A 1950s Schwinn bicycle hung among the lights, adding rusty chrome to the dinge. Nice touch.

A waiter sauntered up. "Get you something?"

Breathe life into my baby brother? Make Dad move back home? Ease Mom's stress?

"A coke, I guess. Thanks." Decker pointed at the ceiling. "Celebrating?"

"Manager left them up for the 2012 Super Bowl on February 5th."

Just before his nineteenth birthday. Whoopee. Frigid wind whistled outside through leftover holiday decorations. They'd probably stay up through February, too.

Lyrics from Katy Perry's "Fireworks" blasted through

1

corner speakers, "...like a plastic bag drifting through the wind..." He was inside that bag, drifting, with no energy to punch his way out. "...one blow from caving in..."

Empty tables squatted around, but anonymous men drank in somber booths planted at the side of the room under dim bulbs strung from the ceiling. A couple guys from school slouched in one booth. He had no desire to socialize and didn't know them anyway. With their hoodies up, cell phones highlighting their shrouded faces, they looked like thirteenth-century monks.

Nobody came here but kids and losers. He wasn't sure why he came.

The front door creaked open periodically, the weak inside light inside barely enough to reorient patrons who came in from the suburban business corridor and melted into the dark, seeking relief from whatever plagued them in the light of day.

A man in the front booth nearest the door crouched in the corner of his booth, stringy hair lapping over his collar, his small-brimmed hat pulled low. Was his hat what they called a Fedora?

A couple empty beer bottles stood on the table. Each time the door opened, he cringed lower, pulled the hat over one eye, and stared warily at the door. Who was he afraid of?

The drug lord he owed money? A cop?

A woman entered, her shadow backlit from outside. The man in the booth straightened. Decker squinted. Who was she? When a sliver of light crossed her face, his breath caught. It was his mother.

Chest tight, Decker slid lower to hide and followed her with his gaze as she made her way to the stranger's booth. He told her he had baseball practice, then would go home to study for tomorrow's English test. The last part was true.

Wide-eyed, he watched her lower herself into the seat

across from the guy who didn't bother to get up. When her mouth curved into a hesitant smile, Decker's jaw dropped. *Why would she meet this disheveled man?*

The waiter came by. His mother shook her head, refusing drinks. She must not intend to stay long. The server swept up the empties and acknowledged the man's nod for another beer.

The man curved toward his mom and began talking intently, his bulk blocking her face from Decker's view. With Adele belting out "Someone Like You," he couldn't hear a word they said. Heads down, they concentrated on each other. He couldn't stretch to catch more of her expression, or she'd notice him.

He thought she smiled once. She hadn't done that in a long time. Why was she meeting a strange man in this murky place? Did he have something to do with their crumbling family? He sat frozen, unable to decide what to do.

He should go up to them and ask the man who he was. Storm up like he was her silly-ass protector and ask the guy point blank who he was and what he was doing with his mother. Ask Mom why she wasn't home. Right. He lied to her. Now he'd embarrass her. He hated confrontation. He always had. He despised his habit of hanging back.

Dad got pissed off when he didn't act. This guy might rear up and clock him. He'd never been good at hand-to-hand combat. They'd probably get thrown out of the diner. That would make the Prospect Heights News.

Decker breathed fast, jaw tense from confusion and anger. He knew he was a factor in his parents' probable divorce. If this character was involved, it would be worse. Could his mother be so fickle? So disloyal to his father to take up with this lowlife? His stomach knotted.

He compared the man's head and shoulders to Dad's. The guy was solid, but not that great a specimen. He squinted daggers at the back of his stupid hat. *She's not your girlfriend, creepo. She's Dad's wife.*

What could she possibly have in common with this man? Maybe she thought Dad was having an affair. This guy was some PI she hired to track Dad, and they were strategizing. His head started to ache. The scumbag shifted his weight in the booth like he was about to stand. Decker tensed. *Was the snake about to leave?*

Before Decker could make a move, two girls bounced into the diner laughing—buddies of Ashley, the girl he liked. *What were they doing here?* This wasn't a place to "see and be seen." They'd recognize him and tell her he was here. It'd be hard to explain why he was sitting alone in this dingy diner spying on his mother.

He had to get out of the booth before anybody recognized him. He slouched farther down, raised his arm to cover his face, and squirmed toward the edge of the seat. From the corner of his eye, he saw the stranger with his mom spring up and shoulder his way toward the front door. He caught surprise on Mom's face. Looking perplexed, she slammed back against the cushion. Her lips thinned and quivered. Then her eyes filled, and she banged her fist on the table. She slipped from the booth, stood straight, took a deep breath, and followed the man outside.

Decker slid his feet outside the booth. As soon as his body cleared the table, he doubled over and headed for the back of the diner.

The waiter hollered at him. "You all right?"

Thank God he didn't know Decker's name. He pointed to his stomach and gestured with a circular hand motion.

"Oh, yeah," the man said. "Nothing worse. Bathroom is back there. Hope you make it."

Decker crossed the room stretching across the back of the diner past the U-shaped booth and plastic-covered table.

Covers of albums he used to like shone through laminate. He swiveled between the booth and nearby pool table and headed for the bathroom, trying not to draw attention.

He spotted a third door on the back wall near the restrooms. If it was an exit and he squeezed through, he could ease around the side of the building and catch the man before he took off in his car. *What if his mom caught up to the guy? What if he grabbed her?*

The thought roiled his stomach. It wouldn't take much for him to throw up. He slipped into the bathroom, made a retching sound, and struggled to quell his nausea. He flushed the toilet and ran water, the force clanging rusty pipes. He made enough racket but waited a few seconds before opening the door in case one of the girls decided to use the adjacent bathroom.

Hearing no footsteps, he cracked the door. Ashley's friends were perched in a booth toward the front of the diner, engrossed in conversation. He slipped out and inched toward the back door hoping it was an exit, leaned against it, and squeezed through.

Moist frigid air attacked his lungs. He pulled up his hoodie and shivered. The temp must have plummeted. The man had trekked around the side of the diner and was plodding steadily uphill. He saw no sign of his mother. If he raced across the vacant lot behind the diner toward the dense wall of trees marking the property line, moonlight shining off the diner roof would highlight him.

He slipped off the back steps, crouched to the right and held his breath, hoping the overhang hid him in darkness. He picked a moment he thought was safe, sprinted across the lot, and hid in a thicket of bushes near the street. Heart pounding, Decker eyeballed the man tromping up the steep hill in freezing weather. He had to follow.

CHAPTER TWO

BETWEEN THE CHURCH ON THE LEFT AND HOUSES ON THE RIGHT, the man leaned up the hill with purposeful strides. Nobody walked in San Antonio's unpredictable winters if they didn't have to. Texans drove everywhere. Didn't the creep drive a car? *Why was he trying to escape on foot?*

Did he ask her to meet? Surely she didn't ask him. He said something to upset her before he stormed out. Was this creep going to meet her somewhere else? Decker doubted he was one of Mom's interior design clients. He didn't bother to fix himself up.

On the left, St. Peter's Prince of the Apostles Catholic Church nestled in soft security lighting. Homes on the right side of the street sat far back from Barilla with steps leading up to elevated front lawns. Prospect Heights was an incorporated upscale suburb with a sought-after school district, a place where crimes were unusual. Tall hedges protected home occupants from curious intruders and noise from Broadway.

As the hill leveled out, cold air hit his lungs. He took shorter breaths and rubbed his hands together. Moonlight outlined the man's body, but with the hat pulled low over his brow, Decker couldn't see his face. Hidden in darkness from hedges, the creep glanced back periodically, eyes glittering like a coyote. He wished he could see those eyes.

Fingering the phone in his pocket, he thought about snapping a picture of the man.

The farther his prey went up the hill, the fewer lights shone from houses. Except for the sliver of suspended moon, the night was black.

Crisp January air revived his eagerness for the trek as his body acclimated to the uphill climb. Wind slapped his face. It might drop below freezing.

Where did she meet this guy? Why did he blast out of the diner? Mom might have said something that freaked him out. If she made him angry, why not stay and have it out with her instead of springing up and charging out?

Was he walking because he feared somebody would recognize his car?

Car lights rounded the corner by the diner and shone up the hill. Decker sensed light on his back. A police car. He ducked behind bushes. He could flag the cop and have him follow the guy, but he might never learn who the scoundrel was or his relationship to his family.

Spooked by the cruiser's lights, the man scurried by the back corner of a house and disappeared. For an old guy, he was amazingly quick.

Decker crouched in bushes and watched the cruiser's taillights get smaller. He leaped to a closer bush and focused on the house where the culprit disappeared. A driveway to the side led to a guest house at the back of the lot.

The patrol car's lights blinked right onto another street, the patrolman making a leisurely reconnaissance of the neighborhood.

Decker stayed still, intent on the corner where the man

vanished. Maybe he was tailing a burglar. When the cop was out of sight, he would break into a house. *Was Mom unknowingly involved with a criminal?*

The patrol car meandered, lights flicking as it swung left onto a cross street. Decker's eyes flipped back to the house. The scoundrel broke from the shadows and charged up the hill.

Crouching behind cover, Decker raced to the corner of the house where he thought the man had been. He cased the area, seeing nothing but shadows.

He looked up the street. Had he lost him? He spotted movement and burst to the next patch of bushes, grabbed his phone, and lifted it toward his face. The man broke from the dark side of a house. When the light from a window caught him, Decker clicked the camera just before he disappeared.

Decker sprang to the next clump of bushes activating motion lights outside the adjacent house. He ducked behind shrubs until they blinked off. The rogue moved fast. If Decker didn't pick up speed, he'd lose him. He stepped on to the street and scurried through shadows until a spotlight blazed his face.

He shielded his eyes as the patrol car rolled alongside. His pursuit was over. The officer leaned out.

"Is that you, Decker? Is everything okay?"

He blinked dark spots from his eyes. "Hey, Sergeant Thorn. I was just out walking...loosening stiff muscles to get ready for baseball season. Getting rid of the jitters, you know? I'm not ready to hit the books yet."

"Is your mom okay?" He had visited them a few times, telling interesting stories about law enforcement.

"She's fine. Had a late meeting with a client, but she's on her way home." He hoped he was right. If he told Thorn the truth, he'd contact her. She would realize Decker saw her in the diner, and he might never learn the identity of the stranger.

"Okay, Decker. I hear you guys have a good varsity team this year. I plan to make some of the games."

"That would be great, Sergeant Thorn." His heart pounded in his ears. He hoped his face didn't break out in a sweat.

Thorn appraised him. "You and your mom call if you have any problems."

"Will do. Thank you, sir."

Thorn rolled away, glanced in the rearview mirror, and waved. He waved back and watched Thorn round a corner. When the policeman was out of view, he dug into his pocket for the phone. It wasn't there.

Licking his lips, he started searching. Damn. The phone was so new he hadn't even put a pass code on it. When his last one slid from his pocket in the garage, he crushed it with his Mustang. This might be the last phone he'd ever have. How could he be so stupid? Besides dropping the iPhone, he lost the sneak he was following.

If the guy was doing something illegal and Decker caught him, then what? If he had the phone, he could call the cops. But they'd press him about why he was plodding around in the dark.

He kept searching. He traced his steps, inspecting every shrub and clump of grass, hoping he didn't trigger somebody's security lights. He couldn't find it. Its guts might freeze overnight. He'd have to search tomorrow.

He turned back toward Barilla and the strip center. From the corner of his eye, he saw house lights flick on. He swirled, glimpsed his target, and squatted behind a shrub. When he was sure the man wouldn't see him, he started moving.

At North New Braunfels, the man turned right. Decker made it to the corner, ducked behind a parked car, and watched. His target walked a block south creeping through shrubs and tree shadows, then dashed across the street and turned left up Elizabeth Road. Decker followed.

From Elizabeth, his target veered right on Cross Lane, then left onto Terrell. In the dark, Decker could barely read street signs, but he knew they weren't that far from his own house on Tuttle Road.

Was the sneak headed there?

Decker hung back and watched the man plod up Terrell. Crouching behind bushes on the right side of the street, he made out a series of two-story brick homes on the other side, widely spaced to insure privacy. *Which one was the burglar's target?*

The houses sat in darkness except for one where a dim light emanated from an upstairs room. He couldn't believe what happened next.

The man strolled nonchalantly up to the dark porch at 303 Terrell and rang the bell. Except for the dim upstairs light, the house was pitch dark. Decker held his breath. No lights clicked on.

The man rang again. Nothing. If he knew the residents, why visit so late? Maybe he called ahead, and the occupants didn't want to see him. Thieves rang doorbells. If they got no response, they knew it was safe to break in.

As he watched, the man stood silently on the shadowed porch, contemplating his next move. Decker slowed his breathing.

His prey slipped around the side of the house and vanished. He caught his breath. He had come this far. He couldn't stop now.

He bolted closer to the house. Moonlight shone on the far side of the house, but his side was dark. Staying close to the brick, shrouded by the roof overhang, he crept through darkness until his eyes focused on a side door where the culprit must have entered. *Did he pick a lock? Have a key?*

Decker sprinted back to a bush and hid thirty feet from the door, breathing fast, his hands sweating. If he followed the man inside, it was criminal trespass. Expulsion from school. The end to his chance for a baseball scholarship. More turmoil in his fractured home.

If he didn't follow the man inside, he'd never learn who the guy was or why he'd been with his mother. His eyes adjusting to moonlight, he realized the door was slightly ajar. His chest heaved.

Could he get his feet to move?

CHAPTER THREE

CONCEALED IN DARKNESS, HE CREPT CLOSER TO THE CRACKED-open door. When a dog barked from a nearby yard, he cringed. Two houses over, lights came on. He inched toward the door and slipped inside. He heard commotion coming from upstairs. Loud voices. Men arguing. One man sounded older. Was the man he followed attacking another man?

They started shouting. His pulse raced. As his eyes acclimated to darkness, Decker realized he was in a kitchen with no place to hide. He sneaked deeper into the house. The snake who upset his mother might be waiting to attack him.

He edged through the dining room into the living room and ducked behind a sofa, hoping he was alone. The room smelled musty. Dust particles floating through the air tickled his nose. He pressed his index finger under his nostrils. He didn't dare sneeze.

Across the front of the house, window shades were pulled down with cracks of moonlight underneath that slivered toward the stairway. His heart pounded. He tried to coax it into a normal rhythm, calm his breathing, and listen.

The cavernous house was deathly silent. Air from a vent stirred a window shade allowing a strip of light to creep up across the bottom stairs. He pinched his nose. Steps farther up were shrouded in darkness. No sound came from upstairs.

Having adjusted to the dim light, he scanned the room. Another sofa and two plushy chairs in drab colors filled the space. He never paid much attention to other people's houses. Most furniture looked like it was either collected at random or arranged for a photo shoot. This room, orderly but lifeless, reminded him of a vintage theater set waiting for somebody to enter stage left and snap it to life. The room smelled like the diner, but with a sweet-smelling overlay, a scented spray or perfume.

He caught the sound of voices upstairs, men talking in low tones. He strained, listening. Did they know each other? Why did the intruder sneak into this house? He began to feel foolish crouched behind the sofa. What if they came down and caught him? The man upstairs, who sounded older, apparently descended steps. Was the younger man reporting to him? Their voices rose. Was the homeowner chewing him out for leaving the diner? Were they both involved with his mother?

Next to the sofa, a photo rested on a dusty table—parents with four children. As he reached to grab it, the voices grew louder. When the older man cried out, Decker's hand jerked and knocked over the frame. A heavy thump on the floor upstairs stopped his heart. He couldn't move. What happened? Did they hear him? He heard only silence.

Hand trembling, he righted the photograph. He heard a moan upstairs, and his heart leaped. The scoundrel could have hurt the other man. Killed him.

How many people were up there?

Could he help? Could he sneak up behind the louse and

attack him? Dad would expect him to rush upstairs and jump the guy. He could go to jail for battery, if the sonofabitch didn't kill him first.

Why would his mother know these people?

Her being implicated in a crime was beyond belief. She would expect him to use his head and call for help, but he lost the damn phone.

Should he stay and try to catch the perp or run for help?

Indecision paralyzed him. He heard the squeal of a siren. The wailing screech grew louder until lights flashed across the front of the house. Maybe cops were after this guy. He crawled to a chair by the window and peered behind the shade. The vehicle had doused the lights and gone black. He heard noise on the stairs and scrambled back behind the sofa.

A car door opened and shut. He heard men's voices. They stomped up to the front porch and pounded on the door. EMTs? Or was that wishful thinking?

A footstep thudded on the top stair. Decker cringed behind the sofa on his stomach, his heart pounding into the carpet. He peeked around the footing. The man crept down the steps, paused before the moonlit step, and looked toward the living room, hat pulled low over his brow. When his eyes stopped at the sofa, Decker stopped breathing.

Voices outside grew louder. Fists pounded. The culprit leaped to the floor and sprang for the kitchen. Decker craned to see the scoundrel moving at a fast clip.

He didn't know who was about to burst through the door, but whoever it was would help the victim. He needed to get out of the house. He sprang across the room, through the dining room, kitchen, pushed open the door and sprinted for the bushes.

Lights popped on at the adjacent house. Behind the

nearest fence, a dog barked. Somebody would call the police. He raced to a clump of bushes and crouched under his hoodie, panting frigid air. He had to get out of the area.

Eyes adapting to the night sky, he scanned for movement and checked the street. No cars. His quarry was gone. He'd lost him. Or he was out there in the dark, watching.

CHAPTER FOUR

D<small>ECKER HUNCHED IN THE BUSHES, EXHALING IN SHORT PUFFS.</small> A dog growled. House lights clicked on. He tried to slow his breathing and consider his next move. When he skirted across a back yard, a security light blared on.

"Hey! Who's out there?" a man shouted.

Decker glued himself to the back fence, hiding in shadow, eyes searching for an opening to the alley. He spotted a gate and slipped through. An eternity passed before he heard a door close and thought the man went back inside. The security light finally went dark.

In the safety of the alley, he squatted to catch his breath. He'd have to weave a circuitous route through alleys and side streets to get back to the Stewart Center. He might as well drive home and try to forget the whole crazy ordeal. He'd search for his phone later.

He could make up some story and go to the cops, say he was driving near the diner when a man burst from the front door and raced up the hill. He heard a siren, so he followed the sound in his car and parked in shadow until an ambulance rolled up in front of a house. When he spotted a man race out the back of the house, he drove to the police station to report what he witnessed. That's what he should have done.

If he remembered all that and kept his story straight, he could at least clear himself.

He walked, staying in shadows. One by one, random house security lights clicked off, and the neighborhood grew quiet. Having dodged the immediate threat, he slipped between two dark houses and wove his way back to Terrell Road where he crouched in thick bushes near the curb.

All remained quiet. Wiping sweat from his brow with his sleeve, he scanned for police cars. Seeing none, he pushed back his hood and coaxed his hair into place with his fingers.

He was drawn to that house. His only way to expose the scoundrel was to learn the identity of the victim.

He took a deep breath and stepped casually onto Terrell. Three blocks down, he saw an ambulance parked in front of the house. He maintained a moderate pace to appear self-assured. He was getting pretty good at making his heart resume regular beats. A driver sat alone inside the vehicle. Other EMTs were apparently inside the house.

He waved amiably to the driver and strolled up to the cab. He considered telling the EMTs everything that happened but quashed the notion. They would call the police, and he left evidence inside. Everybody left DNA wherever they went. If he revealed what happened, he'd have to explain why he followed the man, why he went inside, and why he didn't try to prevent the attack.

The man he followed committed a crime and was somehow involved with his mother, but the EMTs didn't know that. The ambulance driver let down his window.

"I think an old man lives here," Decker said. "I live close by...used to walk some neighborhood dogs when I was a kid."

His route had included the street, but this house was being remodeled when he was walking dogs.

"Cunningham Construction" was painted on several trucks. He passed subcontractors carrying materials in and out and wondered who would live there.

"I heard the siren. What happened?"

"We got a call from Medical Alert. The man inside had one of those gadgets people wear around their necks. We found it on the floor."

"You came right away?"

He nodded. "We were in the vicinity." The driver turned off the device he used to communicate with colleagues inside the house.

"Was anybody else there?" Decker had to know what they knew. With his DNA in the house, he could be fingered as the attacker.

"They don't think so. My team will bring the patient out pretty soon."

Would they notify the police? He didn't dare ask. If they did, he hoped they would say they met some curious neighborhood kid or not mention him at all.

"Maybe I can talk to him," Decker said. "Where will you take him?"

The man paused, considering whether to reveal information. "Medical Center."

Decker thanked him and turned toward the house. The mailbox was on a post three feet back from the curb. "I can check his mail, see if it's somebody we know."

"Sure," the driver said.

Decker opened the box marked 303 Terrell. Correspondence was addressed to Mitchell J. Conahan. He memorized the name and address in case EMTs decided they should take the mail, and he closed the box. "Nope. Don't know him."

The front door of the house banged open, and two EMTs

came out rolling a stretcher. The man lying on it had hair as white as the sheets covering him. His skin looked gray. One EMT paused while the other went back to lock the door.

The victim reminded Decker of Mom's dad, Granddad Hank, who died last year. He missed his gentleness and wisdom, the way Granddad listened with perfect attention when someone talked, like whatever they said was the most interesting thing in the world. If Decker was worried about something, he went to Granddad's house. He sat and listened without comment until Decker was ready to disclose what was on his mind. Somehow, Granddad Hank knew the right time to ask questions and the best way to help.

The old man was out cold with an oxygen mask over his face. What kind of animal would attack this man? Decker blinked away tears welling up.

The EMT tech held a plastic pouch alongside the stretcher dripping something into the old fellow's arm. Decker cleared his throat and walked closer. "Mr. Conahan, can you hear me?"

"He's unconscious, son," the EMT said. "Are you a relative?"

"No. I used to walk dogs by his house. I heard the ambulance and came over. What happened to him?"

"Looks like he fell. Probably hit his head on the way down."

Or somebody hit him. Or he was pushed. A bloody patch of gauze was taped inside a white nest of hair on the side of the man's head. Decker felt queasy. "Nobody else was in there?"

"Didn't look like it. There were no signs of a fight. He might have had a heart attack. Don't worry, son. The hospital knows we're coming. They'll fix him up."

Decker's voice cracked. "Methodist Hospital, right?"

"Right."

Oblivious to Decker, the EMTs opened the back doors of the ambulance and slid the stretcher inside with Mr. Conahan on it. One climbed in with him. The other closed the rear doors and jumped onto the passenger seat. The driver started the engine, and the ambulance rolled away.

Decker opened the mailbox. He grabbed the mail and left a couple of advertisements inside. If he came back, he'd know whether somebody else was interested in Mr. Conahan.

CHAPTER FIVE

DECKER LOPED TOWARD BROADWAY, CLUTCHING MR. Conahan's mail. It felt good to stretch his legs and not creep around hiding. He felt free like when he was running bases. He thought about searching again for the phone, but he wanted to be at the hospital when the ambulance arrived.

He had parked his Mustang across the side street from the diner. Except for security lights in a few stores, the strip center was dark. Few people cruised Broadway at night in Prospect Heights. Nobody would see him get in his car. As he neared Broadway, he glanced at cars parked in front of the diner. Mom's 1998 BMW wasn't there. He hoped she'd gone home.

The distant whine of the ambulance siren told him the driver was going south on Broadway to Hildebrand, then west to the Medical Center. Decker slid into his dilapidated, beloved Mustang, thankful he didn't lose his keys and wallet along with the phone.

He was starving. He took Loop 410 and spied a What-A-Burger with two cars at the drive-through. Stopping would take too much time.

Feeling more clear-headed than he had in weeks, he parked in the hospital parking lot, hoping the man would talk to him and describe his attacker. He'd give him the mail as a friendly gesture.

Nearing the main entrance, he remembered how much he hated hospitals. He wrinkled his nose waiting for antiseptic fumes to hit him, an odor like the athletes' locker room at the beginning of the year when they disinfected it to prepare for the sea of sweaty bodies. How could anybody get better in hospitals smelling disinfectant? Thankfully, the lobby smelled fresh with a hint of pine scent. He inhaled.

He remembered when Mom was in the hospital for what she called "a female plumbing issue," whatever that was. They didn't cover it in freshman science. They talked about human anatomy, animals having sex, and how reproduction worked...duh. Nobody wanted kids or disease, just sex, and he didn't care how animals did it.

He tried it once, on a dare after two beers he didn't want, with some girl who was probably a nymphomaniac. He wanted to forget the fiasco, but painful details popped up at random times. After she stuck out her boobs and he rubbed them, she lifted her blouse and moved his hand down her stomach. He was so fascinated with where she moved his hand and unseen parts she wanted him to touch, he forgot why he was there. She got disgusted and flounced off. He sat there feeling like an idiot.

Sex was supposed to be awesome, but he wanted to care about the girl. Otherwise, it was like two orangutans going at it.

He did think about how it might be with Ashley Montrose. He'd watched her since his freshman year, a pretty blue-eyed blond who knew everyone but never acknowledged him. His junior year, he started talking to her in the hall or in class. They had their first date over the holidays strolling North Star Mall, eating burgers, and watching a dumb Christmas movie.

Later, when he saw her between classes, she looked different. Interested. She stopped him after third period and suggested they get together. She always wore something soft that made you want to nuzzle it. Maybe she liked him better than he thought.

Even she couldn't dissipate the grayness surrounding him, so he said he had to study for a test the next day. She was piqued and produced a hesitant smile. She was usually so busy being popular, he doubted she thought much about him or about sex either.

Every guy who looked at her thought about it, though. Including him. He spotted the information desk and walked toward the receptionist. Without the debilitating gray overlay clouding his perception, the furniture looked bright against the hospital walls.

"Can you please tell me what room Mr. Mitchell Conahan is in?"

She pushed buttons on her keypad and consulted her computer screen.

"I'm sorry. He's not listed as being in a room. Did he come in recently?"

"In the last thirty minutes."

"He may still be in Emergency or in ICU."

"ICU?"

"Intensive Care Unit."

His heart sank.

She smiled sympathetically. "Patients sometimes need to be stabilized before they're assigned to a room."

"Stabilized?"

"They may require emergency treatment or critical care before they're ready for standard care in a hospital room."

"I see." He didn't see, exactly. She was scaring him to

death. What if the man died? He was in the man's house when he was attacked and didn't do anything. His heart thumped.

"I wouldn't worry," she said. "Mr. Conahan will probably be fine. It takes time to admit somebody. Why don't you sit in the waiting room over there and check back in thirty minutes to an hour."

"Okay. Are there vending machines somewhere?"

She directed him to Sub-level 1 where he grabbed two candy bars and a mammoth soda. He polished them off on his way back to the lobby and slogged across the room to a chair as far away from people as possible. Check back in thirty minutes to an hour? They could play an entire baseball scrimmage in an hour. When would they let him see the man? The waiting room started to lose color. His vision grew foggy, gray tones seeping around him.

He remembered when Granddad Hank was in the hospital. He'd been hospitalized a couple times before. When Mom called him at school, he got an excuse from the attendance office and drove to the hospital, expecting to see Granddad and reassure him he'd soon be home. When he approached the room, he saw Mom and Dad at the end of the hall.

Dad looked ashen. Mom was crying. "Granddad died," they said.

He'd already been taken from his room. He was gone. Just like that. Forever. Decker didn't even get to say goodbye.

He slumped in the chair, leaned his head back, and closed his eyes. He sent up a prayer for Granddad and Mr. Conahan. And Mom. And Dad. And Casey.

Noise blasting from the intercom startled him—something about "STAT." He jerked up rigid and blinked at his watch. His neck ached. He must have fallen asleep.

He should call Mom and tell her where he was. He

reached for his phone and remembered he had lost it. Damn. He swiped a hand across his eyes and stood. One leg was numb and tingling. He shook it and limped back to the information desk.

"Is Mr. Conahan in his room yet?"

She looked back at her computer, clicked some keys and looked up. "I'm sorry. He's still in ICU."

"Can I make a phone call?"

"The volunteer can help you." She pointed to the interior of the room where a lady in a blue and white uniform perched behind a desk. He spotted a phone on her desk and walked over. She had a patch on her uniform reading "Bluebird." He liked that.

"Excuse me. Can I call home?"

"Local call?"

"Yes."

"Of course." She smiled. "Dial 9, then your number."

"Hi, Mom."

Bluebird rose and discretely fluttered away.

"Decker, where are you? I've been worried sick."

"I'm sorry, Mom. I didn't have time to call. I was on my way home after baseball practice when I heard a siren east of Broadway, somewhere behind The Broadway Cafe, so I followed the sound. When I jumped out of the car, I lost my phone somewhere. Some old guy was attacked in his home, and they brought him to Methodist Hospital. I'm here now."

"You followed him to the hospital? Why? Who is he?" She didn't mention the diner.

"I don't know him. I watched them wheel him to the ambulance and felt sorry for him. He's old like Granddad and was unconscious. I got his name off the mailbox. Conahan. Mitchell Conahan on Terrell. Do you know him?"

"No, Decker. How would I know him?

"I don't know. He doesn't live very far from us. Are you okay?"

"Yes, now that I know where you are. You need to come home. You lost your phone? For Pete's sake, Decker."

"I know, Mom. It was stupid. I want to make sure he's okay. Then I'll come straight home."

"All right, Deck. Don't take too long."

He was placing the receiver in the cradle when Bluebird settled into view. "Do you have a list of patients with their room numbers?"

"Yes." She smiled. "Who would you like to visit?"

"Conahan. Mitchell Conahan."

She tipped her head back to look through bifocals and scanned her computer screen. "Here it is. Room 627. He's in the cardiac wing."

"Thanks." He found the bank of elevators and punched six. So, it was a heart attack. Caused by the louse who attacked him. At least he survived, poor fellow. He hoped the man could talk. He had to know about the weasel who hurt him.

The elevator door opened, and he stepped out on six, overwhelmed by the odor of disinfectant. Blinking, he scanned a couple room numbers and headed for 627.

As he veered toward it, a nurse stopped him. "Can I help you?"

"How is Mr. Conahan?"

"You are?"

"A friend, Corey Giles." He read the name somewhere. "I used to walk dogs on his street. We visited sometimes. How is he?"

"He's unconscious. I'm afraid he's in ICU. We're doing all we can."

CHAPTER SIX

DRIVING HOME, DECKER FELT LIKE STALE BREAD. HE COULDN'T fathom why his mom would meet with a criminal. Why did the scumbag attack an elderly man? What if the old man died? He'd feel guilty the rest of his life knowing he did nothing to prevent it. He could be charged with assault or accessory to murder, dooming his family and future.

He rolled his creaking Mustang into the garage by Mom's 1998 Beemer, the one Dad bought her when insurance premiums were coming in.

Decker loved his '65 Mustang even though it needed work. He'd wanted one since he was twelve. Dad finally found a used one. When Dad was home, Decker periodically took it to the repair shop. Not anymore. He hoped it kept rolling.

He slipped into the house through the kitchen door, hoping Mom was in bed. Tiptoeing upstairs, he almost made it to his room before her door opened at the end of the hall.

Looking frazzled, she scowled, "Don't worry me like that again, Decker."

NANCY G. WEST

He shook his head. "I'm sorry, Mom. I got caught up in what was happening and forgot to call. Plus, I didn't have a phone." He couldn't tell her the rest.

He thought he had dropped his phone a couple blocks from the house. Now he wasn't sure where he lost it. An investigator searching the vicinity would surely find it. He hoped somebody at the hospital didn't learn the old man was attacked and call the police.

Decker pushed the door to his room slightly open. "I've got to study, Mom."

"Yes, you do. And I've got a long day tomorrow. I'm calling on two new decorating clients. Checking with others to make sure they're happy. We need the money, Deck. And we both need some rest." She turned toward her room and sighed, pivoted toward him, and shook her head. "I love you, Decker."

"I know, Mom. I love you too."

"Another thing, Deck, I can't afford another phone. And your dad? Well, don't expect him to get you one."

"I know, Mom."

She trudged into her bedroom.

He felt like a louse. She had enough trouble trying to support them with Dad gone. He slipped into his room, closed the door, and collapsed on the bed. He fumbled at the back of the nightstand for an emergency Snickers, found one, ripped it open and consumed it in three bites. Too wired to sleep, he got up, showered, brushed his teeth, put on pajamas, and turned on his computer to search for Mitchell Conahan. Granddad Hank had shown him how to use Ancestry.com.

Several Conahans settled in Canada and the northeastern United States. Famous people sprinkled their family tree. One was the ancestor of Herman "Babe" Ruth. He savored the thought. He'd love to have inherited a couple of genes from old Babe. Who knew genealogy was so interesting?

He snagged the baseball from his desk, leaned back and tossed it from hand to hand. He wondered if the Savages or the Johnsons, Mom's family, had any talented ancestors. Granddad found some Johnsons, but he hadn't paid much attention. Mom got her aesthetic sensibility from somebody, maybe a famous architect or designer.

He didn't know of any musicians in the family, but Granddad Hank loved music and played a mean guitar. He remembered him playing and crooning when he was little, the most calming sound ever.

When Decker was older, Granddad's words had the same effect. When they took walks or ran errands, Granddad was never in a hurry, always ready to listen to whatever was on Decker's mind. His questions helped Decker figure out for himself how to handle a problem. He lay his head back on the chair and closed his eyes. He longed for Granddad's questions.

He put the ball down and focused on the screen. He found only one Mitchell J. Conahan in Texas, CEO of an oil drilling equipment firm in Houston from 1990 to 2000, MJC Drill. There was no photograph of him, but the timing seemed right. If he retired ten or eleven years ago, he'd be in his late 70s or early 80s. Ancestry didn't say what the middle initial "J" stood for, John, Jonathan, Joseph, Jason, James? A dozen other names.

Mitchell had two daughters and two sons: Maureen O'Brien (Pennsylvania), Emma Stapleton (Colorado), Murray Conahan (Oklahoma), and Patrick Conahan (California.) His kids scattered all over. He thought it peculiar that not one stayed in Texas. Maybe they weren't tied to the Mitchell Conahan in the hospital. He might be researching the wrong guy.

Decker remembered the English test tomorrow on *The Grapes of Wrath*, and his head throbbed. He grabbed Mom's old hardback copy from his bookshelf and hauled it to his desk. The thing weighed a ton—good thing he liked to read.

He'd really gotten into it over the Christmas holidays. He was moved by people's desperate trek across the desert as they lumbered along trying to escape the Oklahoma dust bowl where no crops would grow. Ways people responded to misery fascinated him. Trudging through his own desert, he connected with their rootlessness, their fear of the unknown.

He internalized their story into his own barren land. His family was like a clay pot abandoned in a scorching desert, crumbling to shards. From inside his gray bubble, he watched helplessly while the shards ground themselves into sand.

He remembered plots, why he enjoyed a book, a few characters, and the author's name. If the test focused on minutia about what the protagonist ate, where a scene was set, or the names of secondary characters, he was dead in the water. He couldn't remember that crap. It didn't matter to anybody but English teachers anyway.

He flipped through pages. Even before the sensation of being bagged in gelatin took over, the world started looking gray, making it hard to study. He used to be proud he could learn. He never mentioned it, especially at school. People— especially girls—were impressed by jocks, not nerds.

He shut the book, turned out the light, and plopped onto the bed. Putting his hands behind his head, he stared at the ceiling. He thought the gray landscape would clear up once school started in January. He liked school. But two weeks into the semester, the grayness persisted.

In the hallways, he walked through a colorless moonscape, stopping at pods of talking people. Talking heads mouthed unintelligible sounds and made gestures unrelated to his life.

He might as well try to sleep and hope his brain stored enough details about Steinway's book for him to pour them out on the test paper.

CHAPTER SEVEN

JILLIAN SAVAGE FLUNG HER VERSACE BATHROBE ON THE coordinating comforter and plodded to the bathroom. The mirror reflected a face with sunken eyes and pinched skin, the face of a woman running a business, worrying about a son, and soon-to-be divorced at forty-one. She rubbed her hand across her cheek, spread moisturizing cleanser on her face and patted it with a damp cloth.

She pushed her hair behind her ears, leaned forward, studied her crow's feet in the mirror, and thought about Decker. He was a diligent, respectful kid who tried to do whatever she and Trent asked. When he was little, if he broke a rule, his vulnerable little face registered so much worry and guilt, she felt worse than he did about his childish infraction.

She shuffled to the bedroom and sighed at her collection of family photos on the dresser. When she picked up the last photo of Casey at age three, her eyes filled. The pain of losing him lodged back inside her chest, and her hand shook. Decker adored his little brother, and Casey worshipped Decker. After Casey died, Decker's open eight-year-old face grew closed and sad. The light escaped from behind his eyes.

She replaced his photo and picked up the latest one of Decker. He looked pensive. He'd been quieter than usual, which was understandable with his family crumbling before his eyes. No matter how often she told him that he wasn't responsible for his brother's death or their impending divorce, he still suffered. His grades went down, and he spent less time with friends, but he still loved baseball. Hitting and running bases was good for him. Nothing else seemed to lift his malaise. She prayed he'd get out of his funk when the season started.

Did he see her car near the diner? She doubted it. He'd have asked her about it.

She couldn't believe she went there to meet that man. If he hadn't called to say he taught at the high school and was concerned about Decker, she'd never have gone. When she first saw him, she thought she might have met him briefly in college. It was funny Decker never mentioned him. He probably wasn't worth mentioning. Besides, Decker was busy chasing an ambulance.

When the guy stormed out of the diner, he still hadn't told her much. He seemed strange, and she was mad at herself for meeting him.

She sat down on the bed, plumped a pillow, and stretched out. Why was Decker so interested in an old man he didn't know? He said the injured man reminded him of Granddad Hank. That might explain why Decker was drawn to him. He and Granddad were closer than Decker and Trent.

In her own grief after her father died, she didn't realize how much his death affected Decker. With Trent having moved out, Decker must be grieving for them both.

Her father was wise, thoughtful, and deliberate in his personal and business dealings. God, how they needed him after Casey died. If only he were here to help. She kissed her fingers and touched Decker's photo.

She was thankful he was taking an interest in someone. If the man recovered, and she liked him, he might be a good influence on Decker. If he was half the man her father was, that would be enough.

Her eyes grew wet. How ironic that she, of all people, would be in this untenable situation. All she ever wanted was stability, not riches, but enough to be comfortable in a secure family with a husband and children who loved and supported each other. She grabbed a tissue from the nightstand and swiped her eyes. Solidarity. Peace. A loving family.

Having known tranquility in her own family with her parents and two sisters, she took harmony for granted. She didn't look hard enough at Trent. With his good looks, charm and dazzling talent, she never bothered to delve underneath.

Trent had no concept of anyone's passion for something that didn't interest him—one of the many reasons they could never cement their marriage. They could never be a team. Odd for someone who played a team sport. Trent craved people around to admire him, but when it came to what he wanted, he flew solo. If anyone wanted to tag along...well, let them tag.

She rubbed her hand over the plush black and cream fabric. They shared this bed for almost two decades. Stretching her neck side to side, forward and back, she tried to relax. She had to sleep. Tomorrow would be nonstop rush.

She plumped a pillow and lay on her side. In nine months, Decker would be in college. She didn't know how she could pay for it. She didn't think Trent would pay for anything.

Could she go through divorcing him, service her clients, and help Decker get through the next nine months?

His grades were good but not stellar. But there was baseball. She was glad he didn't spot her at the diner. It had a reputation as a hangout for kids who weren't plugged in.

With studying and getting ready for baseball season, Decker wasn't apt to go there.

She rearranged the pillow under her head, drew another between her knees, and cuddled a third to her chest. Comforted, she pictured Decker playing college ball and drifted off.

———

JILLIAN WOKE AND LOOKED AT THE CLOCK. SIX A.M. SHE HAD time to make pancakes. She and Decker could eat together before starting their daily sprints. She threw on her robe, brushed her teeth, combed her hair, and pattered down the steps toward the kitchen. When the phone rang, she cradled the receiver between her ear and shoulder.

"Hello. This is Jillian Savage."

There was no answer. She dug the skillet out from under the counter. "Hello."

Still no answer. She thought she heard someone breathing. Not wanting to waste more time on the wrong number, she hung up and greased the skillet.

Decker barreled down the stairs, hauling his backpack. He had his father's dark hair and eyes but was tall and slim, non-confrontational, like she was. Until his third year of high school, he never bulked up no matter how much he lifted weights. Right before his junior year, he started filling out. Girls were undoubtedly beginning to notice.

"I'm making pancakes, Deck. We can actually eat breakfast together."

He sidled up and gave her a quick hug, his hair tickling her forehead. "Sorry, Mom. I've got an English test and have to meet Coach Branson first."

"This early?"

He shrugged. "He said it's the only time he had." He sped through the kitchen door into the garage.

"I hope the coach isn't mad about something," she called after him. There was no answer. She heard the Mustang gurgle to life and the garage door open.

She took the skillet off the heat and stared at it until the phone rang. Probably a client. She took a deep breath, put a smile in her voice, hoping it wasn't another wrong number, and answered.

CHAPTER EIGHT

THE MAN NEVER THOUGHT HE'D GO TO THAT HOUSE.

Years of frustration and dissension propelled him relentlessly toward it. It was time he took care of business.

He sensed someone tailing him. A !ash of light. The sensation of movement behind him. Periods of unnatural stillness.

Anger welled up until it controlled him. Things escalated and got out of hand until...it happened.

Once inside the house, he thought he heard something downstairs. What if someone caught sight of him entering? Followed him in? He had to find him.

The screech of a siren startled him. Was it the police car he'd seen earlier? He couldn't be caught inside. He raced down the stairs. He sensed movement in the living room and stopped mid-step. He spotted motion near the sofa. He stared at it, straining to discern a body or a face.

In front of the house, sirens quit wailing. Somebody cut the vehicle's engine. The silence was deafening. Car doors slammed. Cops? He couldn't explain his presence in this house. Not with the old man upstairs lying on the floor.

No one must know he was here. He tensed to charge for the sofa and drag out the culprit.

The doorbell rang. Voices shouted. Men pounded the door. He had to escape.

He jumped off the stairs, raced through the dining room, kitchen, and out the door.

He slipped through the darkness to get as far from the house as he could.

CHAPTER NINE

DECKER NEEDED TO COMB THE WHOLE AREA WHERE HE MIGHT have dropped the phone. From home, he drove down Garraty Road, but instead of continuing toward New Braunfels, he turned left on Eldon, and then on Terrell, Mr. Conahan's street. He slowed but didn't spot anything on the road or in the grass. He must have dropped the phone earlier in the chase.

Decker took Eldon back to Elizabeth and cruised slowly, searching for spots where he'd hid behind bushes. In the daylight, none of the houses looked the same. When he was pretty sure he was in the right block, he turned around to park his car near the corner on the south side of the street and got out to search.

He remembered running from a corner house to a series of hedges near the street, so he looked for clumps where he might have dropped the phone. Heading for a batch of shrubbery, he peered down one shrub, then another, and felt the ground around every bush.

"Help you, son?"

"Oh." He straightened. "Uh, no thanks."

A man stood at the end of his sidewalk in pajamas, holding a newspaper. Porcupine quill whiskers poked from his face. He peered suspiciously at Decker with beady eyes over smudged glasses that slipped down his nose.

Decker cleared his throat. "I may have dropped something around here and thought I might find it. But thanks."

"Dropped what?"

"A phone. I was walking up the hill past St. Peter's Church the other night when I lost it."

"This is pretty far from St. Peter's. What night was it?"

"Uhhh...I'm not sure. Tuesday or Wednesday. I walked quite a while."

He pointed to the Mustang. "That your car?"

"Yes, sir."

"You weren't driving your car?"

"No. I parked it at Stewart Center that night and decided to do some jogging and walking before I drove home—you know, to loosen up and get in shape. Baseball practice starts next week." He knew his answers were stupid, but he couldn't think of anything else.

Furrowing caterpillar eyebrows, the old guy was giving him the third degree. Maybe the attacker spotted Decker near Conahan's house and told this man about it. He sure couldn't ask if he knew Mr. Conahan.

He bent intently toward a shrub hoping to end the conversation. "I'm sure it'll turn up. Thanks for asking."

He heard a car roll to a stop at the curb. When Sergeant Thorn leaned out, Decker's stomach lurched. Good thing he wasn't full of pancakes.

"You guys are out early. What's up?" Thorn said.

"This fellow lost his phone," the old man said, curling his lip in a doubtful sneer.

"It's no big deal, Sergeant Thorn. I thought I lost it around here somewhere, but it's probably at home. I'm bad about misplacing it."

Thorn grinned. "I thought you guys never lost a phone. Homework, maybe, but not a phone."

Decker shrugged and tried to grin along with him. "I got away early this morning—have to meet with Coach before first period English."

Thorn studied Decker's face. "Okay, then. Better get going."

"Yes, sir. Thank you, sir." Thorn glided the patrol car into the street, and Decker wheeled toward his Mustang.

"Hey." The old man stopped him with a bark. Peering over coke-bottle lenses, he looked like he could clamp that quilled jaw onto something and never let go.

"If I find your phone, I'll hold it for you. What'd you say your name was?"

"Uh. Sam Shupbach. Thanks for keeping an eye out, sir. I'll check back. I'll look in a couple more places later today. I'll probably find it." He conjured up a friendly smile, hoping the man might respond in kind. He didn't.

He spotted another clump of bushes but was reluctant to search with the guy staring at him. He might have heard the patrol car the other night and caught sight of him hiding behind the bushes. His heart pounded like it did that night. If his prey was this man's friend, they might put two and two together.

Decker jumped into his Mustang, waved thanks, and coaxed the car into action. If this grizzly guy suspected it was a lie, he might report it to Sergeant Thorn. Why did he give a false name? Thorn knew Decker and his family. If he found out Mr. Conahan was assaulted, he'd ask Decker why he gave a false name, and where he was going when he dropped the phone.

Why not just tell Mom he was going to look for his phone

and give his real name? Her sitting with that stranger and the house thing totally spooked him.

What if the attacker spotted him in the house and identified him? If Thorn linked the time of the assault to Decker, he was toast.

He tried to concoct a plausible story. He heard the ambulance, ran in the direction of the siren, dropped the phone somewhere, saw the ambulance stop at the house and decided EMTs would take care of the problem. So, he went back to his car and drove home. He discovered later his phone was missing.

He was getting a lot of practice making up stories. It reminded him of *Huckleberry Finn*. He checked his watch. He had better get to school and start thinking about *The Grapes of Wrath*. His grades used to be good, but not lately. He didn't have the crispness of thought to wrap his mind around anything. Mrs. Pritchard insinuated he better do well on this AP English test.

The only parking spot left at school was the farthest possible distance from Decker's class. He sprinted toward the building. When he charged in panting, everybody was seated. Mrs. Pritchard glared at him. With the stance of a general, she pointed straight-armed to his chair. The test lay on top of his desk.

It was a shame to waste her talent on a bunch of kids, even if they were in AP English. Some of them didn't care if they never read another book. He grabbed a pen from his backpack, slung the pack over the back of the chair, and tried to catch his breath as he slid in. Pritchard looked at her watch.

"Open the first page of the test," she commanded. "There are two essay questions, one on the first page and one on the second. A shoddy answer on either one means a grade of fifty. Go."

Decker closed his eyes and tried to put himself back into John Steinbeck's *Grapes of Wrath*. Caravans of desperate families hauled their belongings across the desert to California to escape the barren Oklahoma dust bowl. They heard California was a promised land of endless crops and plentiful jobs. But despite reaching the lush state with its rich land, they found barely enough work to feed themselves. And more misery. Cruel landowners were determined to perpetuate their poverty, which robbed them of their dignity.

"If you need more space for your answers," Mrs. Pritchard said, "you can use the back of the pages." She had taught him before. He mentally translated her meaning: *Think about your answers before you write. Make them succinct; don't pad your writing.*

He read the statement preceding the first question. It looked familiar. She probably lifted it from Spark Notes.

"In the beginning of the book, men make the decisions, and women obediently do as they're told. Pa Joad, increasingly distraught by their hopeless circumstances, withdraws from his role as leader and spends his days tangled in thought. In his stead, Ma Joad assumes responsibility for making decisions for the family. By the end of the novel, the family structure has undergone a revolution. The woman figure, traditionally powerless, has taken control. The male figure, traditionally in the leadership role, has retreated."

Her statement reminded him what happened after Casey died. The air crash murders of 9/11 shocked the country. Dad's business faltered. He withdrew from his family and spent time away from home. When he was there, he stared at TV.

Mom was stunned, devastated, and sad, but she grew increasingly dogged in her determination to jump start her decorating business and steer them back toward normality.

Mrs. Pritchard cleared her throat. "Think about what the main characters did."

He pulled his mind back to the first question. "Which woman, among the strong women in the book, stands out as especially courageous and compassionate?"

Decker thought about Ma Joad. Determined and loving, she emerges as the center of strength. Pa Joad, crushed by their dire circumstances, becomes less effective as leader and provider. Despite great turmoil, Ma meets obstacles unflinchingly.

Ma Joad's daughter, Rose of Sharon, has a stillborn child after the long journey. Yet, despite her personal tragedy, she offers a dying man her breast milk to sustain him. Even though Rose acts at Ma Joad's suggestion, Decker decided that, in offering life to the dying man, Rose of Sharon was the most courageous and compassionate. She also embodied the promise of a new beginning.

Mom, by reigniting her business, tried to steer their family toward a new beginning.

He wrote down his answer and points to support it. He finished, sighed, and looked at the ceiling. He thought he did a pretty good job on Question 1.

The next question asked, "What character in *The Grapes of Wrath* is the novel's guiding voice?"

His first thought was Tom Joad. The story revolved around him. After spending four years in prison, Tom is ready to dedicate himself to the present moment. He's strong, thoughtful, and has moral certainty.

His friend Jim turns Tom into a social activist who wants to help people. Jim is so selfless, he resembles a Christ figure. What was his last name, this champion of the poor who dedicated himself to helping fellow sufferers? Jim could be the novel's guiding voice. What was his last name? Decker had to at least know the man's last name to compare the two characters and reach a conclusion.

His brain fogged. Why couldn't he remember the dude's

last name so he could answer the stupid question? He looked around at classmates agonizing over idiotic details. There was no use. A lot of characters in the book helped each other through unimaginable hardships. Who cared which one was the most devoted to helping others?

He was done. He slammed the pen into his pocket, slapped the notebook closed, slid it off the table, and strode to Pritchard's desk. She looked up over horn rims, her eyes following the path of his notebook to her desk.

She lifted her eyes, studied him, and kept her voice low so as not to disturb the other students. "You can't be finished, Decker. I've read your excellent answers to test questions before."

"Yes, ma'am, I am." He clenched his teeth.

"This is an important test, Decker. It sets the tone for the rest of the year."

"I know."

"And...?"

"That's it." He set his jaw. "That's all I've got."

She leaned forward, put her elbows on the desk, clasped her hands under her chin, and peered up over her rims. "You read the entire book?"

"Yes, ma'am."

"And that's all you've got. You're sure?"

He nodded.

"I see. She leaned back in her chair. "Meet me at the counselor's office after class."

"But my next class..."

"Is what?"

"Statistics."

"Do you have a test?"

"No, ma'am." He hoped not. So far, he hadn't understood much of what the teacher said.

"Meet me at the counselor's office. Decker. I'll give you an excuse for being late to statistics."

He closed his eyes and sighed. He didn't need this. What could a counselor do about anything? He turned on his heel, grabbed his backpack off the chair, and trudged out of the class and down the hall. He had intended to make good enough grades to get into college and learn enough to help Mom and Dad with expenses—give them hope they seemed to have lost. One thing he counted on was his ability to learn. Not anymore. He'd end up with some crummy job, be useless to his family, and add to their hurt.

He was halfway to the counselor's office when the bell rang. Ashley Montrose stepped from her class into the hall and smiled. Her attentive expression held him.

"Hey. Where are you going?" She gazed at him, bewitching and soft in her pink sweater. She had expectant blue eyes as though she was asking a question, but he never quite knew what it was. Without his permission, his eyes slipped to her chest.

He blinked and managed to focus on her face. "I've got to pick up something at the office before statistics." He didn't want to delve into the counselor thing.

The corners of her mouth slid up when she was delighted, turning her mouth into a Cupid's bow. The corners were down now. She blinked thick lashes over unreadable eyes.

"I'm going to Frank Sweeney's tonight," he lied. "What if we hang out later, like after baseball practice Monday?"

He hadn't talked to Sweeney yet, but mostly his brain was too frazzled to take on Ashley Montrose.

She hesitated. Did she expect him to ask her out this weekend?

"Sure. Monday sounds good." She gave her bouncy hair a casual flip. "Like, maybe, seven?"

"Perfect. I'll pick you up." As she turned and finger waved, he watched her swish nonchalantly down the hall, blonde hair bouncing. Every boy in the school would love to date Ashley. And he put her off until Monday. Was he nuts?

He sighed. At least he had something to look forward to. He slogged to the main office and approached the receptionist. "I'm waiting for Mrs. Pritchard."

"Sure. Have a seat."

He shambled across the room and plopped into one of the chairs. Metal with a thin padded seat. Institutional. Maybe the whole place was an institution. He hoped the counselor was too busy to see him. He didn't need a lecture, and he wasn't about to tell her about feeling like he was floating in a bag of gray smog. He put his head in his hands.

"Decker."

He jerked up, stood to face Mrs. Pritchard, and remembered. "It was Jim Casy," he blurted. "That was his name, Casy. He had this selfless devotion to others, and he inspired Tom Joad to join him. He gave his life for the rest of them and lived on through Tom Joad. He's the novel's guiding voice—the answer to the second question."

She nodded and produced a knowing smile. "You do remember."

"Yes, ma'am."

She put her hand on his shoulder and peered at him through her glasses with kind eyes he never noticed before. "I know you're having a rough time at home right now. Maybe the counselor can give you tips to help you recall information."

Geez. Did everybody in the whole school know his parents were getting a divorce? He felt his face flush.

She withdrew her hand. "You do know the answer, Decker. I'll consider giving you partial credit." She pivoted toward the receptionist. "Is Dr. Sanborne in?"

"Yes."

Mrs. Pritchard gave him an encouraging smile. "Go on in, Decker. She's free to see you."

CHAPTER TEN

AFTER HIS SESSION WITH THE COUNSELOR, DECKER WAS exhausted from trying to be polite and engaged while revealing as little as he could about his life with a gray pall hovering around him. She expressed sympathy about their tragedy losing Casey. That's when Decker said he'd better go eat before class started.

He slogged to the cafeteria and plodded through the line, selecting the least miserable-looking food. He carried his tray to a table away from everyone. At least the fog surrounding him helped block incessant chatter exuding from other tables.

He dragged his body through afternoon classes and went home, glad the school week was over. He raided the fridge, grabbed some cheese, and decided he couldn't wait until Sunday to see Mr. Conahan. He left a note for his mother about where he'd be.

He parked in the main lot, went straight to the Bluebird's desk, and smiled at her. He never thought he'd be glad to enter a hospital. "Can Mr. Conahan have visitors? He's in 627."

She looked at her screen. "Yes, until nine when visiting

hours end." The clock on her desk said 5:30 p.m. Plenty of time.

"Thanks." He turned to leave. *Was there anyone he should call about Mr. Conahan? Family? Friends?* He swung back to the Bluebird. "Has he had other visitors?"

"I'm afraid I don't know. You can check with the charge nurse on his floor." He nodded, walked toward the elevators, and pushed six.

He tapped lightly on 627, heard a guttural grumble, and eased open the door. A medicinal odor tickled his nose. Mitchell Conahan lay propped on pillows, an oxygen tube clipped to his nostrils and an IV bottle dripping liquid into his arm. Leads on his chest communicated with a screen across the room producing intermittent beeps. A food tray rested on a stand near his bed.

Mr. Conahan looked over. "Who are you?"

Decker was surprised by the dark, penetrating eyes sizing him up.

"Corey Giles." He thought he should use the name he gave the nurse, not the one he gave the snoopy old man when he searched for the phone. He hoped he could remember all the names he used. He'd never lied so much in his life.

"Why are you here?" Conahan asked.

The patch, half buried in Conahan's white hair, was smaller than he remembered. A bruise below his temple was purple and swollen. His black eye made him resemble a scruffy pirate. A splotchy growth of white and dark gray patches covered his chin from ear to ear resembling an untended lawn in various stages of drought.

"I was walking down your street when I heard the ambulance and saw it stop at your house. I wondered how you were."

"Not too damn good. Why did you wonder? I don't know you." His dark eyes pierced Decker's.

54

"You remind me of my grandfather, I guess."

"Where is he?"

"He's dead."

"Oh." He looked straight ahead. "Well, he's in a better place." He swiveled his head back toward Decker. "You might as well come in. There's a chair by the window."

Decker felt Conahan's eyes track him across the room and watch him settle into the chair.

"So what about your parents? Or are you some kind of orphan?"

He swallowed and cleared his throat. "My mom knows I came to see you." He paused. "I haven't mentioned it to Dad."

Conahan studied Decker's face. "He's not around?"

Decker looked at his lap.

"Lots of dads aren't around much. I wasn't around much." He turned his attention to beeps on the screen.

"Do you remember what happened?"

Even though it was dusk outside and hard to see much, Mr. Conahan stared out the window. "I remember being surprised. I remember a lot of yelling. Thinking I might fall." He looked up at the ceiling, sighed, and looked back at Decker. "That's about it. I don't remember coming here."

A nurse entered smiling. "I'm sorry, but Mr. Conahan shouldn't have visitors for long periods. You can come back tomorrow, Mr...?

"Corey Giles."

"You can come back tomorrow, Corey." She smiled.

"I have baseball practice. The season starts next week."

"You're a baseball player?" Conahan said. "I'm a big fan. I follow the Red Sox and the Cardinals. The Astros are getting better." He turned to the nurse. "Talking to Corey about baseball will be good medicine."

"All right. For a while, I guess." She walked to the food tray and lifted the cover. "You didn't eat much, Mr. Conahan."

"The meat tastes like shoe leather. I ate the mashed pota-toes and the pudding."

"You drank the liquids. That's good."

Conahan gave her a sour look.

"I'll ask one of the orderlies to bring you a snack in a couple hours." She smiled and swished toward the door.

"See if they have any ice cream," he bellowed after her. "Chocolate!" He was gruffer than Granddad Hank. Decker liked him.

He studied Decker. "So, you play ball. What team?"

"Prospect High School. Second base. Varsity."

"I played second and third. They kept moving me around. When somebody better showed up, they'd put me someplace else. Sometimes it didn't work. They put me in the outfield once and I jammed my middle finger catching a fly. Had to wear a splint on it for two weeks."

"Where did you play?"

"Katy High School, southwest of Houston."

Decker thought he'd found the right Mitchell Conahan. "This is my first year on varsity. I don't have to try out, but the scuttlebutt is they have a couple hot shot players coming in from a big school in New Braunfels. I hope I can keep second base."

"Been practicing?"

"Over the holidays with my dad."

"So, he's not always gone."

"No, sir. But he and my mom..." Decker looked down and shook his head.

"Getting a divorce?"

Decker looked at his lap and nodded. "Separated, but she filed. Dad already moved out."

Conahan nodded. "I see."

Decker wanted to get back to baseball. "I'm going to practice tomorrow with a friend, show him some of the Matt Antonelli drills from YouTube that Dad and I used."

"Antonelli was good at second base. He fielded for a lot of teams—the San Diego Padres, Washington Nationals, the Yankees, Orioles, and the Cleveland Indians."

"You know a lot about him."

"Yeah. I liked to watch him adjust his play for the different teams."

"He's a good teacher on YouTube. Now he coaches varsity at the high school where he played. I watched his video about ten unwritten rules of baseball."

"Like not bunting to break up a no-hitter?"

"Yes, sir. And like not showing up the umpire even if you're furious over a call by yelling straight at him. Or like it's okay to steal signals if it's not obvious you're doing it."

Conahan coughed out a laugh and reached up to hold his head near the bruise. "If it's obvious you're stealing signals, somebody's going to drill you."

"The bruise, sir. Is the bruise from when you fell?"

He pressed his eyes closed. "I'm not sure. I remember being surprised. And arguing...there was yelling and shoving. I yelled back. Maybe I fell and hit something, or...I don't know." He frowned and stopped talking. "Thinking makes my head hurt."

Decker scooted forward in the chair. "Who were you arguing with?"

Conahan squeezed his eyes closed and leaned back against the pillows. He threw up his hands. "I don't know."

"I understand, sir. Maybe I should go."

He sat with his eyes closed for a minute. He opened them and looked at Decker. "When the ambulance stopped at my house, how did you know I'd come here?"

"I asked the EMTs where they'd take you. I told them I walked dogs in the neighborhood, and we talked sometimes."

Conahan pursed his lips and nodded. "I see. Well, I guess those were harmless lies."

Decker looked at his lap. He didn't know the difference any more between harmless and harmful lies.

Conahan perceived his concern. "It's okay, son. Besides, we're talking now."

"Yes, sir." He was glad Mr. Conahan didn't know what else he had done.

The nurse came in and stood holding the door open. "It's almost seven. I think you should leave now."

"Yes, ma'am." He looked back at Conahan. "Is there anybody I should call, sir, to let them know you're here?"

"No." He peered out the window into the darkness. "There's no one."

"All right. Take care of yourself, sir."

Conahan looked back and nodded. His mouth turned up. "Guess I'd better do that, son. Come back and we'll talk more baseball."

"Yes, sir. I'd like that, sir."

Decker bounced to his car and whistled driving home. He'd call Sweeney first thing.

CHAPTER ELEVEN

EXHAUSTED BUT EAGER TO SEE HER SON, JILLIAN WAITED FOR him in the living room and admired her sofa. She remembered the first time she sat there. Trent's insurance agency had a big year, and they moved to Prospect Heights. After their beds, this sofa was her first purchase. She rubbed its soft suede surface, glad she majored in creative design.

Her degree led to work with a prestigious designer. After Decker was born, she left to start her own business. It grew by word-of-mouth until she had a thriving enterprise.

When they moved to Prospect Heights after Casey was born, business exploded to the point where she had to cut back. She barely managed to service the clients she had. But she was thankful. Hopefully, she could maintain the energy to sustain it.

She inhaled deeply and walked to the tall bookcase with its gleaming wood and glass front. She scrolled titles, proud that she and Deck had read most of them. The exquisite case was a fitting backdrop to hold ideas and treasures precious to them.

She strolled to the glass tables by the sofa with

photographs of the boys when they were little. Reflections off the glass accentuated their innocent beauty. Eight-year-old Decker loved school and was eager to learn. In this school district, high-achieving parents wanted the best for their children. Decker's brother Casey, about to be four, would start kindergarten and grow up in the neighborhood.

Trent was more interested in golfing at the San Antonio Country Club than he was in his sons' educations, but she supposed both were possible. They entertained Trent's insurance prospects at home, and he bragged about whatever new piece of furniture she found. This room was especially inviting with its gleaming book display case, inviting upholstered furniture, and glass-topped tables.

Casey never reached four. She crossed her hands against her chest to contain the ache. He toddled away to a neighbor's pool. It was too long before they found him.

Trent began to lose clients, and the insurance agency suffered. She shook her head, sadness replacing the smile. Her gaze moved to the lamp table that held the last item she bought for their home: a bronze miniature statue of two young boys playing.

After Casey died, Trent resented her buying anything for the house. For him, the house completed their family and validated his success, his shield against the competition of the world. Without their foursome, the house lost its luster. He couldn't stand it when she wanted to embellish it.

For her, the house grew in importance. Her home was the one thing she could cling to and make her own. With her family in disarray, she invested in other people's homes, feeding off integration and harmony, and comforted by her connection to clients.

Enough self-pity. Decker would be home soon. She pushed off the sofa and walked to the kitchen.

After the coach said Decker might be college baseball

material, Trent started practicing with him. She was thankful and amazed. Never having played baseball, Trent searched You Tube for major league players giving online tips. He found a slew of informative videos and coached Decker, who was so glad to have his dad's help, he'd have practiced for hours. Things between them were better for a while. When school started in January, Decker would practice with the team.

She and Trent reached the point where they either squabbled or didn't communicate at all, and he moved out. She took a deep breath. She and Trent let Casey and each other down. She couldn't let Decker down. Being a mom overrode everything.

When the kitchen door slammed, she jumped. Decker burst in smiling.

She gathered herself and stood, expectant. "How is Mr. Conahan?"

"He seems okay. A lot sharper than I expected. He used to play baseball, so we had stuff to talk about. Maybe he'll be all right."

"And your English test?"

"Not so good. I'm starving." She followed him toward the refrigerator and sat at the kitchen table.

He reached inside the refrigerator and grabbed the milk. "I screwed up. Couldn't remember some of the stuff I read." He poured the milk, gulped it down and peered inside the fridge to see what else was available. "Is this chicken dinner for me?"

She nodded. "I brought it home for you from Church's. I understand about the test, Decker. It's hard to remember details when you're under stress."

He didn't reply. He zapped the fries in the microwave and tore into the chicken.

"Are you and your dad practicing baseball tomorrow?"

"No. I'm going to call Sweeney. I'll eat a burger later with Dad."

"I'm glad." She watched him devour the dinner. At least his appetite was still good.

His stomach finally full, he leaned back and closed his eyes. "I'm beat, Mom. I'm going to hit the sack."

"Me too. I love you, Deck. Things will get better. Your baseball uniform is clean. It's hanging in your closet."

"Thanks, Mom. I love you too."

CHAPTER TWELVE

DECKER SLEPT LATE BEFORE EATING A LAZY BREAKFAST WITH his mom.

"It's nice not having to rush," she said. "I've got a pile of work today, drawing plans and pulling fabric samples to show a new client. This project might be a major boost for us, Deck."

He loved seeing her excited about her work.

She covered his hand with her small one. "I hate it that we can't do more fun things together."

"It's okay, Mom. I've got a little homework. Since Coach called our first baseball meeting for Monday, Sweeney and I need to practice drills this afternoon. I'll show him some of the drills Dad taught me."

"That's good, Deck. That's good. I'm going out with clients for dinner."

He hoped one of them wasn't the dirt bag he followed from the Broadway Cafe.

Decker liked going to his buddy's house. It didn't look as beautifully planned as Mom arranged theirs, but the Sweeneys' furniture was plushy and soft, stuffed with something he sank into. Sweeny's younger brother and two sisters bounded all over the place, chasing, running, and laughing like animated bouncing balls.

He remembered tussling around on the floor with Casey when they were little. He wasn't that much bigger than Casey, but he felt like he was. He was careful not to hurt him. Dad chased them around the house, acting like a monster.

In the background, Mom would call, "Be careful, boys. Don't hit the glass tables." At some point, she wrapped them all in a giggly hug.

Decker never felt happier than when he was enveloped in their cocoon. His family was everything. He couldn't bear to lose it.

Sweeney's mom, plump and cushy like the furniture, wore a satisfied smile as though she breathed better in the middle of chaos. If Sweeney's dad was home, he'd be whistling or singing, cheerfully fixing something that was broken, teasing Mrs. Sweeney or one of the kids, concocting some weird combination for lunch, or looking for a ball to toss around with the kids after they ate. Mrs. Sweeney loved his teasing. They all did. It was the kind of pandemonium Decker remembered at his house, not the silent disharmony they endured.

No wonder Frank Sweeney usually smiled or looked like he was about to. He had unruly, sandy hair flecked with red, and freckles that faded in winter, popped to life in spring, and spread in patches during summer. He was tall like Decker, but when he played ball, his body was tight and purposeful.

The only gangly things about him were his arms, long and rubbery when he fielded balls. Right before he made an amazing throw, he tucked them to his tight body. After making a great throw, Sweeney laughed like it was a delightful surprise. He seemed to think life itself was a series of unexpected marvels.

Mr. Sweeney and the kids were flipping a ball around the front yard when Decker pulled up to their house. The trees were bare and most of the leaves were still on the lawn.

He remembered Dad tossing a football to him and Casey. They rarely caught it, but if Decker caught it, he'd give it to Casey to toss back. Sometimes Casey would dive into a pile of leaves seconds before it was his turn to catch the ball. Decker would tear in after him. Dad would come roaring after them like some lion and they'd thrash around in the leaves until they were all exhausted.

The Sweeney kids had varying shades of red and blond hair and fewer freckles as they descended in age, as though freckles had been sprinkled on top of Frank and scattered as they landed on the other kids. The three-year-old reminded him of Casey.

"Hey, Deck," Sweeney shouted. "You ready to go to the field?"

"Yeah. Get your stuff." He waved. "Hey, Mr. Sweeney."

"How're you doing, Decker? I can't wait for you guys to start playing."

"Me too, Mr. Sweeney."

If only Dad was as enthusiastic. Dad always wanted him to play football. When Decker made varsity, he finally got excited. He started watching the Padres' major leaguer Matt Antonelli illustrate infield drills on YouTube and offered to work with him to practice Antonelli's drills. Over the holidays, they used the Olmos Park Fields.

Frank Sweeney came loping up to the car, threw his gear into the back, and jumped in beside Decker. "You going to show me those Antonelli moves?"

"He's got some pretty good drills. We can try them."

As varsity players, they didn't have to try out.

Decker remembered how excited he was to make varsity as a junior. He had wanted to play varsity ball since he was six. He played second base. The coach hinted that if he played well, he might have a chance to play college ball.

He turned on the radio and lowered the windows halfway. Sweeney leaned back, closed his eyes and let music and crisp air roll across his face, his arms rubbery and limp, the wind flipping his hair.

Remembering Dad's intensity when they practiced, Decker smiled. They interacted as father and son for the first time since the bleak years after Casey died.

He remembered Dad's expression when he said. "Kneel on the turf about six inches back from where the turf meets the dirt. Now, lean forward over the dirt so you can field ground balls without a glove. I'll roll you a jillion balls. The idea is to feel the ball roll on to the index finger of your left hand every time. Cover the ball with your right hand, then bring it back to the same place at the middle of your chest, elbows up, and think how you'll position your feet to make the throw."

They repeated the move a hundred times, another hundred with Decker keeping his glove flat, a hundred more with Decker cupping his glove. Antonelli said the idea was to imprint "fielding the ball over your index finger until scooping up a ground ball was automatic."

Dad never tired. Decker thought he could field any ball coming toward him.

He wished marriages worked that way. *You do this, I do that, and from then on, it's automatic—everything is bound to work.*

When Dad leaned down, Decker caught sight of a bald spot the size of a quarter on the top of his head. It was hard to imagine his father getting old.

When Casey was there, Dad seemed perpetually young. After Casey was gone, time leaped ahead for his father. Life itself divided into BCD and ACD, before and after Casey died.

His parents' bickering escalated last fall when school started. After the Christmas holidays, Dad moved out. Decker knew it was coming. He tried to ignore the new hole growing inside of him and concentrate on baseball. With Dad gone, he needed a steady practice partner. His pal Sweeney fielded a lot of balls at third base.

They pulled up to Olmos Park Field.

"Let's do it," Sweeney said. They spotted a vacant field and took their gear to the outfield behind second and third.

"Okay, here's the deal," Decker said. "I roll you a bunch of ground balls. You bend down to scoop the ball imprinting it over your index finger. Bring it mid-chest every time, elbows out, thumbs down, ready to throw left, right, or straight to a base."

Sweeney grinned. "You going to go shag all the balls I miss?" He walked a few yards away, spread his legs, and bent slightly forward, hands out, ready to scoop Decker's grounders. Decker threw him a low ball. As Sweeney swooped the ball to his chest, Decker called out a base. Sweeney reared back, ready to throw.

Every time he planted his feet, Sweeney smiled, as if he knew the ball would go precisely where he threw it. Decker rolled ball after ball to Sweeney, left, right, hard, short, or right at his feet.

Watching Sweeney move to the ball and scoop it up was like watching a dance—every step purposeful, graceful, perfectly executed.

"You look like a damn dancer," Decker said.

"Right," Sweeney said. "I bet you can dance." He started drilling balls around Decker's feet.

Decker jumped out of the way and started laughing.

"Ready for me to roll you some?" Sweeney said.

"Yeah." He took his stance. After fielding twenty or thirty

balls, he thought he was coming close to Sweeney's fluidity. He was sweating when they finished.

"Guess we ought to bat a few," Sweeney said.

"Yeah."

Sweeney took the pitcher's mound with Decker in the batter's box.

"Down the middle," Sweeney called, pitching Decker a ball high and inside. If Decker pulled the ball to right or left field, Sweeney called out "middle" until Decker hit two or three drives straight down center field.

Sweeney mixed up his instructions and varied his pitches, so Decker never knew what was coming. At least he had an idea of what to prepare for and could adjust, unlike what was happening in his life.

They switched places and pitched and batted until both were worn out. It was great.

"Doubtful we'll make the majors," Decker said.

"Yeah, but we'll do okay Monday when the new guys are there."

"Know anything about them?"

"Only that they're supposed to be all-district infielders moving here from New Braunfels." He shrugged. "Maybe it's hearsay."

"Great." Decker sure didn't need some hotshot fielder vying for second base. This was his only chance. They walked the field picking up practice balls and hauled them to the car. Rolling down the windows, they sang with George Strait until they pulled up to Sweeney's house.

"Come on in," he said. "Dad gets fried chicken every Saturday. There'll be plenty."

Decker followed him inside. He smelled chicken the whole time he was washing up. He and Sweeney were last to sit at the big table.

"Welcome, Decker. Let's give thanks," Mr. Sweeney said."

They grabbed hands around the table. When Sweeney took Decker's hand, he realized Sweeney was the closest thing he had to a brother. The closest he'd ever have. He ached to hug Casey.

When Mom and Dad grew apart, they hardened like concrete pillars at both sides of a locked gate. He was outside the gate, and Mom and Dad were too solidified by grief and memories to open it.

Mr. Sweeney prayed for their family and friends, their health, their wisdom to make good choices, thanked God for their food, and said "Amen."

Decker was glad the prayer was short. During a longer one, he might have teared up. He looked around the table. Everybody was smiling or laughing. They all talked at once, but nobody seemed to mind. It was disorganized, loving, wonderful chaos. Decker could hardly bear it.

After lunch, he and Sweeney helped Mrs. Sweeney clean up the kitchen while the little kids raced outside to play. Mr. Sweeney and Frank's brother Todd stretched out on the sofas and turned on TV to watch sports.

"You want to hang out? Watch TV?" Sweeney said.

"No. I think I've had enough noise."

Sweeney stared at him, puzzled. "What? What did you say?"

"I've had enough noise for one day. Thanks for the chicken. I need to go home where it's quiet."

Sweeney shook his head and followed him outside. As Decker plodded toward the Mustang, he felt Sweeney's eyes on his back. He turned the key in the ignition, knowing Sweeney still had a puzzled look on his face. Mixed with hurt.

Decker couldn't explain. He only knew he had to leave.

CHAPTER THIRTEEN

DECKER DROVE HOME AND THREW HIS STUFF ON HIS BED. WHEN he came downstairs, his mother was all dolled up, her auburn hair flipped up at the ends.

"Wow, Mom. You look fantastic."

"I have to look my best." She whirled around. "Otherwise, clients wonder how I'm going to make their houses look better." She kissed his cheek. "We're going to Biga on the Banks."

"Big deal, huh?"

"Yes. Downtown on the River Walk."

"Dad and I are meeting at What-A-Burger."

"Okay. That works. Gotta' run. See you tonight." She sashayed through the kitchen. "Don't forget to lock up when you leave."

After he checked his email and showered, he slid into his Mustang and drove to What-A-Burger on Walzem Road near Dad's apartment. He recognized Dad's white Ford 150 pickup at the back of the lot, parked and walked inside. Dad waved to him from a booth.

"Hey, son." He stood and hugged Decker.

Dad hadn't hugged him since he was a little kid. It felt good.

He slapped Decker on the shoulder. "You're getting big... look like a football player."

Maybe the football/baseball barrier would eventually crumble. Decker let the remark ride and slid into the booth.

"How's baseball? Have you started practice?"

"Coach called the first meeting for Monday. There's supposed to be two guys transferring in from New Braunfels. One of them plays second base."

His father leaned forward and frowned. "You're not going to let some interloper push you out, are you?"

"No, sir." Decker hoped it didn't happen.

"That's my boy." Dad settled back. "Let's get something to eat." They settled on Double Meat What-A-Burger meals. Despite eating three pieces of chicken at Sweeney's, polishing off a burger was easy.

"Sorry I couldn't practice with you today," Dad said, chewing. "Had some paperwork to catch up on." He attacked the burger like he hadn't eaten in a week.

"It's okay. Sweeney and I practiced. We used some of those drills you taught me from YouTube."

Dad looked up from his burger. "No kidding. That's great. What did he think of them?"

"He liked them."

"Is baseball practice at three on Monday?"

"Four-thirty."

"You'll work on hitting and fielding?"

"Probably."

"I'll come watch. I want to size up this loser from New Braunfels."

"You don't need to watch practice, Dad. Won't you be working?"

"I can take off a couple hours." He chomped the last of his burger. "How's your mom doing?"

"She's working a lot. Her client list is growing. It keeps her real busy."

"She likes to work. Keeps her from sitting around moping."

"I don't think she's moping, Dad."

"Well, that's good. You want to come check out my pad?"

"Sure." He and Dad never talked about how they felt, what they believed, what they hoped for. Except when Dad urged him to play football.

He followed Dad's pickup down Walzem, a wide, busy, thoroughfare with small businesses huddled together in clumps of strip malls, one after another. Behind the commercial area, lines of apartment complexes ribboned the street on both sides like never-ending railroad tracks. They wound back to the second group of apartments.

Dad called out the window. "Park anywhere. I have to park in my slot. Meet me upstairs at 237."

Decker trudged up the steps. The wood buildings reminded him of a ski lodge in Winter Park where they went as a family, sturdy but well worn. The deck he walked on leading to 237 needed re-staining. He imagined an ad for the place. "Come home to Tanglegrove Glen, where comfort doesn't cost much."

Dad stood in the doorway. "Welcome to my pad. It ain't fancy, but it's home."

When he walked into his father's living room, sadness overwhelmed him. A worn, matching sofa, chair, and rickety coffee table sat across from a television squatting on cheap tweed carpet. The room smelled musty. Every piece of furniture looked like it had been abandoned and would never be reclaimed.

To the left, a Formica table and two chairs flanked a galley kitchen with vinyl floors. Empty beer bottles and a fifth of Jack Daniels lined up by the sink.

"My bedroom is in there."

Decker crossed the living room and peered through the door. A queen bed hunkered on the same crummy carpet. Blinds in the only window were overlaid with cheap-looking curtains hanging from a bent brass rod. "You even made the bed."

Dad stuffed his hands in his pockets and grinned. "Yeah. Well, special occasion."

Unkempt compared to his old self, he still had the winsome smile and demeanor that won people over.

On the bedside table was a picture of him in his football uniform. The other frame held an old photo of Mom and Dad looking incredibly young. He looked away.

A used desk and chair crouched under the window, the desk scattered with papers. A two-drawer metal cabinet leaned against the desk.

"Are those your business files?"

Dad stuck his hands in his pockets. "I work at home now. It's more convenient."

Decker studied him. "What about your office?"

"I really don't need it. Insurance clients don't know where you're calling from."

"But it was nice, a few steps down the corridor from Mr. Hall." Hall Insurance Company owned the building, and Dad was the company's chief operating officer. He wouldn't have had to pay rent.

"You had more space and a secretary, and you were close to our house and the club where you play golf."

Dad's hands flew up like he was warding off painful facts he'd already fought through. "I don't need those things anymore, Decker. I go to the club occasionally if somebody asks me to play. It's not that far."

His father was delighted when his friend got him into the San Antonio Country Club. He must have forfeited his membership.

"That's a shame, Dad."

"Things happen." Dad shrugged.

Like losing a son, splitting with your wife, leaving your home, losing most of your business. Which things randomly happened, and which did a person cause?

Dad pointed to the door off the bedroom. "Bathroom's in there."

"Okay." The sink was stained from whatever Dad last poured into it. The wall-hung glass medicine cabinet had a comb, brush, deodorant, toothbrush, paste, and a razor. When Decker returned to the living room, Dad was sprawled on the sofa, feet propped on the scratched coffee table, slugging a beer while he watched TV.

"Sit down," Dad said. "This is a pretty good sofa." He patted it. "Comfortable for sleeping. I've slept here a few nights. You can stay over sometime and try it out."

"Sure." Decker plopped into the matching chair. He wondered if Dad drank himself into stupors and passed out on the couch. He had tossed a blanket over the sofa arm.

"They're showing highlights from this afternoon's NFL's Senior Bowl. Top college seniors and some juniors get to showcase their talent in front of NFL scouts, coaches, and executives."

"That's super. A good opportunity." A couple scouts might watch their baseball practice on Monday. Spring practice was a big deal. Members of the faculty came to watch. When practice was well underway, colleges always sent scouts. If his grades didn't get better, baseball might be his only route to college.

Dad went to the kitchen and returned with another beer. "It's the only football game on today. I looked. The Senior

Bowl unofficially kicks off draft season." He swigged his beer. "It's the last time NFL teams get to watch their top prospects play. You want a beer? You're almost nineteen. Close enough."

"That's okay, Dad. I'm pretty full. I told Mom I'd be home when she got there, so I better head out."

"Oh, yeah? Where'd she go?"

"Biga on the Banks, a restaurant on the River Walk. She's with clients."

"Hmm. Much be rich clients."

"I guess." When he rose to leave, Dad lumbered to stand. Decker leaned over and squeezed his shoulder. "I'll let myself out, Dad. Thanks for the burger."

As Decker plodded to his car, he saw a few people emerge from vehicles, home late after work. They looked tired. Most of them drove pickups, none of them new and shiny. *How many singles from broken families existed behind these dry wood walls?*

He pulled back onto Walzem and headed home. Apartments had sprung up everywhere in San Antonio, but down Walzem Road, apartment units continued for miles. *Were these batches of apartments temporary lodgings or interminable tracks to nowhere?*

He wanted to get home before Mom did. Maybe he'd learn something about her clients. He hoped one of them wasn't the creep he followed. If he was, it would be easy to check him out.

CHAPTER FOURTEEN

TRENT SAVAGE WATCHED MORE SENIOR GAME HIGHLIGHTS. Several kids were amazingly skilled. They'd be drafted for sure. He realized Decker was disappointed with his apartment, but he didn't think it was so bad. He swigged his beer.

Decker and Jillian knew if it wasn't for the football scholarship, his family couldn't afford to send him to UT-Austin. Even so, he had to work at some menial job every summer.

Fortunately, he was smart enough to keep up his grades. But he had to struggle like crazy. When he pledged the jock fraternity, he couldn't afford a car or partying like the other guys.

He closed his eyes and pictured the University of Texas campus. Big imposing buildings. Huge trees. Self-satisfied frat boys in cool clothes strutting across campus like the Lion King on Daddy's money. Fortunately, jocks got away with a lot in the fashion department. He would remind himself he was lucky to be there at all and head for football practice.

He made another trip to the refrigerator and grabbed a cold beer. He had tried to explain to Decker how valuable it was to play football, but the boy wasn't interested. He wiped his hand across his mouth.

Baseball wasn't cool. It was slow. Dull. Not much physical contact. He loved tackling. He shrugged and plopped back on the sofa. He hoped baseball worked out for Decker. A scholarship might be his only ticket. The kid was smart, but his grades weren't great.

He sure couldn't pay Decker's college tuition. His assets were kaput. He paid half the mortgage on their house and would probably lose it in the divorce. Jillian had already filed.

He managed to put most of the money he borrowed back into the company's reserve fund, but premiums for new policies weren't coming in. To bring in business, he had to continually rally agents to sell, and he hadn't been up to it. Jillian was making money, but she wasn't likely to share it with him.

Slogging to the bedroom, he picked up their dating picture and thought about how he met her. At a Friday night mixer with the Zetas, she looked like the girls in Vogue magazine his sister read. Slender. Regal. Shimmering auburn hair streaked with gold in the summer. Blue-green saucer eyes. And sweet. Oh, so sweet. So as not to scare her off, he took his time with her.

So she wouldn't long for dates with affluent guys, they did fun stuff, like driving twenty-five miles in a friend's borrowed car to eat the "World's Best Apple Pie" or watching planes land and take off from the airport and imagining where passengers were going and why. He chuckled at how inventive he'd been.

She was impressed that in addition to playing football, he had a job. Most guys she dated attended law school or medical school or were going for finance degrees to be investment bankers with their fathers paying for their education. He couldn't afford any more school.

If he managed to graduate from UT with a business

degree and emphasized his jock status, he might get a decent job and make some money, enough, he hoped, to win Jillian and keep up with her sorority sisters and his frat pals.

He wandered back to the sofa to check on the game. After graduation, he studied to get his real estate license. A well-known firm wanted to hire him, and licensing was a prerequisite. He passed the exam and started selling real estate. When a jock friend taught him to play golf, he took to it easily and impressed his friend's country club crowd. He smiled recalling their expressions as they watched him play.

When it looked like he and Jillian were a sure thing and set a wedding date, he got a job offer from the father of his buddy's friend, a guy who owned an insurance company. His agents sold medical insurance, life insurance, and liability insurance to building contractors. Things were looking up.

Since he was new to the business, he had to borrow money to contribute a buy-in. He figured he could sell a substantial amount of insurance, enough that the premium income he earned would cancel the buy-in.

Of course, there was the perpetual temptation to play golf with his friends, which took a lot of time. He took a swig of his beer. He couldn't believe the company suggested he work his way up to Chief Operating Officer. He had no idea what to study for that.

One buddy suggested he join the San Antonio Country Club and got him in. The initiation fee nearly broke him, but after a lot of rounds of golf, some of the guys bought insurance from him. He leaned his head back on the sofa and closed his eyes, remembering how the commissions rolled in. He thought he had it made. Easy job, beautiful wife, and a slew of golfing buddies. He got up and started for his bedroom closet to grab a club and practice his swing. He hit a couple balls toward a cup but stopped and returned to the sofa. He couldn't hit squat.

At least they were able to buy a house in Prospect Heights and put the kids in a good school. They liked inviting his buddies and their wives over to show off their house. Jillian decorated it tastefully, and her beauty and charm were always a hit. The Texas economy was on the rise, so business grew, and his premium income increased.

Some insurance policy premiums were set by the State Board of Insurance, so that made it easy. He wasn't sure how other rates were set. He'd quote a rate, and most of the time they'd pay it. He only knew that when he sold policies, he received commissions.

The boss knew how to run the company, and he reaped the benefits. Sure enough, he worked his way up to Chief Operating Officer, second only to the boss' son, CEO Stephen Hall.

Then the company president died unexpectedly. A real punch to the gut. Trent slouched on the sofa. He found himself in charge of company finances and virtually on his own. He didn't know what to do. He was a full-fledged member of San Antonio's high society with a large house and plenty of bills.

After a few months of dwindling income, he could hardly afford to play golf at SACC, much less pay the monthly dues.

He got up and started to pace. He started borrowing funds from the insurance company's reserve fund, at first, a small amount. It was only temporary, and he planned to pay it back.

The bills kept coming. Then Casey died, and the bottom fell out. Trent put his head in his hands. He couldn't pull himself out of depression.

When Jillian recovered enough to want to be with friends, he never felt like going. His response caused a rift. He'd be remote and silent the next day or fuss at her for spending too much money. They didn't agree on anything, and the distance between them grew.

He grabbed the beer off the table and gulped. Fate hadn't been kind to him. Some guys had all the luck. At least Decker hung out with him. He would be sure to make ball practice Monday.

He meandered to the window and gazed out. Cars were tucked in slots except for one parked near the fence, a Mazda. He'd always liked that model. He squinted. The windows were tinted. Was somebody in it? Why was he sitting here? Waiting for somebody? He stepped out onto the walkway to study the Mazda. As he turned toward the steps, the Mazda made a U-turn and rolled toward the exit.

Trent turned back to his apartment to get his keys. He needed to buy more beer.

CHAPTER FIFTEEN

He cruised down Walzem Road.

Damn, he liked driving this Mazda. He should make it a point to take it out and cruise someplace new every week. There wasn't much to look at in this area. Nothing but strip centers and apartments far as the eye could see.

If Trent Savage lived around here, he must have really gone to pot. He still couldn't believe she had any interest in Savage. He must have fooled her...hid who he really was. Guys who played football with him in high school said he was totally egocentric, more interested in showcasing himself than working with teammates. He did or said whatever he wanted...to hell with the effect it might have.

With college girls, he was Mr. Charming. They swarmed around him, reinforcing his distorted view of himself. He thought with his looks and charm, he could have almost anything. For the most part, he was right. Several girls liked him, but he had to choose Jillian.

Savage wanted to be the center of everything. The star. As long as everything went his way, he was amiable and charismatic. When it didn't, he was insufferable. With women, he played the reticent, sweet, somewhat needy guy, an insecure but kind, jovial fellow they wanted to mother. What a crock.

This was the right block. He must be getting close. There it was, Tanglegrove Glen. He pulled into a section of apartment units and looked around. Lines of two-story unpainted wood apartments all looked alike.

He'd found Savage's address earlier and drove slowly up to the first building looking for numbers. This was the 100s section. He cruised back to the 200's. There it was on the top floor, 237. Savage's domicile. Sure, was different from his fancy house in Terrell Hills.

Why did he bother to come here? Maybe to size the guy up after all these years. He wasn't sure Savage was even here, and he didn't know what kind of car he drove. Knowing where he lived didn't solve anything, but somehow it made him feel better. Maybe he should follow Savage home one day. Anything could happen.

He parked near the outside fence between the two rows of units, cut the engine and sat in his car awhile, thinking what he might do. He got bored and decided he could ponder better at home with a drink. He started the engine and wheeled the car around toward Walzem. In his rear-view mirror, he saw Savage standing on the walkway, watching him.

CHAPTER SIXTEEN

DECKER WAS IN HIS PAJAMAS WATCHING TV WHEN MOM breezed through the front door and sashayed into the den, flushed and bouncy. He hadn't seen her this happy for a long time.

"Wow. You must have had a great evening."

"I did, Deck. Fabulous place." She took off her heels and put them on the table by the sofa. "The food was delicious. I had Red Snapper Pontchartrain."

"Sounds fantastic, whatever it is."

She threw her head back and laughed.

"So, who was there?"

"Two couples and their friend who builds homes. Laura Handy invited me. She's the one who hired me to decorate their house. Her husband is a lawyer. Her friends, the Parsons, might be interested in my help decorating the home they're building!"

"That's great, Mom. And the builder?"

"He and his partner built the Handy's home and are constructing the Parsons'."

She was practically bouncing off the walls. "He also builds spec homes in The Dominion."

"Is that good?"

She stepped toward him, her eyes growing huge. "The Dominion is full of million-plus dollar homes, Deck. He builds a slew of homes out there. He's already sold four houses. What if he recommends me to decorate all of them?"

"That's fantastic, Mom. What's his name?"

"Michael Connelly." She wiggled her toes. "No. Wait. That's the mystery writer. It's Michael Cunningham. That's it. Mike Cunningham."

Decker went on alert. The man's name was similar to Mitchell Conahan. He tried to appear casual. "What does he look like?"

She cocked her head to one side. "Michael? I don't know, Decker. Average height, a little shorter than you. Brown hair. About Dad's age, I guess."

"His wife didn't come?"

"He didn't say if he had one." She raised her eyebrows. "This wasn't a date, Deck. It was a get-acquainted business dinner."

"No, right. I get it. I just wondered."

"Since I'm decorating Laura Handy's house, she invited him. As their builder, he checks out interior designers to help clients who want decorating help." She sat beside him and glanced at the TV. "What are you watching?"

"Some stupid sitcom. Dad and I had a good time. He's still into football and beer. His apartment isn't the greatest, but he's doing okay. He might come to our first practice on Monday."

"I'm glad, Decker." She yawned.

"Bet you're ready to hit the sack," he said. "Why don't you sleep late in the morning? We can have breakfast whenever you get up."

She sighed and closed her eyes. "That sounds perfect. You're the best." She reached over and hugged him. "I love you, Deck. We're all going to be all right."

"I know, Mom."

She grabbed her shoes and walked back toward the stairs. He followed as far as the kitchen.

"I'm getting some milk, Mom. I'll turn off the lights."

"Good night, Deck."

———

THEY SLEPT UNTIL TEN O'CLOCK SUNDAY MORNING. WHEN THEY meandered downstairs, Jillian got a bowl to stir her pancake mix and plugged in her waffle iron. They stuffed themselves with homemade waffles.

"I think this will hold me until dinner," He grinned. "Maybe."

"Me too. I'll be working with Annabelle Parsons' plans all afternoon—pulling furniture catalogues and fabric samples to give her ideas about the home Michael is building for them. She gave me a copy of the plans. They're in my car."

"It's great to see you so excited."

She leaned toward him and held out her hands like she was holding a world globe. "This could be it, Deck. The big push we need to be financially stable. I could help you with college. If Michael likes what I do for the Parsons, I might decorate a ton of houses in The Dominion."

He was already sick of hearing about Michael Cunningham. Mom couldn't stop talking about him. He reminded himself the man probably had no connection to Mr. Conahan.

"I'll clean up and let you get to work." He carried dishes to the sink. "I've got some reading and computer work to do. Then I want to go see Mr. Conahan."

She bounced into the garage to retrieve house plans from her car and pranced through the kitchen waving blueprints. "See?"

She spread the plans on the dining room table and held down corners with furniture catalogues and fabric sample books, humming. She used to hum, fixing dinner while he and Casey played on the floor.

He walked over to look at the plans. "Wow. That's one big house." She nodded, smiling. Decker pecked her on the cheek. "Have fun, Mom."

He raced upstairs to his computer and found what he needed in the *Dictionary of American Family Names*. The name Conahan was Irish, "a reduced Anglicized form of the Gaelic O'Connachain, Cunningham." Conahan and Cunningham were the same name—altered when an Irishman came to America. He had a lead. They could be related. Maybe they met at some group for Irishmen. He drilled his fingers on the table.

Cunningham probably noticed his mom around, heard she was separated from Dad, and asked Laura Handy to invite him to dinner. He might have told Laura he planned to meet with Mom privately to discuss her decorating approach. He pushed back from the desk and swiveled around to stare at his bookshelf on the opposite wall.

Meeting Mom at the Broadway Cafe was a strange way to impress somebody, but men did strange things. Especially predators. He didn't know why the jerk would go to Conahan's house in the middle of the night. He had to determine if these men had a connection.

He swung back to the keyboard, Googled San Antonio Custom Home Builders and found their website, Cunningham and Sloan. No pictures of the men were on the site. He'd never seen the face of the man he followed, so how would he recognize him anyway? He might have captured his image with the phone, but it was dark, and the man was moving.

Decker looked at other builders' websites to see if they included owners' pictures. They did not. He wrote down Cunningham and Sloan's business address. Maybe he should pay them a visit. He threw up his hands. Thinking there was a connection between Conahan and Cunningham was a long shot, but he didn't know where else to search.

He needed to find his phone, but first, he wanted to go to the hospital. If Mr. Conahan was okay, he'd try to glean information about this guy with the similar name.

Decker grabbed the mail he retrieved after school from Conahan's mailbox and headed out.

CHAPTER SEVENTEEN

HE SHOULDN'T HAVE STARTED DRIVING BY HER HOUSE.

It might foul up everything. He'd already called her a couple times and hung up. He didn't know what to say.

He made sure he cruised by at random times, usually after dark, to check on her. If he parked, it would be in a secluded spot and not for long. If another car drove slowly down the street, he'd start the engine and, after a reasonable time, pull in behind. Since Trent had moved to the place on Walzem, he wouldn't be a problem.

He watched her emerge from her house one night and followed. He realized she was going downtown. and tailed her to Biga's Restaurant. He found a parking spot and managed to slip inside the restaurant before she arrived.

He asked for a secluded table in the back, studied the expensive décor, and brooded about why he originally asked her to meet him at that crummy diner, a kids' hangout with loud music. He doubted she'd ever set foot in there.

When the waiter came up, looking snooty, he decided he better order something that would last a while.

"*Calamari as an appetizer,*" *he said,* "*and a Long Vodka.*" *Both arrived quicker than he expected, and he sampled.*

He'd about decided he made a terrible mistake when she came through the door. His breath caught. She was as beautiful as she was in college.

The only change he noticed was that her skin looked taut. Her eyes had developed a permanently thoughtful look. She was worried about her boy. The more she talked at the diner about her grief and hinted at Trent's self-absorption after their younger son died, the more his anger welled up. When he couldn't stand it anymore, he blasted out of the diner. It was time he took care of business. Find out once and for all what he desperately needed to know

At Biga's, he watched the two couples and the single man who was obviously flirting with her. Who was he?

He positioned himself so she couldn't see him and settled in to watch the party. Jillian was vulnerable now. It wouldn't take much for some sweet-talking SOB to lure her in. Where would she and the boy be then? He needed to carefully plan his next move.

CHAPTER EIGHTEEN

DECKER STOPPED AT THE SIXTH-FLOOR NURSES' STATION. "Is Mr. Conahan okay?"

"He's doing very well." She grinned. "He's getting cranky. Go on in, Corey."

He was glad she said his name. He'd forgotten. He remembered some critic saying *Huckleberry Finn* was the best liar in literature. He might top him. He hurried to 627 and knocked.

Conahan sputtered, coughed, and barked, "Who's that? Come in."

He craned his head around the door frame. "Hi, Mr. Conahan. Is this a bad time?"

"Come in, son." The blinds were open with weak sunlight seeping in. The room smelled fresh, not so much like a hospital. "I've been remembering some of those unwritten rules in baseball."

"That's awesome, sir."

He looked closer to seventy than eighty. His hair looked like it used to be bushy. Now it was thinning and mostly white. His eyes were penetrating. He had a big frame, boney with sharp points at his shoulders and elbows. Big scrawny feet stuck out from the bottom of the bed sheet.

"Sit over there, son." He pointed to the chair under the window. "You know not to ever step on the pitcher's mound when you enter or exit the field?"

He sat. "Yes, sir. Coach told us."

"And not to talk to the pitcher when he has a no-hitter going."

"We don't see many no-hitters in high school."

"I guess not but watch the major leaguers. When the pitcher's team is in the dugout and he's got a no-hitter going, say, at the seventh inning, he comes back to the dugout and sits at one end. Everybody else is down at the other end." He stretched one bony paw to his left, the other to the right.

"They don't want to talk to him and jinx him?"

"That's right. He'd really be pissed if somebody got chatty, broke his concentration, and he went back out on the mound and screwed up."

"I can see that. Did you toss baseballs with your kids when they were growing up?"

Conahan turned toward the window, sadness settling on his face. "No. I should have. I should have. I was constantly busy working."

Decker remembered all the flowers in Granddad's hospital room. The sweet smell nearly overpowered him. There were no flowers in this room. He had never seen any here. Four kids and no flowers?

"I mean when you had time to toss balls to them."

He turned back to Decker. "I was CEO of a Houston oil field service company. I never had time. Drilling was in full swing all over Texas. I thought if you made a lot of money and were important to a lot of people, it meant you must be loved. I was wrong about that." He looked back through the window.

Decker thought Conahan's eyes filled with tears, but nothing rolled down his cheeks. He needed to change the subject.

"Coach told us something else a while back—not to pimp a home run. I didn't know what he meant."

Conahan turned back toward Decker and grinned.

"He said not to sit there and stare at the ball you just hit," Decker added, "not to wave it goodbye—that kind of thing."

"Yeah. There's some major league player, can't remember his name, who flips his bat some kind of crazy way if he hits a homer." He shook his head. "He's a jerk."

"A showoff."

"Yeah. Teammates don't like it."

Decker didn't want to be cruel, but he had to find out about Cunningham. "Your kids probably watched games with you on TV? When you didn't have to work, I mean."

"The girls never cared about it. I watched with the boys occasionally. Until they moved away."

"None of them live here?

He looked out the window again. "They're scattered all over the place. I managed to push them away." He closed his eyes.

How could this man push his family away? He was lonely. Decker wanted to hug him and tell him it was okay. He reminded himself this wasn't his grandfather.

"Maureen married Doctor O'Brien, who went for training in Pennsylvania." He took a deep breath as if gaining strength to divulge painful truths. "They stayed there. Emma married Mark Stapleton. They met studying environmental science at UT and went to Colorado to save the planet. They work for some non-profit outfit." His lips curled into a wry expression. "It wasn't non-profit that paid for their educations."

"Nobody went into the oil field business?"

"Murray studied petroleum engineering and worked in

the Oklahoma oil fields for a while. Then he went back to school to study education. He decided he wanted to teach at some college. So I guess he's the closest." Conahan threw up his hands like he couldn't comprehend such a choice but had to accept it. "Patrick partied his way out of school and went to California to become a hippie."

He was disappointed in his kids, and they had to know it. Decker knew how that felt.

Gloom overtook Conahan as he gazed through the window.

"But you loved them."

Conahan nodded.

"If they knew you now, they would realize it."

"I guess so. I'd like to tell them." He shook his head. "I used to have all the answers. Now I don't have any."

The nurse pattered in, smiling. "You should probably rest, Mr. Conahan."

That was Decker's cue to leave. He'd have to come back to learn more. He cleared his throat. "Do you know somebody named Cunningham? Michael Cunningham?

Conahan pondered. "Yes. He used to play ball in Houston. We met once at a game. He's a lot younger than I am. I heard he came here to start a home building business, so when I decided to move here and buy a house, I hired him to update it before I moved in. He did a nice job. Ours was primarily a long-distance relationship."

"That's interesting. My mom knows someone with that name. It's a common name, though." He waited for a response, but nothing came. He stopped short of asking if Conahan knew his mother. If he hadn't given Conahan a false name, he might have asked.

He had to eliminate the remote possibility that Cunningham was connected to the man he followed, and whether he had some reason to do his mother harm. He steeled himself, then jumped in.

"Do you know my mother, Jillian Savage? That's the business name she uses." He held his breath.

"No, but I'd like to meet her. Lovely name."

Decker scrutinized his face. It held no hint of dishonesty. He exhaled. The nurse cleared her throat, his second cue to leave. He stood and moved toward the door. "It's nice talking to you, Mr. Conahan. I almost forgot. Here's your mail. I'd like to come sometime next week and let you know how practice is going."

"You do that, son. I'd like to hear." Conahan's eyes followed him out the door with the mail still lying on his stomach.

Decker strode to the parking lot, started the engine, and listened to the old motor rattle into action. He liked Mr. Conahan and didn't know a shred more about how to find his attacker.

Conahan's kids weren't even around to help. The creep might be somebody from his oil business who held a grudge, but he had no way to track him down. If he went to the police, they would contact Houston PD to investigate Conahan's associates. But he might implicate himself.

Why, with his kids scattered in other states, did Conahan move from Houston to San Antonio?

Decker pulled out of the parking lot. He could probably eliminate Cunningham, but he didn't know where to go from there. He was still following the mystery man around in the dark.

CHAPTER NINETEEN

DECKER HAD A HARD TIME CONCENTRATING ON ANYTHING IN class. Monday, January 30, was the first day of baseball. University Scholastic League rules made them wait until today to start practice.

After school, he raced home, grabbed snacks from the kitchen and barreled upstairs to suit up. He couldn't believe he forgot to put the uniform in his school locker. Brain fog. He sprinted back to his car and headed for Olmos Field. Their first meeting would include practice drills, and the coach would hand out the spring schedule of practice days, scrimmages, and games. This was it...finally...the game he loved...his chance to win a ticket to college.

Fresh air forecasted spring and invigorated his lungs. He jumped from the car and bounced toward the field, kicking the red dirt and breathing it in. He wanted to roll in it.

Near the dugout, his teammates grinned and horsed around giving fist bumps, high-fives, and slapping shoulders. He relished getting into the mix. He belonged here.

The new guys stood off to one side, grinning and shuffling their feet. One was slender and about his height, the other was chunky and a couple inches shorter. Which one would challenge him for second base?

Behind home plate, spectators crouched expectantly on bleachers behind the screen—diehard fans who relished Prospect Heights ball. Dad waved. He recognized other dads and faculty, including the vice-principal. At least one staff member attended the school events. There were several men he didn't recognize who could be faculty, parents, fans, or scouts. They all relished this season. This was the strongest team they'd had in four years.

Coach Branson checked his watch. "Okay. It's 4:30. Let's get started. Pick a place on the fence and warm up with your J bands. Get your legs loose. When you finish, start running bases."

The coach liked to place guys at least two deep at each position. Guys who lined up at first were "Speedy" Parker, who made Varsity as a junior, and backup, Jim Acorn. They were both good. Sweeney was at third with two guys behind him, junior Lenny Schwartz, and the tall guy from New Braunfels. He doubted either one could play like Sweeney. He put Trey Segura at shortstop.

Todd Messner, a kid he played ball with since fourth grade, lined up behind Decker, and behind him, the chunky New Braunfels guy. He wore his cap turned a little to the side. With hooded eyes and a thrust-out jaw, he reminded Decker of a turtle.

Coach Branson blew the whistle. "Go to your positions. We'll take ground balls with outfielders running the bases, and we'll try to get in some swings. Coach Scott will hit fungo, and we'll play it live with the runners."

Coach Scott hit a hard-line grounder to second. Decker darted right to read it. It fell short and took a bad hop to his left. Segura scooped it up, saw the coach signal to first base, and heaved it.

As Decker rotated to the back of the line, Turtle from New Braunfels smirked. "Gotta' watch those short hops, Duckfoot."

Decker sneered at him like he was a worm and lined up behind him. Coach Scott whacked a zinger to Todd. He drew it to his chest and fired it to third.

Turtle got a grounder with a weird hop. He scurried in, snatched it on the upward bounce and effortlessly threw it to first. Decker's stomach flipped. He hustled to the front of the line.

"You know yours will be a grounder that will try to eat you up," Turtle said. "Try not to muff it this time, Dumbass."

Decker felt blood coursing through his body. He told himself to calm down and focus on the ball. Coach Scott hit a fly. Decker ran to get under it, stumbled, and bobbled the ball. Off balance on his back foot, he rushed his throw to first, and Speedy had to leap two feet off the bag to retrieve it. Turtle turned his back. Decker knew he was laughing. He felt like grabbing the nearest ball and drilling him.

"One more round," Coach Branson shouted. On his way back to second, Decker glanced at Sweeney and pounded a fist into his glove. He hadn't mentioned his home turmoil. Sweeney gestured safe at base..."be cool."

Decker concentrated on the fluid moves he'd practiced and managed to shut Turtle out of his head. Coach's next grounder was a deep shot to the four holes. He got his feet under him, fielded it cleanly and drilled it to third.

"Okay," Coach said. "Outfielders to the cages. Infielders get ready for live batting practice on the field." They grabbed bats and started practice cuts. Decker tried to ignore Turtle, but the weirdo managed to get behind him in the batting line.

"Coach Eggars is going to pitch each of you three balls. Hit the first one to center field, the second to left, and the third to right."

Nearly every ball was hitting its target. His team was good. He trotted up to the plate. He got a good pitch and pulled it left of center. The next pitch was in front of the plate. He reached for it and popped it into foul territory. He was supposed to hit the next one to right field. He glanced to right field, and smoked it. On the mound, Coach Eggars ducked the line drive to his head. The center fielder came up to shag it near the infield dirt. He heard a voice behind him.

"When did right field mean center?" He knew who said it.

Pitching coach Eggars wiped his mouth, shuffled his feet on the mound, and straightened his cap. "Let's try another one, Decker," he said

He heard the voice behind him. "Hope you don't screw up again, Dimwit."

The ball came high and outside. He swung hard and missed. Anger welled up until he thought he would explode. He banged the bat to the ground, breathing hard. His forearms clenched, and he grabbed the bat and flung it backward. It whacked up against the backstop.

He realized what he'd done and spun around in horror. Behind the screen, spectators sat with eyes wide and mouths open. Faculty. Fathers. Scouts. Dad.

Coach Branson stormed toward him, his hat pulled down over his eyes. He growled through his teeth, trying to keep his voice down. "What do you think you're doing? What's the matter with you, Decker? We don't throw bats around here. Ever. You got that?"

He nodded.

"You got that?"

"Yes, sir. I'm sorry, sir." Tears backed up behind his eyes. If they leaked out on his face, he didn't want anybody to see. He was breathing hard, so hard. He blinked.

Coach Branson's voice changed. "You don't do crap like

that, Decker. I know you don't. Can you get your stuff together? We've got a team here, Decker."

"I know, sir. I'm sorry, sir. I'll get it together by Wednesday."

"Good." He nodded. "Good. By Wednesday. I'll count on it. I know you're going through rough times, Decker. We can get through this. We'll get through this."

"Yes, sir."

Coach Branson's voice softened. "Here's the schedule, son. We'll get through this."

"Yes, sir. Thank you, sir."

The coach turned to the field. "Come get your schedules. And be here Wednesday at four-thirty. Sharp."

CHAPTER TWENTY

THE KID MIGHT BE LOSING IT—HEAVING A BAT AT SPECTATORS THE first day of practice.

He could get kicked off the team for that. He must be seriously upset. By what? Did he follow the ambulance? Did he find out where the old guy was?

He had called the hospital himself and said he was an interested relative, Nate Gunderson. The nurse said the old fellow was in ICU, but that's all they would tell him. His heart probably acted up. That was the usual ailment of old age. He felt guilty—until he thought about the past. Anger engulfed him.

Maybe the old man improved, and the kid went to visit him. He told the boy about the attack and who he thought did it.

Should he make a personal trip to the hospital? He could not be fingered for trespassing and an attack. Not now. He didn't intend for the confrontation to come to that, but it didn't matter. A revelation like that would ruin his career. Might even land him in jail.

He had to change this kid's trajectory, but how?

CHAPTER TWENTY-ONE

THE COACH'S WORDS RANG IN DECKER'S EARS. HE MANAGED TO swallow tears that collected behind his eyes and clogged his throat. His face must be crimson. His back felt like hot steam rose from it. He hurled himself into the Mustang and slammed the door before anybody could talk to him.

He'd told Ashley he'd meet her after practice, but he was too roiled up to go home and change. He would probably see his mom, and he was so angry, he might say something he'd regret. He was an idiot to let that Turtle-faced kid get in his head. He played like a numbskull and acted worse.

Closing his eyes, he pushed his head back on the seat. Startled faces from people in the stands rolled across his eyelids. His heart pounded like a hammer. Could somebody have a heart attack at eighteen?

He decided to shower in the gym locker room. Cool water might calm him down. He pulled up to the gym, grabbed his clothes off the seat, and strode around the basketball court to the locker room. When he stomped in, three guys in towels turned around—the two guys from New Braunfels and Sweeney, his unruly hair standing up.

Guys on the team called Decker "skinny ass" and popped him on the arm or the butt. He'd make a joke, dress fast, and go. He was good at making jokes and moving fast enough to get out of there before they started pounding him. Today he didn't feel like making jokes.

"Well, if it ain't Screwup," Turtle said. "Did Coach kick you out yet, Doofus?"

Decker dropped his clothes on a bench and strode toward him like the Hulk, ready to destroy this weasel. He got in Turtle's face and snarled down through clenched teeth.

"You'd like that, wouldn't you, Asshole? My disappearing so you can teach your sorry ass how to play second base."

The guy's friend and Sweeney took a step toward them.

"It's not going to happen," Decker growled. "Not today. Not tomorrow. Not ever!" He was going to pummel the guy.

When he reared back to take a swing, Sweeney grabbed his arm. "The guy isn't worth it, Deck. Don't waste your energy. You're going to need that arm."

"Deck? I thought it was Dick." Turtle sensed his opportunity and swung a punch that landed under Decker's chin. Decker's neck snapped back.

Turtle's buddy grabbed his arm. "Hey, Pal. You gotta' make the team. This ain't the way. Don't louse it up."

Turtle shook him off and squinted reptile eyes at Decker. "Nice bat shot at the spectators, Screwup. By the way, anybody up there in the stands scouting for college ballplayers?"

Adrenalin welled up until Decker couldn't see anything but a tunnel to his loud mouth. He lowered his head and charged, butting Turtle in the chest. He grabbed him around the back and pulled him down. The guy was chunky and hard like a punching bag. They rolled on the cold concrete and tried to throw punches.

Decker's arms were longer. He landed a right to Turtle's

Adam's apple and a left to his cheek. He felt the guy's shoulder jerk, and a fist pounded into his right eye.

Turtle's friend and Sweeney jumped on top of them. Wet liquid rolled down his check. He curled his tongue around the taste of a rusty penny.

"Break it up! Break it up! You want to fix it so neither of you can play ball?" Sweeney's yell sounded far off like background noise.

Looking through his right eye, Decker could only distinguish shapes. He stopped flailing and rolled off Turtle. Between coughs, Turtle muttered obscenities. His buddy helped him up.

"I'm going for your spot, Bozo," Turtle growled, his lips curled into a jeer. The right side of his face was changing color. "Shouldn't be hard since you field like a girl."

"Oh yeah? Try it." Decker strode toward him. "Try it, Shortwad. I'll show you how to play ball." He drew back his arm and Sweeney caught it.

Decker shook him off and whirled around. "Leave me alone, Sweeney. I don't need your help." He clenched his fists, banged his locker open, snatched his clothes, and headed for the shower.

The last words he heard were Sweeney's. "Yeah? You don't need any friends? Well, forget it, Decker. Just forget it."

CHAPTER TWENTY-TWO

DECKER LAID HIS HEAD BACK AND LET THE COOL SHOWER RUN over him. The stream cooled him off outside. Inside, he churned. Blood stopped dripping off his face, but his eye closed to a slit. His eye socket and cheek throbbed.

It grew quiet in the locker room. When he peered from the shower, they had all cleared out. He dried off and pulled on his clothes.

He drove to Wendy's on San Pedro where nobody knew him, sat in a corner booth and tore through a bacon-and-cheese burger.

He wanted to throw a saltshaker or pound the table. He ached to run ten miles or pummel a punching bag. He needed to strike out at somebody for the whole mess, but there was nobody to blame. Except for the asshole he knew couldn't play second base as well as he could. And the illusive bastard he couldn't find.

Could he succeed at anything? Baseball? Grades? Patching up his family? Finding the sleezeball who hurt an old man? Fat chance he'd ever be Big Man On Campus and get a girl like Ashley Montrose. The room started to look gray.

She wasn't really his girlfriend when they saw the Christmas movie at the mall, but lately she acted like she really liked him. Maybe it was because it was baseball season, and he played varsity.

He looked at his watch. Time to pick her up. He still felt wired, but he didn't want to stand her up. Maybe her softness would settle him. He got into his car and found a country music station.

He rolled up to her house, killed the engine, took a deep breath, and strolled toward the door. When he rang the bell, she opened it wearing a blue sweater that matched her incredibly blue eyes and a jacket thrown on her shoulders under a fluff of light hair. It was hard to keep his eyes off the soft mounds on her chest. He swallowed.

"Hello, Ashley."

"Hi, Decker." She smiled seductively before her eyes widened. "What happened to your eye?"

"Had a fight with a new guy after baseball practice. No big deal." His cheek and eye pulsed. He wished he had a painkiller.

Her dad stood behind her. Decker reached around Ashley to shake his hand. "Hello, Mr. Montrose."

"How are you, Decker?" Montrose looked him up and down. Every inch. He should have changed clothes. "Looks like you have the makings of a good shiner."

"Yes, sir. It'll be okay."

"Hmm. How's your mom?"

"You know my mother? How?"

"Jillian and I went to the same college, you know."

No. He didn't know. "Did you date her?" Was this the jerk he followed?

"I tried. She had her mind made up for Trent. Neither of us attends parents' meetings, so I haven't seen her in a long time."

If Montrose didn't attend the meetings, how did he know she didn't?

Ashley moved to precede him out the door. As she passed Decker, she winked and batted her lashes. An intoxicating scent assailed his nostrils.

"We won't be late, sir."

"Good." His face was stern. "I'm sure you both have homework."

As they walked to the car, he felt Montrose's eyes on him. He held open the passenger door. "Hungry?"

"No," she said. "We've eaten." She smiled.

"Me too." He walked around the car, slid in, and started the engine. Flipping around the dial, he landed on Lady Antebellum's "Need You Now." "Why don't we drive through Brackenridge Park, near the zoo?"

She turned toward him, eyebrows raised. "You want to go to the zoo?"

"Maybe. It's open at night and the weather has warmed up. It's a pretty spot. Calming, you know? You sure smell good. Why don't you slip out of the seatbelt and slide over. I'll drive carefully, I promise."

He flashed what he thought was his most engaging smile. His face must be swelling under his slitty eye. She clicked open the belt and slid closer, so he put an arm around her. "That's better."

They drove in silence. He sang along with Lady Antebellum, hoping he was on key. He reached a secluded spot not far from the entrance to the zoo, pulled to the curb and cut the engine.

He pulled her closer. With his other hand, he drew a finger around her face. "You're so pretty. And you smell delicious." He kissed her, drew her closer and kissed her again. Her face touched his and he winced.

"I'm sorry your face hurts, Decker. Let's go sit on that bench."

He backed away and dropped his hands into his lap. "Right."

He got out and opened her door. Pulling on lightweight jackets, they walked to a softly lit area not far from the car. Soft grass and steppingstones led to a bench for people waiting to enter the zoo.

"It's nice here," she said.

"Yeah. I wish we had music. I could turn on the car radio, but the battery might die."

She snuggled next to him and looked up. "You could sing."

"You'd be grossed out. Say, aren't you dating a football player?"

"I was. We broke up after the season ended."

"Oh." *Well, now it was baseball season...who knew?*

She grabbed his hand. Fortunately, it wasn't the sore one from when he clocked Turtle.

Maybe they could talk about school. Turned out she didn't take AP classes, so he couldn't discuss *Huckleberry Finn* or *Grapes of Wrath*.

She said she didn't like to read much. "Math is okay."

"I don't know how to talk about math."

"Do you ever watch *Dancing with the Stars?*

"No."

"There's a new one, *Skating with the Stars.*

"They probably have fewer contestants for that," he said, grinning.

"I guess...*The Simpsons* are good. Do you ever watch them?"

"No. I don't watch much TV. Baseball and studying take a lot of time."

"I guess."

He looked down at her and kissed her nose. "Why don't I take you home and we'll go on a date later when my face isn't swelling up."

She nuzzled into his side and kissed him. "That sounds good. Very good."

He put his arm around her, wanting to let his hand drape down over her breast. Instead, he stood, took her hand and walked her to the car. He held open her door, trooped around to his side, cranked the engine and turned on the radio. They sang along with Taylor Swift belting out "Shake it Off" all the way to her house. He'd seen Taylor perform it on YouTube.

He walked her to the door and pecked her cheek in case her father was watching.

Back in his car, he thought about Montrose. Geez. His mother knew everybody. No surprise. She was pretty and personable. He knew Greeks and sorority girls had Friday night mixers at UT. She probably met him there, along with hundreds of other guys. He couldn't scour four UT yearbooks and track down every man who knew his mother.

How could he find out if she and Montrose were more than acquaintances? Ashley wasn't going to tell him.

Montrose said he tried to date his mother, and Decker thought he'd gone to some parents' meeting hoping to catch her there. If he managed to eliminate Cunningham as the sleaze he was tracking, there was still Montrose.

Mom probably met lots of guys working with Mrs. Handy on her house...builders, contractors, realtors. He couldn't quiz her, make her suspicious and dampen her enthusiasm. At least she seemed happy. He drove around aimlessly, wishing he could talk to Granddad Hank.

He turned the Mustang toward Loop 410 and Methodist Hospital. It would help to get his mind on something else.

CHAPTER TWENTY-THREE

DECKER WAVED AT THE CHARGE NURSE, WENT STRAIGHT TO Conahan's room, and knocked on the door.

"Come in." Conahan sounded like a general summoning his aid. He sat straight against the pillows in a commanding posture that made Decker smile.

"How are you, sir? You look a lot better. Stronger."

"It's about damn time. They're finally bringing me decent food. How's baseball going?" He tapped a chair, gesturing Decker toward it.

"Not so good, sir. I screwed up big time at practice."

"Looked like you took some punches. What happened?"

Decker leaned forward in the chair. "Remember I told you about two players transferring in from New Braunfels?"

"Yes, I do."

He remembered their conversation. That was a good sign.

"Well, one of them wants to play second base. He kept needling me until I got angry and made lousy plays." Decker paused. "I even threw a bat."

"That so?"

"Yes, sir. Parents, faculty, and maybe some scouts were there. My bat hit the backstop. The coach was furious."

Conahan frowned. "That how you got the shiner?"

"Oh no, sir. Coach would never hit us." He touched his cheek and winced. "We had a fight later in the locker room, the two guys from New Braunfels and Sweeney and me. One of the New Braunfels guys wouldn't shut up. So, I charged him. We rolled around and threw punches."

"...and one of them landed on you. So who won?"

"I think I did, sir. He has a long face kind of like a turtle—like Crush in *Finding Nemo,* an animated movie I used to watch about a fish. I landed a couple of punches, so he probably has a big bruise down one side of his face."

"He looks like a turtle?"

Decker nodded, thought about Crush, and started laughing. A laugh erupted from deep in Conahan's belly. Once they started laughing, they couldn't stop.

The nurse stuck her head in the door and smiled. When they finally stopped laughing, she turned to Decker. "Corey, your eye must hurt. Would you like an ice pack?"

"That would be great, ma'am." She returned with the ice bag and gently placed it on his eye and cheek.

"That feels good. Thank you."

Conahan had laughed so hard, tears splotched his cheeks. He grabbed a tissue and wiped his eyes. "Baseball is a head game, son. If you can keep them out of your head, you can do your business."

"I know, sir." Decker swiped another tissue out of the box on the hospital tray and dabbed his eyes.

"You want it so badly, don't you? To play well."

"That's it, sir."

"I wouldn't worry about the new guy if he looks like a turtle."

"Why not?"

"Turtles can't talk. Have you ever heard a turtle make a sound?"

"Uh...no, sir."

"Whenever he spouts off, remember that. His lips might move, but he can't make a sound."

Decker pictured Turtle moving his lips with no sound coming out.

Conahan pushed himself up straight and leaned forward, his big hands extended, ready to gesture. He squinted at Decker. "Every time he moves his lips, you hear Antonelli telling you to watch the ball and move into position."

He leaned forward and twisted his shoulders. "How to scoop under the ball and feel it roll over your index finger into your glove." He spread the fingers of his left hand like a glove, curled his hand around the imaginary ball, and coiled his index finger over it.

The way he did it, Decker practically felt the ball roll into his glove. "I see what you mean. I think I can do that, sir. I practiced it about a thousand times. I should be able to do it in my sleep."

"Practice it a hundred more times and you'll do it every time there's a grounder. The movements become automatic."

"I'll do it, sir. I'm glad you remembered Antonelli's videos."

Conahan nodded. "I'm remembering better."

Decker leaned forward in his chair until their heads were four feet apart. "What do you remember, sir, about what happened at home before you came here?"

Conahan fell back against the pillows and closed his eyes. He was still for so long, Decker grew fearful.

After an interminable time, he opened his eyes. "I was reading in bed and had fallen asleep when the doorbell rang. It was late. I thought the neighborhood kids were playing pranks, and I wasn't about to answer. The paperback must have fallen off my chest to the floor. I closed my eyes and must have dozed off with the bedside lamp on."

Decker remembered weak light coming from an upstairs window.

Conahan closed his eyes again. "I remember hearing footsteps."

Decker's breath caught.

"I got out of bed and stood there deciding what to do when a man came through my bedroom door. He was in shadow. I made out his outline but couldn't see his face. He said something. I remember it angered me. We argued and —" He sank back into the pillows.

Decker watched him take short breaths. "Are you okay, sir?"

Conahan licked his lips. "I'm okay, son. I simply can't remember." He took a ragged breath.

"Should I call the nurse? Do you want water?"

Conahan nodded. "Water."

Decker poured water into a glass from the bedside pitcher and brought it to Conahan's lips. When Conahan took the glass, his hands shook. Decker was terrified. Conahan's heart —what if trying to remember was too stressful?

"It's okay, sir. Just relax. You don't need to tell me anymore." He watched Conahan's breathing slow. "I think I should call the nurse."

"Don't do that, son. I'm all right. She said I might go home in a few days. I don't want to louse that up." His voice was stronger.

"But sir..."

Conahan adopted a commanding expression. "It's okay," he said, putting down the glass. "There was something familiar about him, the man who came in."

Decker's eyes widened. "Someone you knew?"

"Maybe. Or he reminded me of someone." He shrugged. "I'll probably remember more later."

Decker was relieved that Conahan appeared calm.

"Maybe he looked like someone I worked with in Houston." His eyes rolled to the ceiling, then back to Decker. "But why would some guy come from Houston to chew me out in the middle of the night?"

He was all business now, weighing facts. "Why didn't he call me first or come in the daytime? How would he know where I lived? Or that I lived alone?" He frowned and dropped his hands on the bed. "Wish I could remember why he was so angry."

"It's okay, sir. Maybe you will later."

A voice over the loudspeaker announced the end of visiting hours.

"I better go, sir."

"Are you coming back?"

"I hope so." He thought about his schedule. "We have practice Wednesday." He remembered throwing the bat, puffed his cheeks, and blew out air. "I better make some good plays. I could come after dinner."

"You'll do well, Corey. Practice Wednesday exactly like Antonelli said. Listen to Turtle."

Decker grinned.

"I imagine I'll still be here but call the nurse's station before you come."

"Yes, sir." He wished he could tell Conahan his real name. He wondered if he'd ever be able to tell him.

Conahan offered his big hand. When Decker went to shake it, Conahan put his other hand on top. "You'll do well, son. I'd bet on it."

Decker got back into his Mustang, glad to have a friend who liked baseball and who believed he could play. He cranked the engine and drove out of the parking lot onto the freeway. Halfway home, the steering wheel started pulling to the left. He had a low tire.

Taking the next off ramp, he pulled into the first gas station on the access road. Rolling to a stop at one side of their driveway, away from the pumps, he got out to check. His left front tire was nearly flat. Another quarter mile and he would have had a blowout on the freeway or be bumping along on the rim. He could have lost control, rolled the car, caused a pileup. It could have been the end of him.

He opened the trunk. The spare looked okay. He retrieved the jack and lug wrench and went to work releasing the lug nuts. When they felt loose, he slipped them off and jacked up the car, finished taking them off, and removed the tire.

He looked at the flabby tire and carried it into the shop where the mechanic worked on a car. "Will you have a look at this tire?"

"Looks like you have a flat."

"Happened real fast right there on the freeway. I was going about sixty. I check these tires regularly."

"Let me see." The mechanic turned the tire in his hands. "I can't tell anything. Let's put it in this tub of water and see what we get." They watched it settle in the water. Bubbles popped up on one side. He grabbed it at the spot near the bubbles and pulled it up.

"There." Decker looked where he pointed. "See that slit in the sidewall? That's a clean gash. If I had to guess, I'd say somebody stuck a knife in your tire."

Decker stared at the cut, his neck tingling. "Who would do that?"

The man shrugged. "You'd know that better than I would. Need help getting the spare on?"

"No, but I might get you to tighten the lug nuts and check the air pressure. I'll pull over there."

The man nodded and walked back into the mechanic's

bay. Decker got the spare on, replaced his tools inside the trunk, eased the car near the bay where the man worked, and cut the engine. The mechanic came out, tightened the nuts and checked tire pressures.

"Looks like you're good to go. Need some gas?"

"No, but I'll get it here when I do. Thanks a lot."

"Sure. Drive safe."

"You bet."

Decker pulled onto the freeway, getting in sync with fast-moving cars. Would Turtle slash his tire over a fight? It didn't seem likely, no matter what kind of turd the guy was.

Did the man he followed find his phone and discover who he was? Follow him to the hospital? Was he determined to keep him away from Mr. Conahan because Conahan might pin him as the attacker? Would that guy slit his tire? Ice went through his veins like it did when the culprit froze on Conahan's step and stared at the sofa where he hid.

He could have been killed. What had he gotten himself into?

CHAPTER TWENTY-FOUR

JILLIAN SAVAGE WOKE AT 6:30 A.M. TUESDAY, FULLY functional with a sense of anticipation. She rushed through her bathroom routine and focused on her upcoming day. She would call on Annabelle Parsons whose large house was nearly finished and needed furnishings.

Tingling with excitement, she hoped Annabelle had a flexible budget. What if she earned enough to pay their bills and finance the first year of Decker's college, even if he didn't get a baseball scholarship? He said he played terribly and lost his temper the first day. One practice didn't predict anything, especially the first one. He might play great ball tomorrow. Who knew?

She tripped downstairs as the kitchen phone jingled on the counter. Before she could get there, the ringing stopped. She snatched the phone to her ear, but the line was dead. Probably a wrong number. These incomplete calls were disquieting. They unhinged her, made her feel fractured like she did after Casey died.

She crumpled into a chair at the kitchen table. She needed to call Annabelle but couldn't make herself move.

The familiar pain of losing Casey descended around her like hardening cement. She never knew when the pain would grip her.

For months, she despaired over her crumbling family and struggled to keep going, despite her debilitating isolation. She felt detached from her sense of self.

When the terrorists hit the Twin Towers on 9/11, and aimed for the Pentagon, only a few months after Casey died, everyone grieved for the victims and first responders. The Savage family's personal grief was overwhelmed by the country's massive collective grief.

Trent disconnected from his office. For hours, he stared at TV pictures of police and fire fighters rushing into burning buildings. Mesmerized, he couldn't tear himself away. He grew hard with Decker. Why didn't Decker play football, like he did? Baseball wasn't a contact sport. Why didn't Decker stand up, speak up, accept a challenge? He seemed to want Decker to be a perpetual first responder, a big, burly, aggressive hero.

She pushed up from the table, angry.

Trent must have wanted to be one himself, a fearless and effective savior. Since he'd been unsuccessful molding Decker into a carbon copy of himself, he pinned his hopes on Casey, tossed him footballs at age three. Imagine. But he couldn't save Casey from reality. He couldn't save either of his boys.

She inhaled deeply. Maybe she could bolster Decker. She was finally beginning to coalesce into a whole person. Little by little, her dismembered parts began to reinvigorate and reattach themselves. *I'm still here. The whole me is intact.* She wasn't previously able to help Decker much because there was so little left of her. There was more of her now. Enough to share.

She put her hand near the phone, picked up the business

card she kept there, held it with both hands and read it aloud. "Delectable Designs. Jillian Savage, Owner." She'd managed to increase her bank account by adding sales to the money Trent sent every month. It was easier to pay her half of the house mortgage than try to get him to pay it. Paying her way gave her a sense of pride and relief.

With business booming and new prospects at The Dominion, her income had the potential to blossom. She put the card back in place. The miracle was she had regained enough self-esteem and stamina to plunge into the demands of her business and move forward.

She brewed three cups in her Cuisinart and leaned back against the counter, breathing in the aroma while it percolated. It was a new year, with new prospects and new hope.

If only Trent sold new insurance policies and saw more premium income coming in. It would boost his self-esteem and help lift him from melancholy. She no longer wanted to be part of his life, and she didn't want to depend on him financially, but she'd like to see him bounce back to his enthusiastic self.

Sipping coffee, she strode to the kitchen window and peered out. People were backing out of driveways, going to work. A lone car parked down the block. She discerned a figure behind the tinted windows, but the car never moved. Strange. This was the second time she'd seen the car.

When she told Decker about meeting clients at Biga's, she didn't mention that on her drive downtown, she noticed a car in the rearview mirror that appeared to be following her. She spotted it twice. Probably a coincidence. A lot of people went downtown. She squinted at the car. The driver started the engine, and the car pulled away.

She whirled to look at the kitchen clock and frowned. Did Decker oversleep? If she didn't wake him, he'd be late for school.

She started up the steps. "Decker! Are you awake? It's seven-thirty."

Massive tennis shoes clomped down the steps leading Decker, shiny-faced and eager. "Got to go, Mom. I'm late."

"Wait a minute, Deck." She stopped him at the bottom of the steps. "What happened to your face? Your eye is nearly shut."

"It's nothing, Mom. No big deal. I threw a few punches with a new guy."

"A fight?" She came closer, scrutinizing the damage and studying his expression. "That's not like you, Deck. Can you see through it? What was the fight about?"

"I can see okay. A new ball player from New Braunfels hassled me about the way I played in practice. I got tired of his big mouth and popped him."

She put her hands on her hips and tilted her head. "Was that all?"

He shrugged. "We rolled around in the locker room and punched each other a few times."

She nodded. "I see." She started to touch his face. "Does it hurt?"

He backed away. "Not unless you poke it."

"I have some makeup that might cover the bruising. Want me to get it?"

"No, Mom. That's not cool." He grabbed an apple off the kitchen counter and poured milk. She followed.

"I get it. You're proud of it. A badge of honor."

"Sort of. He probably looks worse. I think half his face is bruised." He pictured Turtle's face with one side discolored and grinned. "I can't wait to see it."

She couldn't help but grin with him. "Do you still feel like playing ball?"

"You bet! I'm going to practice after school and tonight. I know exactly what to do. We have practice tomorrow. I told

Coach I'd be more than ready." He threw the backpack over his shoulder.

"Okay, then. How about an ice pack? You can put it on your face on the way to school and take it off when you get there. It will reduce the swelling."

"Okay."

She went to the freezer for ice cubes, crushed them in the blender, and put them into a small Ziploc. "Here. Hold it on your face every time you stop. You need two hands to drive."

"Okay, Mom. Thanks. I love you."

"I love you too, Deck."

He pecked her on the cheek and whirled, a cyclone of bone, muscle, and vigor. She stepped back to avoid his backpack. When had he grown so tall? They might make it, she and Deck. What was a little fighting? Some scuffling was probably good for him. It appeared he enjoyed it.

She smiled hearing the familiar gurgle of the Mustang grinding to life in the garage and poured more coffee.

She grabbed a tablet and pen from the kitchen table, took them to the dining room and moved fabric books to the end of the table, some for Annabelle, some for Laura. She flipped through them again to make a list of what each woman liked and decorating strategies she would propose. She was weighing her ideas when the phone rang.

Absentmindedly, she sauntered back to the kitchen counter and lifted the receiver. "Jillian Savage."

"Mrs. Savage, I'm Kathryn Sanborne, the School Counselor at Prospect Heights. Decker came to see me recently. Do you have a moment to talk?"

"Sure. By the way, did you call earlier this morning?"

"No."

"I guess somebody called the wrong number." Jillian shivered.

"I guess so. I'm calling about Decker."

She sank onto the kitchen stool. "He said he had a scuffle at school. Is that what it's about?"

"I'm afraid it's more than that."

She couldn't believe Decker did anything terrible. "Go on."

"As you know, his grades have slipped. Most of last year he had a 3.9. His grades slipped to 2.8 toward the end of the year and this year...well, he's unable to remember what he read. Mrs. Pritchard said he couldn't recall things on her test that he clearly knew. She told him to come see me."

Jillian knew he'd had a rough time concentrating and sometimes seemed to be in a fog. But he seemed better... motivated again. Then there was the baseball bat. She slumped down on the stool and waited. Surely, he didn't hit somebody.

"After missing a pitch at practice yesterday, he threw his bat into the screen that protects the fans."

Her limbs grew weak. Decker had been somber and introspective, but never violent. "He didn't hurt anyone?"

"No. The bat hit the screen and bounced off. But it showed he was out of control."

She knew he had a fight, but he didn't seem to think it was a big deal. She would remain calm. "I see. And you learned this how?"

"Mrs. Pritchard heard about it and mentioned it this morning. The coach was furious, and spectators were astonished—faculty, parents, possibly college baseball scouts."

This woman was describing Decker like someone she didn't know.

"How did your visit with him go?"

"Actually, I did most of the talking during our time. I asked what was bothering him," she said. "I told him sometimes things that happen outside of class can make it hard to remember schoolwork, but he didn't really say what that might be. He said he had his mind on baseball, that baseball meant everything to him. He said he'd start studying more… things like that." She paused. "I'm so sorry, but I have a student coming in five minutes. We could talk more later. Maybe you and Decker could come in together?"

"I'd like to think about what you told me. If I think we should come in, I'll call and make an appointment. And thank you for letting me know."

"Of course. Decker has a lot of potential."

She thanked Kathryn Sanborne again and hung up. The counselor painted a different picture from what she saw. She put her head into her hands and squeezed tears from her eyes.

She remembered how Deck changed after he went to the hospital to visit his new friend. He was purposeful now with new enthusiasm. He even showed interest in her new clients, especially Michael Cunningham. Maybe he was perceptive enough to sense her interest in Michael.

He'd hinted they should meet again to discuss her decorating approach. Although attractive, tall, and successful, he meant nothing to her. She hoped she convinced Decker of that.

She meandered to the window, gazed out, and reviewed what she knew about her son. He had always been a thoughtful, intelligent kid, but not a fighter. He seemed to enjoy this one, his first fight since age eight. Throwing a bat was completely unlike him, but he was eager for Wednesday's practice so he could play ball again. Apparently, the coach hadn't thrown him off the team. He was upset about his family breaking up, but he was the same kid he'd always been. And now he could fight.

She unknowingly shook her head against Kathryn Sanborn's evaluation. She would wait to see how practice went. She knew teenagers. Their moods changed on a dime.

She wouldn't mention the counselor's call to Decker. She would simply wait.

The phone rang again. Now what? She picked up the receiver. "Jillian Savage."

"Jillian, this is Mike Cunningham. I know we discussed your decorating approach, but I'd like to know more. Do you think we can set something up? Dinner in a nice place?"

CHAPTER TWENTY-FIVE

JILLIAN THOUGHT TRENT WOULD BE AT DECKER'S BASEBALL practice, but neither of them had called to report. She hoped they were out celebrating.

She checked the bathroom mirror to put final touches on her makeup. She used to get compliments on her skin, but stress had sapped her glow. Her auburn hair hung limp. She usually pulled it back into a professional looking bun but decided to brush it until it shone.

She couldn't remember the last time someone took her out to dinner. Despite the permanent fatigue that had taken up residence in her body, she still looked good.

She told Michael Cunningham she was running late because of work. The truth was she wanted to be home in case Decker bounced in euphoric after a good baseball practice.

She looked at her watch. Seven-thirty. He should be home by now. She hoped he wasn't moping around somewhere. He might be out with friends. Whichever it was, she couldn't stall much longer. Mike must be starving.

She clicked his number on her cell. "Sorry to keep you

waiting, Mike. I'm finally ready." Over the click of her heels descending the stairs, she remembered the eagerness in his voice when he called. She wasn't at all sure she should be going out with him.

When she opened the front door minutes later, a broad smile lit his face. The sheen of his silk blend suit complemented his tan skin and wavy black hair. His blue eyes danced with pleasure. She had to admit he was striking.

"You look fantastic, Jillian. You should wear your hair down more often."

"Thank you."

He stepped close, swung his arm through hers, and leaned toward her neck. "Hmm. Smell good too."

She gave her hair a casual flip and discretely drew her arm back. "I usually wear it up for work." She tried to resurrect the tenor of their business meetings. "Where did you say we were going?"

"I didn't. Do you like surprises?"

"Umm, not usually."

"How's Frederick's Restaurant? Have you been there?"

"Yes, but not in ages. I remember the food is wonderful."

Then Frederick's it is." He opened the car door for her, brimming with pleasure.

Like his black, low-slung BMW, everything about Mike Cunningham reeked of class. No wonder he sold gargantuan houses in The Dominion. She desperately wanted to decorate them. She hoped he wasn't expecting more.

Her priorities were to get her life in order, grow her business to support herself and Decker, and give him the emotional support he needed to deal with their divorce. She didn't have the energy or inclination left over for an affair with Michael Cunningham.

It wasn't like she'd been totally faithful to Trent. There was that one grievous night.

She had cared for the children all day in the throes of struggling to decide which bills to pay. Trent made a good living, but he spent a lot. He came home late, long after the boys were in bed. After playing golf with his buddies and drinking at the club, he was insufferably loud and boisterous and totally oblivious to whatever minutia had occupied her day.

He sloshed her with a kiss. "Hello, Gorgeous. Whatcha' been doing?" He weaved toward the bedroom. "I was such a stud on the course today. You should've seen me beat those sorry no-good asses I call friends."

She stood there fuming and took another sip of her wine. She got herself under control and was anxious to flee. But where? With whom?

She thought about the man she knew in college who obviously liked her and recently called unexpectedly. He was divorced, had a daughter, and had moved back to San Antonio.

She strode purposefully to their room where Trent passed out on the bed. She showered, dressed, went downstairs, and picked up the phone to call Lee Montrose. "Hello, Lee."

"Jillian, is that you?"

"Yes, surprise. I haven't seen you in a long time. But I still remember the nice dinner we had...plus a lot of good wine."

"We could do that again. Anytime."

"Hey. Why not tonight? We can catch up."

Shame and disgust plagued her over their brief time together, although she didn't recall much of it. Trent wasn't the only one who drank too much that night.

In the days that followed, Montrose called her several times. She always managed to be too busy to talk.

Later, when she and Trent were enjoying a neighborhood barbecue, her cell phone rang. Thinking it was a client, she went into a bedroom to answer. Montrose was on the line.

She made sure he knew never to call her again. She had no further contact with the man.

Trent was inside the house sloshing himself with another drink when she heard Decker cry out. She dashed from the bedroom and ran toward Decker's voice. She saw Decker struggling to get his brother out of the pool, tears streaming his face.

She ran to them screaming. She and Decker moved Casey's lifeless body away from poolside. She struggled to revive him with CPR. Unsuccessful, she collapsed beside him on the concrete.

She didn't remember much of what happened after that.

She didn't think Trent ever knew about Lee. His business began slipping, he was distant, and she didn't protest when he decided to move out. After they lost Casey, nothing else mattered.

———

FREDERICK'S WAS SMALL, DARK, AND INTIMATE, COMPLETE WITH candles on the tables and ardent, syrupy waiters. After they shared brie and goat cheese on crackers, she sighed and leaned back in the chair, rolling the Chardonnay around in her mouth.

She knew Mike Cunningham was watching. It was nice to be pampered and admired. They ate red snapper with lemon butter sauce that practically slid down her throat and compared notes about memorable clients.

Romantic music drifted from invisible speakers. They talked and laughed until they were the last patrons to leave the restaurant.

"I haven't enjoyed myself like this in a long time," she confessed.

He covered her hand with his. "I'm glad you're enjoying yourself. You deserve it."

While he paid the bill, she took stock of their evening. It was a joy to be appreciated. As much as she liked Mike Cunningham and wanted his business, she wasn't some Hollywood starlet ready to audition on the couch. She had stopped loving or even liking Trent very much, but she wanted him to get back on his feet and be a father to Decker.

When she found herself alone, depressed and feeling worthless, she tried very hard to break from her sadness and recapture her self-esteem. At last, she was succeeding, both as a person and as Decker's mother.

She was bone weary of demands. It would be nice to have a man to share her journey, someone she could talk to about her business. Mike drew people like a magnet, including her. She sighed. It was up to her. Weary though she was, everything was up to her.

On the drive home, Mike looked over and smiled. "Why don't we go to my house for a nightcap?"

"I'm afraid I can't," she said, smiling regretfully. "I have a killer day tomorrow. And my son is expecting me home soon."

"That's too bad," he said, grabbing her hand off the seat. She allowed him to hold it a few seconds, then slowly withdrew it. They arrived at her house, and he walked her to the door. When he leaned down to kiss her, she offered her cheek, put her hand on his arm and looked up at him.

"Thank you for a perfectly delightful evening, Mike. I think we'll be good friends and wonderful business partners."

She slipped into the foyer, maintaining an agreeable mask on her face while she watched indecision and irritation slip around on his. She gently closed the door and silently clicked the lock.

CHAPTER TWENTY-SIX

DECKER CRUISED TO SCHOOL, STEERING MOSTLY WITH HIS LEFT hand unless he had to turn. The ice pack on his cheek felt good, but he was seeing mostly through one eye. He didn't want to completely erase the shiner. He didn't think there was much chance of the damage disappearing this fast.

He stopped at a light and checked the mirror. Yep. Closed, swollen eye and purple cheek. The light turned green. It didn't hurt if people knew he had a rumble. Especially since he figured Turtle looked worse.

He pulled into the school parking lot and thought about his tire. The mechanic might be wrong about the slash. It wasn't unheard of to run over glass or metal. Spotting a parking space, he pulled in and cut the engine. Except for the tire, things looked pretty good. Mom didn't go ballistic over the fight. Coach seemed sympathetic, so he didn't think he'd get kicked out of school for throwing the bat.

Plus, he'd get to see Turtle's face. The guy would probably watch his mouth in the future. If not, Decker knew he could block out his drivel. He grabbed his backpack, got out and locked the door. He knew exactly what to do in practice. He was going to be killer Wednesday afternoon.

Mom was jubilant about her new prospects. What if she made enough money to afford his college, baseball or not? Just knowing it was a possibility would help him relax and play better.

She didn't seem interested in Michael Cunningham, who apparently was not related to Mr. Conahan.

Decker ambled toward the school. Mr. Conahan loved baseball and knew a lot about it. He was getting better and remembered more about the attack. Before long, he might be able to remember enough to help police catch the guy without unfavorably involving Decker. But he didn't want to push him to remember and upset him.

He needed to find that phone. What if the bastard stumbled upon it and came after him? He was glad he hadn't turned on the app that showed his location.

He sauntered down the hall whistling. Vice-Principal Tensel walked toward him with a friend. The kids all liked Mr. Tensel. He didn't recognize the man with him, probably a new teacher.

"Hello, Decker. How are you doing? This is Josh Baker, one of our new faculty members this spring. He teaches freshman science."

"That's great, sir." He offered his hand. "Decker Savage. I'm taking European history instead of another science class. I like reading about World War II, especially about Churchill."

Mr. Baker smiled. "Ah. I'm a diehard Churchill fan. He was an amazing man."

"I was thinking this morning about something he said, 'Success is not final, failure is not fatal. It is the courage to continue that counts,'" Decker said.

Joe Tensel pointed to his face. "That quote wouldn't have

anything to do with baseball practice, would it, Decker? The shiner?"

"Yes, sir, it does." He wished Tensel hadn't been at practice to see him act like an idiot. "Monday was awful."

Tensel nodded.

"I played like a bonehead and threw the bat."

"That wasn't like you, Decker."

"I know, sir. I told Coach I'd never do it again. Do you know if any scouts were there?"

"I met one from Abilene Christian. He might be there Wednesday...maybe scouts from other schools. Coach has big hopes for the team this year, so colleges are showing interest early."

Decker nodded. "I'll be better on Wednesday."

"You'll get there, Decker," Baker said. "Like Churchill said, 'Every day you may make progress. Every step may be fruitful. Yet there will stretch out before you an ever-lengthening, ever-ascending, ever-improving path. You know you will never get to the end of the journey. But this, so far from discouraging, only adds to the joy and glory of the climb.' I love that one."

Decker nodded. "Me too, sir."

"Maybe we should have a Winston Churchill powwow."

"I'd like that, sir. If you get one up, count me in."

Tensel checked his watch. "We enjoy watching you guys play." He turned to Baker. "Are you free Wednesday after school?"

"You bet."

"We'll see you there, Decker. Better get to class."

"Yes, sir. Nice meeting you, Mr. Baker."

"Same here, Decker. See you around."

Tensel headed toward the main office, and Baker turned toward the Science wing. It was nice to be encouraged.

Decker was determined to concentrate at practice and be deliberate with every play.

He strode into English class checking the expression on Mrs. Pritchard's face. She was in instructor mode, all business with no evident irritation or empathy.

"Today, before we begin our preliminary discussion of *Huckleberry Finn*, I'm going to return your test papers on *The Grapes of Wrath*. Since the questions were open-ended, and what people glean from literature is variable and subjective, I was lenient on grading. I looked primarily for your depth of understanding of the text and whether your examples supported your conclusions. Of course, if your writing was illegible or full of grammatical mistakes, I deducted points."

With each question worth fifty points, and his leaving a whole question blank, the best he could get was a failing grade. She handed the first row their papers, and Decker saw a lot of dismal expressions. She started down his row.

"You'll have a grade at the end of each section with comments and total points on the last page." She placed his test on his desk, glanced at his black eye and proceeded down the row without pause. "If you have questions about your grade, come see me."

He stared at the bottom of page one. "Fifty points for excellent recall of major characters and themes in the book. Fifteen points for comparing/contrasting characters and logically supporting evidence of how the author depicted Rose of Sharon as the most compassionate and hopeful character." He didn't expect more than fifty points, but sixty-five points was still failing.

He cringed and flipped to page two. After skimming over a sea of blank space, he read, "Fifteen points for excellent late recall of the importance of Jim Casy and Tom Joad with supporting reasons why the former was the novel's guiding voice. Grade total, eighty points."

He passed. She had listened. He actually got a B. Barely. He leaned back in his chair and blew air at the ceiling. He sat up, put the paper into his backpack, and followed the class out of the room, a smile forming on his lips.

Mrs. Pritchard stood by the door and peered at him, stone-faced, over her glasses. He stopped, afraid she had changed her mind.

"There's a one-time benefit for remembering late."

"Yes, ma'am. I understand. Thank you." He bounced out of the room and whistled going down the hall.

Ashley came out of her class and watched him, a smile spreading across her face. "You look happy.""

"I thought I failed a test in English and got a B. It's amazing."

"Awesome. Do you want to tell me about it?"

He told her about going blank on the English question, remembering the characters and their actions later, telling Mrs. Pritchard and getting credit. Ashley hadn't read *The Grapes of Wrath,* but she smiled all the way through his description.

He told her about throwing the bat at practice and how he was determined to play well today. He talked more than he had in weeks.

"I know you'll play well, Decker. I have faith in you. You can do whatever you set your mind on. I'm sure of it." She tiptoed and kissed him on the cheek.

He hadn't felt so good in months. He believed her. He would study more, smoke out the mystery man, and protect Mr. Conahan. Ashley might prefer TV shows to studying, but she understood him. She liked him. He might be B.M.O.C. after all.

CHAPTER TWENTY-SEVEN

Decker could hardly get through classes Wednesday. He couldn't concentrate on what the teachers were saying. All he could think about was sliding his glove under the ball and feeling it roll over his index finger into his glove.

When the last bell rang, he loped to his car and pointed the Mustang toward Olmos Field. Windows down, he took a deep breath of crisp January air. He was fine-tuned to the weather, invigorated by gusts of wind, and uplifted by the fresh smell of rain. He was glad to be past the debilitating, disheartening pressure of humid summers.

He checked the view for trees breaking up the gray landscape. Sturdy trunks rose into spindly spokes—slashes of black crayon splayed against the sky.

Most people, knowing the trees wouldn't leaf out until mid-March, saw a dormant, stagnant vista, but he sensed their calm, thoughtful waiting in January and February. He liked this secretive, quiescent interlude with time to think and plan. With all he had on his mind, he needed it. Baseball season would give him a boost.

He rolled down the windows, turned up the volume, and belted out "Here For a Good Time" with George Strait.

Decker rolled up to the practice field, cut the engine, and grabbed his uniform off the seat to change in the dugout. Suited up, he ambled back to his car, threw his clothes in, and waited for coaches to drive up with the gear. He bounded over to their cars to help carry equipment and picked up a bucket of bats and J-bands.

Guys started dribbling in. He dumped his load by the fence and fist bumped Speedy Parker and Jim Alcorn. He'd be zinging balls to one of them at first base.

A couple players asked about his eye. "Just a dust up," he said. "No big deal."

He went to Coach's car for another bucket of balls and met Sweeney carrying another load. "How's it going, Sweeney?"

"Great," Sweeney mumbled as he kept walking. "Just great."

Sweeney had no clue what was going on in his life, Decker thought. No wonder his buddy snubbed him.

Lenny Schwartz and the new tall guy Randy Waller plodded after Sweeney like ghouls hoping he'd trip over his feet. Wasn't going to happen. Sweeney was wedded to third base.

Decker laid balls behind home plate, grabbed a J-band, and went down the fence line looking for a spot to pull it through a hole and stretch his arms. He needed to be loose and, he hoped, powerful. He passed Todd Messner and gave him a thumbs up.

The next guy on the fence was turtle-faced Crush. He learned his actual name was Charles Crocker. Crush Crocker. That worked. Crush had his hat turned almost sideways with the brim pulled low over the purple side of his face. He read somewhere that the direction a guy turned his brim indicated the direction his life was heading.

Decker couldn't resist. He stooped, level with the purple bruise, stared at it, and raised one eyebrow, not saying a word. Crush glared and curled his upper lip. If Crush wasn't stretched out clutching a band, Decker knew he'd pop him.

Coach gave them plenty of time to stretch. "Okay, guys," he called. "Line up three deep at the batting cages. The rest of you go onto the field and ease into long toss."

Decker was close to a batting cage and lined up in third place, eager to warm up more and focus on watching the ball. He swung two bats, waiting his turn, and glanced at the spectators. More people had come to watch than on Monday. He recognized some of the parents, including Sweeney's dad.

A couple of new guys he didn't recognize sat by faculty members Tensel and Baker. Other guys he didn't know. More new faculty? Scouts? Officer Thorn sat in the bleachers, out of uniform. Dad waved to him from high in the bleachers, so he waved back.

Inside the cage, Decker stood in the box, planted his feet, shifted his weight back, and gripped the bat. The first ball came out of the machine fast. It took him a few pitches to get his timing down. He finally entered the zone, seeing every ball like it was a beach ball.

When he heard, "Okay, next," he relaxed. He felt good about his swings and knew he could concentrate.

He left the cage, grabbed his glove, scooped a ball off the ground, and jogged onto the field, tossing the ball into his glove. He spotted Todd and pointed at him. They backed up and threw long tosses. As the cages emptied, more guys filed the field and eased into long, hard throws. Decker felt his body loosening up and his blood pumping.

The coaches stood in a semi-circle, watching, planning

the practice segment, and deciding who to put where. Coach stepped forward.

"Okay, listen up. We're going to break into teams and work live situations. Paco, you're playing first. Savage, you're on second. Sweeney, you're at third, Segura, you're center field, Finger, you're shortstop."

They trotted to their positions. Decker grinned. This was the A-team. His team. The guys he'd be playing with most of the season. This was their chance to win State. They almost won it last year.

Alcorn, you're the runner already at first," Coach said.

Alcorn would try to steal second, drawing a throw. Sweeney, at third, would be ready to tag a runner out or throw to the catcher if anyone tried to steal home. Nothing like competition. What would Coach do with Crush Crocker?

"Crocker, you're playing left field." Decker was damn sure not letting any balls go by in that direction. He didn't want to see Crush Crocker's ugly face.

"Rives, you're pitching, and Hofman is catching. Pandera," he pointed. "you're in right field. The rest of you guys will take turns running to first base after Lenny hits the ball. Hanson, you're first runner up."

Rives was their team's best pitcher, and Lenny Schwartz could hit the ball to China. Coach was sharpening them up real quick. This was going to be good.

Everybody took their positions. Runner Hanson leaned toward first base. Rives delivered to the plate, and Lenny cracked a short grounder to second that took a high hop. Short stop Finger ducked. Alcorn was halfway to second when Decker jumped up, caught the ball, and tagged Alcorn out. But Hanson was safe at first. Decker was sluggish with a guy charging at him. He had to think ahead where to throw the ball.

Second runner Todd Messner leaned toward first base.

While Rives fingered his pitch, Hanson barreled to second. Messner slid in at first.

Before Rives threw the pitch, Decker saw Lenny turn his body slightly left. He was determined to catch it before Crush Crocker got a glove on it. When Lenny blasted a grounder to left field, runner Sam Hays made it to first. Decker waited for the ball, caught it on the upward bounce, and chased Hanson to tag him before he could get a good lead to third. Todd rounded second and was headed for third. Decker threw the ball in a fluid motion to Sweeney, who waited for Todd at third base. Out three. Their part of the inning was over.

Decker jogged off the field, trying not to smile. Even with his face throbbing, everything was perfect. He loved baseball. You were tagged out or not. You scored or you didn't. If you practiced, you got better. It was foreseeable. Expected. Logical. Fair. If only the rest of his life could be so predictable.

Next, Coach put Crush Crocker playing second base with Alcorn and Messner on first and third. Jim Handy would pitch to Trey Segura. Decker, Paco and Sweeney were the first three runners.

Handy pitched a curve ball to Segura. When he smacked it to right field, Decker took off for first. Crush ran over, caught it, and threw Decker out. He walked to the back of the runner's line, breathing hard. "Just one play," he told himself.

Segura bunted Handy's next pitch, and Paco scrambled toward first. The third baseman picked it up and made a wild throw. Alcorn went scrambling for the ball, so Paco barreled around first, shot toward second, and slid in. Safe.

While the catcher signaled the next pitch, Paco took his lead and flew toward third.

Lenny hit the next pitch to left field. Runner Sweeney barreled to first.

Crush Crocker stretched for the ball and missed. Decker managed not to grin.

The outfielder scooped it up and heaved it home, but it was too late. Paco slid in, and Sweeney took off for second.

Decker was dying to run again, but he never got the chance. The infield turned a double play to end the inning.

He longed to be back on second base. Coach put him there, put Sweeney on third, and sent Crush Crocker to first. Decker wished he'd sent him to Mars.

Handy pitched a fast ball to Messner, and the runner behind him took off. Messner got a clean hit, and the ball sailed into the outfield. Two guys scrambled for it, but the runner was safe on first.

Handy's second pitch drew a grounder to Decker's left. He thought it would bounce high. He backed up, stretched for it and drew it into his glove. He ran forward to tag the guy hauling to second base, spun to first base, and heaved it. Crush Crocker caught it and tagged the runner at first. Two outs.

Trey Segura planted his feet and gripped the bat. Handy wound up and drilled him a fast ball. Segura connected with a center field zinger that flew to the outfield. Decker watched the ball sail left. He ran over, jumped for it, and tagged the guy charging toward him. He squeezed his glove around the ball and tossed it to first. Out three.

It was quiet for a minute. Dead silence. Then spectators started talking and clapping. Decker felt like he'd won the World Series. He jogged to home plate trying not to smile, scooped up a ball near the catcher, and pummeled it back and forth between his hand and glove. It felt right. Everything felt right. He saw Crush out of the corner of his eye and walked by him. There was no need to say anything.

He heard his name and looked up to see Dad clomping down the bleachers wearing a big grin. He'd like to be with Dad after playing well, but he had a date with Ashley in a couple of hours.

"Big date," he shouted to Dad. "Get together later."

He showered in the locker room. He had put his best pants and shirt inside a locker before the scrimmage. As he expected, there was no sign of Turtle. He checked his face. The ring around his eye was still yellow. He looked like a raccoon, but when he touched his face, it didn't hurt. That was the main thing. He wanted to get close to Ashley.

First, he needed to do a thorough search for his phone. He ambled to his car, developing his search plan. He heard a ball zing toward him, inches from his head, and ducked. It bounced off the hood of the Mustang. Crouching beside the car, he looked around. Nobody was there. Everyone had left. There wasn't a car in sight. Not many trees encircled the ball field. Nothing moved. He looked at the substantial dent on his hood. A ball to the head could kill.

Whoever threw the ball could aim and was powerful. Crocker? Maybe. He looked around, didn't see anyone, and picked it up. It was a regular ball like dozens they used in practice. He opened his car and tossed the ball on the seat. Could police get fingerprints off a ball? It probably had prints from every guy on the team.

He walked to the driver's side, slid in, locked the doors and sat, thinking. Had the man he followed come to practice? Was he trying to scare him off from seeing Mr. Conahan? From baseball? Was this only general harassment? Decker decided he had better leave the area. Maybe finding his phone would provide answers.

He drove back to the vicinity where he thought Thorne's police cruiser spotlighted him, parked the Mustang, and tried to recall the sequence of events. After Officer Thorn left him standing in the street, he remembered checking his pockets for the phone. If Sergeant Thorne found it, he would have heard from him by now.

He remembered how the culprit, spooked from the patrol

car lights, hid behind a house near the driveway leading to a guest house in the rear. He thought he recognized the house and walked toward it. He had checked around the house for clues after the creep left. He could have dropped his phone there.

If the occupants of the house found it, they would have given it to the police, especially after hearing the ambulance scream a short time later. Maybe they didn't see it.

Suppose Grizley found the phone. He might turn it over to Thorn, or he might not. It had no pass code. Curiosity might have led him to search through, but there wasn't much to see except photos. If the perp was recognizable in the photo he snapped, and Grizzly knew him, he might contact him. Were they in cahoots? Did both men know Conahan? If the photo image was indistinct, the old man might be conducting his own investigation.

Did he mention baseball in front of the neighbor? Maybe he was at the game and threw the ball at him. Grizzly didn't look like he had that much power, but you couldn't always tell. Decker didn't know why the guy would do it, but he looked like the type who would enjoy it.

What if the guy he followed found the phone and recognized himself. Could he trace it to Decker and remain anonymous?

Dusk was descending. As he contemplated where to search, lights came on inside the house. He'd have to stop. Somebody would see him. He went back to the car, started the engine, and rolled into the street.

He remembered the pull of his car when the tire went flat on the freeway, the swish of the ball zinging past his head. A bolt of terror shot through him.

In searching for the man who hurt Mr. Conahan, had he put himself at risk?

CHAPTER TWENTY-EIGHT

Trent Savage was glad he came to practice. Decker played ball like he used to. Confident. Strong. In control. Maybe they should celebrate. He caught up to him on the field. "Hey, Deck. Nice job! Want to go get a burger?"

"I can't, Dad. I'm meeting a girl. Give me a rain check?"

"Okay, son. I should catch up on paperwork anyway." He slapped him on the back. "You played great ball, son. Great ball. Next time, then."

"Thanks, Dad. I'll call you, okay?"

"Sure, son. See you soon."

Sticking his hands in his pockets, he slouched toward his car. He doubted the kid had a real date. There might be a girl involved. Who knew? At least the kid performed well. He could play college ball after all. He was glad to be here, even if Decker didn't want to hang out. He pressured Decker so much to play football, the kid must think he couldn't possibly be proud of him playing baseball. He hoped to remedy that. When the time was right, he'd reassure Decker again that he wasn't responsible for Casey's death.

He got into his truck and cranked the engine. Could the

kid possibly fathom how much football meant to him? He and Jillian gave Decker everything, whereas he grew up with so little that football was his only way up.

Trent aimed the car east toward IH 35 and Walzem and thought about his jock fraternity's Friday night mixer with the Zetas—the night he met Jillian. She was the most beautiful, sweetest woman he'd ever met. He couldn't let her get away. After that, he saw her every chance he got and turned on the charm.

Pulling into Tanglegrove Glen, he was surprised to see a gray Mazda 3 with tinted windows pull in not far behind him. He always liked the 2003 model, pretty snazzy for a compact. The guy must have restored it. Was that the same car he saw before? He hadn't gotten a good look at it. It was probably a tenant's guest; that's why he parked by the fence. He slid into his designated space and started his trek up the wood stairs, remembering the first seven years of their marriage.

The economy was strong. People built homes. Contractors bought liability insurance. Homeowners bought life insurance, and he was happy to sell it to them. Between 1993 and 2000, the United States had the best economic performance in thirty years. A sweet time.

He reached his door and fumbled for the key. The 2000 recession didn't hurt insurance companies much, but when President Travis Hall died that year, his son, Stephen, grieving for his dad, left Trent pretty much on his own. He didn't know much about variations in policies, or which ones were best for different types of prospective buyers.

Before he went inside, he turned and glanced at the Mazda. It hadn't moved.

He stepped inside his living room. What a contrast it was from their home. How different their lives were after Casey died. He poured himself a scotch, plopped on the couch and closed his eyes, reliving the fateful day.

They had gone to the Walden's summer neighborhood barbecue. Decker and Casey were there earlier until Jillian walked them home to put Casey down for a nap. She put eight-year-old Decker in charge, instructing him to go to Casey's room the minute he woke up. Decker, mature for his age, always followed instructions.

When she returned to the party, they were talking to his golf buddies and their wives when Jillian's cell rang. She left the group and went into a bedroom to answer her stupid iPhone. It was probably one of her clients. Couldn't it wait? Her actions irritated him, so he left the conversation and went to the kitchen to pour himself a drink.

He returned to the gathering and was speaking to other people to avoid Jillian when he heard Decker yell for them and charged outside toward the screams. Jillian flew out of the bedroom and raced with him toward their son's cry.

Decker found his brother floating face-down and pulled Casey from the neighbor's pool. He and Jillian bent over him poolside, Jillian desperately trying CPR. Somebody called 911. Three more of them tried CPR.

But Casey was past reviving.

Trent looked at his empty glass and slogged to the kitchen for more. The grief that descended crushed them. As they dragged through the motions of burying their youngest son, they couldn't look at each other.

Where were you when Casey wandered to the pool? They blamed one another in silence, desperate to alleviate their own pain. He slugged the drink and stumbled back to crumple on the sofa.

———

SOMEHOW, THEY MADE IT TO SEPTEMBER, 2001. THEN THE attack on the Twin Towers shattered everyone and reopened their wounds. The tragedy of thousands of lost lives collapsed under the weight of their own grief.

They dragged around like zombies while the Dot-com bubble crashed, the Dow hit bottom, and the recurring refrain was a "jobless recovery." The year 2002 began with worries about events in Iraq and possible war.

He flopped his arm over his eyes to shut out the light. People didn't have money to buy insurance and premium income plunged. He didn't know enough about which policies to offer under the circumstances or how to motivate the sales force. He knew he should learn more about the business, but inertia debilitated him.

Since he was chief operating officer and supposed to know more about bookkeeping than CEO Stephan Hall, he convinced Stephen to raise premiums on some of the policies. Everyone in the office got angry phone calls, and the company lost more customers. They started losing control of the company.

Jillian and Decker grew increasingly distant. He didn't know how to connect with them. Eventually, he lacked the energy to try.

By the time the economy began to surge in 2004, it was too late. He was dipping into the company's reserve fund to stay afloat. He felt nauseous. If he lay still, maybe it would pass.

Jillian jumpstarted her decorating business and was largely supporting them. When her business took off, he was impressed. He didn't care for her new aggressive side, but there wasn't much he could say.

He didn't know how to approach Decker, and he would never have the chance to know Casey.

They rarely saw friends. He felt sad, lackadaisical, and didn't want to socialize. If Jillian wanted to go somewhere, she went alone. His stomach churned. The next day he'd be distant or critical.

Dipping into the reserves was only temporary; he intended to pay the money back, but it took a toll.

He barely made it to the bathroom before throwing up. He heaved until he grew weak. He splashed water on his face and neck, blew his nose, and swished his mouth with water and toothpaste.

Staggering back to the sofa, he lay down and closed his eyes. He hid his feelings from Jillian. They talked even less. He felt like a fraud, a dead man walking, and began making up reasons to stay away from home. He wished they had watched their son play ball today. Together.

Pushing himself up, he traipsed to the kitchen, grabbed a glass of water, and meandered back to the sofa. He had to eat something. He needed to drive somewhere for food. He didn't think he smelled like alcohol. If he got one more DUI, the cops would arrest him.

He stepped out on the walkway hoping brisk air would revive him. He spotted the Mazda parked not far from the entrance to the complex. Why wasn't the car in visitor parking? He slipped inside the apartment to grab his key and stomped shakily down the stairs. As he wheeled toward the car, the driver revved the engine and executed a quick exit on to Walzem.

The guy obviously saw him. Who was he? Some PI Jillian hired? Somebody from the State Insurance Board checking him out, ready to yank his license? Or the company's license? That was the last thing he needed. He turned, strode inside his apartment, and slammed the door.

CHAPTER TWENTY-NINE

After Decker picked up Ashley, they went for pizza. She was in turquoise this time, looking even softer and cuddlier than usual.

It would be a shame when spring came, and she stopped wearing sweaters. She probably ate something at home, but he was famished. Plus, he hadn't seen her in a while and wanted time to talk with her, watch her smile, light hair framing her face, and look into her eyes. She was a good remedy to ward off punctured tires, baseballs, and confusion.

Back in the car, he grabbed her hand. "Why don't we head for our bench at the zoo?"

She looked at him lovingly and nodded. His previous fiasco popped in his mind.

He parked the car and rolled down his window a couple inches. "It's colder than I thought."

He slid toward her, clicked her seat belt, pulled her to him, and shivered like he needed warming up. She giggled. Holding her face with one hand, he slid his other arm around her back underneath her coat. When he kissed her, she let out a sigh, turned her face up, and kissed him harder.

Coats open, their chests touched. She kissed him deeper and relaxed into him. He started breathing fast and let his hand on her cheek drift down her neck. Pressing her against the seat with strength he didn't know he had, he let his hand wander down over her breasts.

He was considering how far down he should go when she stiffened.

"Hey," he said. "Relax." He tentatively moved his hand down her stomach.

She hesitated, then gently pushed him away.

He paused, then tightened his grip around her back, kissing her cheeks and neck. "I thought you liked me," he said, finding it hard to talk.

He nuzzled her neck, fondled her breasts, and pressed his hand down her body.

She pushed her hands firmly against his chest. "I do like you, Decker, but you're scaring me."

He heard fear in her voice and backed off, his breath coming in short bursts. "You've been smiling all over the place, wanting to go out." He swallowed, then kissed her neck. "What did you plan to do? Just tease me?" He kissed her cheek.

She kept her palms on his chest. "I like you, Decker. I do want to go out with you. But I can't—I'm not ready... You're scaring me, Decker. I didn't know this would be...an attack. You better take me home."

He released her, panting, and stared at her. "It's not an attack. You've been flirting with me for weeks. Giving me inviting looks."

He looked at her with disbelief. "You acted like you couldn't wait to be with me. Wearing that...that..." He looked down at her chest. "Oh, forget it."

He fell back against the seat, enervated. He sat there, hoping she'd come kiss him, but she sat still and rigid.

He took a deep breath, wiped the back of his hand across his mouth, and started the engine.

She clicked on her seatbelt, cracked her window, and gazed out. He turned on the radio to fill the silence and flipped to another station. He looked over and reached for her hand. She pulled away.

"So that's the way it is."

"I like being with you, Decker," her voice quavered, "but I think you might be looking for...somebody else."

He calmed down, his anger dissolving to chagrin. Even though she was a flirt, he must have gone too far, too fast. Dang.

They drove to her house in silence. Without waiting for him to open the door, she got out and started walking. He could hardly catch up as she scurried to her house and fumbled with the lock.

"I'm usually not like this," he said. "I didn't mean to scare you. Can I call you?"

She didn't answer. Stone-faced, she turned the lock and stepped inside, never once looking at him.

He threw up his hands. "Never mind."

He wheeled around and headed for his car. Behind him, he heard Montrose's door lock click.

He started the engine, rolled the window all the way down and stomped the accelerator. The date was a total R-bomb. The Mustang jumped forward. He wanted the wind to blow away this crummy ending to a mostly good day. He drove home, scribbled Mom a note, and headed for the hospital.

CHAPTER THIRTY

DECKER HUSTLED TO ROOM 627 AND PEERED IN. MR. CONAHAN sat upright in bed, hair combed, with his eyes half closed and a contented look on his face. A fresh scent assailed Decker's nostrils. Flowers burst from a vase on the windowsill.

"Mr. Conahan, is it okay to come in?"

He turned toward Decker and grinned the smile of a young man. Granddad Hank did that, looked old until something piqued his interest, and a smile faded away the years.

"Sure, come in. Good to see you." He reached out and patted Decker's arm. "Have a seat."

Enjoying the robust sound of Conahan's voice, Decker made his way to the chair by the window, grinning. He glanced at the TV screen.

"You're watching basketball?"

He nodded. "College basketball. Kentucky's playing the Kansas City Jayhawks. They'll probably make the NCAA playoffs in March, but I'll be watching baseball then." He winked. "It's either basketball or five days of hype running up to the Super Bowl. I hope the Patriots beat the Giants, but I can't take five days of pre-game blather. How was practice?"

Decker broke into a smile. "Awesome."

"You were able to concentrate?"

"Had to. Coach had me fielding second with Crush Crocker—that's Turtle—playing left field. I wasn't about to let him get a glove on anything."

"Good. So, you fielded well?"

"Yep. Caught everything. Felt like every ball had my name on it."

Conahan grinned. "How did he play?"

"In one drill, the coach had me running to first and Crush threw me out. But it was only one play."

"That's right."

"The next round, Turtle played second base. He jumped for an easy fly and missed it."

Conahan put out his hand to high-five Decker, both of them grinning like ten-year-olds. "So, you got Turtle out of your head and played like you know how."

Decker sat back in the chair and nodded. "Yes, sir. My eyes were glued to the seams on the balls."

Conahan squinted. "Shiner looks good, only a little yellow around your eye."

Decker touched his face. He'd forgotten about it. "It was worth it."

"Maybe that's why you played so well? Riled up after the fight?"

"It was only a short rumble in the locker room, but I'm glad I pummeled him. Before baseball today, I worked on Antonelli's moves. Who sent you the flowers?"

"My daughters. I didn't want to call and worry them until I had some good news."

"Oh?" Decker leaned forward.

Conahan clasped his hands together and rocked back against the pillows looking smug. "The doctor says my lab work is good. I might be able to go home Friday."

The news hit Decker like a basketball to the gut. "No kidding? That's great!"

"Yep. The old boy still has some life in him."

Has he forgotten about the break-in? The assault?

"What about your head?"

"It's fine. It's sore, but there's no lasting damage."

Decker leaned in closer. "You live alone, right? Who's going to take care of you?"

"Just me." Conahan grinned. "I've been doing it for years."

"Of course, but—"

"My housekeeper said she'll come the day I get home. I'll ask her to stop in every couple of days."

What about the days she didn't come? His attacker would watch the house. He'd know Mr. Conahan was alone. He'd come back.

"What about the man who attacked you?" Decker blurted.

"I think he had his fun. Got it out of his system. I don't think he'll come back."

"How can you be sure?"

"I can't be totally sure." He paused. "I can't remember every word, but I feel like we had our yelling argument and it's over." He smacked his lips and nodded. "Yep. I'm pretty sure it's over."

There must be some memory in his mind, something too painful to pull to the surface and express, but he was still in danger. Decker put his elbow on the chair arm and rubbed his chin. "So, what time will you go home Friday, Mr. Conahan?"

"The doctor makes rounds before lunch, so probably around noon."

Decker leaned back and exhaled. "That's good. That's my lunch hour. I can drive you home."

Taking Conahan home might connect him to the break-in, but he had to risk it.

"From school? There's no need, son. I can take a cab. The

housekeeper said she'd meet me there. I'll call her before I leave."

Decker felt his heart speed up. *The housekeeper would only be there a few hours, then Mr. Conahan would be vulnerable to another attack. This couldn't happen. He couldn't let this happen. He had to think of something.*

"You might need something, and I could go get it, check your locks, make sure everything works."

"Tell you what, son. I'll call you on Friday before I leave. Who knows? The doc might change his mind about my going home. If he discharges me, I'll call you. How's that?"

He had given the nurse his home phone number and a false name.

"My cell phone broke," Decker said. "I'll borrow a phone and call your room about eleven-thirty Friday to see if you're still going home and if you need a ride or anything." He went to the bedside phone and scribbled the phone number to the room.

"That's fine, son." He settled back into the pillows and closed his eyes.

"You won't leave until I get here? "

"No, son."

A nurse popped her head in the door. "Nine o'clock. Visiting hours are over."

"I know. I'll call you, Mr. Conahan."

He gave Decker a short wave. "I guess you better let an old man rest. Don't worry, son. I'll be fine."

Decker walked to the nurses' station. The duty nurse was one he hadn't seen before.

"I'd like to leave you my phone number in case Mr. Conahan needs a ride home this week." She handed him a tablet. "And visitors upset him. No one should be allowed in his room unless Mr. Conahan says he knows them."

"I have a written request about Mr. Conahan for that. I just found it."

"That's great. Thanks."

"Actually, a man did come by and ask for his room number. "

Decker froze.

"I said Mr. Conahan was in ICU and after that, they would move him to another room. We didn't know where that would be. He thought about it awhile, paced around, and eventually left."

"Okay, perfect. If anyone else asks, you won't give him Mr. Conahan's room number, right?"

"Yes, now that you reminded me."

"Good. That's good. Thanks."

He walked to the parking lot, thoughts bouncing inside his head like ping-pong balls. Mr. Conahan needed someone home with him. What did he remember to make him think his argument with the attacker was over? A clear recollection of the event might upset him and burden his heart. He should be in the hospital when he remembered the details, with professionals around who could help him. He was a cardiac patient, after all. *Who came to the hospital looking for him?*

Decker stopped near his car. *Did somebody follow him to the hospital?* He checked the tires. They looked okay. He glanced around the parking lot, got into the car, and drove to the exit.

———

HE PULLED INTO THE GARAGE BESIDE MOM'S CAR. HE WANTED to tell her about practice, but his head swam from Conahan's news. If she'd gone to bed, he could concentrate on what to do next.

He saw his note still on the kitchen counter and grabbed the pen. "I'm home, Mom. I'm pooped from practice and visiting Mr. Conahan in the hospital. See you in the morning. Love, D."

He tiptoed upstairs. The door to her room was closed. He slipped inside his room and quietly closed the door. Since he showered after practice, he wouldn't have to make shower noise. He put on a clean T-shirt and shorts, brushed his teeth, and flopped on the bed.

He would have to tell Mr. Conahan his real name. When he did, the man might not want a ride home. Eventually, he'd have to confess his involvement in the break-in. He only followed the man inside the house because he was concerned about the occupant, but he should have called the police. If the attacker hadn't been sitting across from his mother, he would have. He couldn't explain that to Conahan without involving her.

Decker was pretty sure breaking and entering was a felony. He put his hands behind his head and stared at the ceiling. He didn't steal anything, so maybe he was only guilty of criminal trespass, which was probably a misdemeanor.

What if the assailant took something? If he saw Decker following him, he could claim he followed Decker inside and that *he* was responsible for the theft. How could Decker prove otherwise? They both left DNA in the house.

Unsettling scenarios tumbled through his brain. He doubted he'd sleep much. He had until noon on Friday, a day and a half, to figure something out. He thought of something Churchill said: "Success is stumbling from failure to failure with no loss of enthusiasm."

He tried to sleep. Would he conk out from exhaustion and wake up with an idea?

CHAPTER THIRTY-ONE

DECKER WOKE, DRESSED FOR SCHOOL, AND CLOMPED DOWN THE stairs. Mom sat at the kitchen table, warming her hands around her coffee cup. She looked up and smiled.

"Good practice, huh?"

"I'm into it, Mom. Handling the ball feels totally natural. Like I never stopped playing since last season. I don't think I have to worry about anybody taking my spot at second base."

"That's great, Deck. No more shiners?"

He laughed. "Nope." He popped two pieces of bread into the toaster. "I think Turtle got the picture."

"Turtle?"

"That's what we call him, Mr. Conahan and me. He's much better. The doc says he might leave the hospital. I'm worried about his going home."

"Why?"

"He's old and lives alone. And his heart isn't up to par."

"Maybe we can check on him. I'd like to meet him."

He wasn't sure how that would work. "That's a good idea, Mom. Butter and grape jelly?"

"Sure."

"So how was your date?"

"Very nice. Mike and I had a lot to talk about, and the food was delicious." She ate a bite of toast. "Hmm, good. I'm not sure we'll be going out anymore, but I *would* like to decorate some of his houses."

It appeared Mike Cunningham was out of the picture except for business. Good. "You'll decorate some huge houses, Mom. I know you will. Your clients love what you do."

She jumped up to hug him. "You know, Decker. I think I *will* get to decorate big homes." She handed him her plate. "Spread more peanut butter on my toast, will you? By the way, I got an early morning call the other day. I heard somebody breathing but they didn't say anything, so I hung up. Did anyone you know mention it?"

His throat constricted. "No, Mom. Nobody I know would do that."

They settled at the table while Decker described the finer points of Wednesday's practice. Basking in his excitement, she couldn't stop grinning.

He finished gobbling his toast and raced upstairs to brush his teeth. *Who called Mom and didn't speak?*

He catapulted back down with his gear and threw his backpack onto the kitchen counter long enough to pour milk and gulp it down. He unzipped the backpack and took out the history book.

"Too heavy to haul around until third period." He pecked her on the cheek, noted she was still smiling, and whirled through the kitchen door into the garage. "Bye, Mom. See you this afternoon."

He threw his backpack on the seat, put the history book beside it, and sent a sheet of paper flying to the floor. *What was that?* He didn't remember leaving loose paper in the car. He'd retrieve it later.

He bounded to the driver's side, jumped in, cranked the engine, and cruised to school. Things were rocking.

His shiner was gone, he was back in baseball groove, and he didn't care what Crush Crocker said or did. He was keeping up with schoolwork. Mom and Dad seemed okay, and Mr. Conahan was decidedly better. Whoever tried to visit him at the hospital apparently changed his mind. If only he could figure a way to keep Mr. Conahan safe when he went home.

He found a decent parking place and sauntered into the building. He saw Ashley down the hall and caught up. She looked up at him and glared.

"Ashley, I'm sorry." He walked fast and talked softly. "I'm sorry I scared you. I was just...I don't know. I acted like a jerk." She stopped, looked up at him, nodded curtly and kept walking.

Well, he said he was sorry, and he meant it. That was all he could do. Did her nod mean she accepted his apology?

He trod into class feeling optimistic. He was good in English because he loved to read. He had redeemed his status with Mrs. Pritchard and thought his head was clear enough to do well all semester. He liked *Huckleberry Finn* and *Grapes of Wrath* and counted on her to make *The Crucible* palatable.

He was thinking about Mr. Conahan when she interrupted his thoughts.

"Today, we'll discuss Huck Finn's words and actions in opposition to society's expectations. Huck keeps wrestling with his conscience because he's torn. Is he helping an innocent man escape slavery or stealing Miss Watson's property? He does a lot of lying to himself and others while he walks this tightrope and tries to decide what to do."

Decker appreciated Huck's dilemma.

Mrs. Pritchard picked up the book. "We know that lying will play a major part in the book from these first few lines.

'That book was made by Mr. Mark Twain, and he told the truth, mainly. There was things which he stretched, but mainly he told the truth.'"

"It's immediately obvious," she said, "that truth, or the lack thereof, is a major theme in the book. Huck Finn is a liar throughout the whole novel, but unlike other characters, his lies seem justified and moral to the reader because he's trying to protect himself and Jim and doesn't intend to hurt anybody."

Decker squirmed in his chair and mentally listed his lies, the first one to Officer Thorn about walking down the street at night "to stretch his legs before baseball." Thorn had to know that was ridiculous, but there was no law against walking. He'd never been in trouble. No harm, no foul. Then he gave a false name to Grizzly.

He told the EMTs he was Mr. Conahan's neighbor and neighborhood dog walker. He gave the nurse and Mr. Conahan a false name. *Did he use one false name or two?* The one he remembered was Corey Giles. He hoped it wasn't the name of some serial killer.

None of the lies hurt anybody. They were only meant to protect his mother while he sneaked around trying to determine what was going on. Trouble was, the sneaking and lying hadn't helped anybody or produced results.

Mrs. Pritchard talked about four kinds of lies Huck Finn used, self-serving, harmless, childish, and noble. Decker's lies fit several categories. If the truth surfaced about his entering Conahan's house, the types of lies he told wouldn't matter. Most people would conclude that everything he said or ever would say was a lie.

When the bell rang, he moseyed down the hall to get water from the fountain. He dragged himself into statistics class prepared to be bored to death. After previously suffering through algebra and geometry, he thought he was through with mathematics. Then he learned he had to take either statistics or calculus. He hoped he never saw another math book.

Miss Folkes pranced back and forth discussing various industries that used statistics. Okay. All companies large enough to afford it used statistics at one time or another. He was slightly more interested when she gave examples of how companies used the stats.

His mind wandered to the old neighbor with the porcupine quill whiskers who caught him digging through the shrubs. *Did the guy grub around later and find his phone?* He recalled it needed charging. He hoped the man fumbled with it long enough for the battery to die. Mom and Dad's numbers were listed under "M" and "D" but without names. He didn't think the man would know to ask Siri to call Mom or Dad.

Phones had IMEI numbers like cars had vehicle identification numbers. IMEIs were used to call the carrier to trace the phone's ownership. He doubted Grizzly knew that. If he'd memorized the IMEI number for his own phone, the carrier could help trace it. If, if, if. He had nothing but "ifs" and no answers.

If the man left the phone on, hoping somebody called, he'd be out of luck. He didn't get that many calls, and the battery would poop out.

He was relieved when the bell rang. Once he got through statistics, he could look forward to European history. Maybe he could get Mr. Mack on the topic of Winston Churchill and World War II. Decker loved war stories, spy stories, and accounts of the French underground resistance.

He'd read *A Separate Peace, The Diary of Anne Frank, Band of Brothers, The Book Thief,* and a short biography of Winston Churchill. He'd read pre-publication publicity about *The Code Talker* coming next summer and would read it.

Churchill fascinated him for the way he withstood opposition politics and rejection and stayed focused on saving England. He wanted to be like him; not a politician, but a man who didn't back down from what he believed. He wanted to read longer biographies of Churchill to learn the source of his courage. When his mind fogged, even his favorite World War II heroes receded into oblivion.

He could use Churchill's wisdom about now. It was odd the new science teacher Josh Baker was the Churchill fan instead of Mr. Mack. Maybe Baker would loan him a book. His own small volume of Churchill's quotations was dog-eared.

Decker wished he had baseball practice after school to breathe some fresh air. If he could concentrate on baseball a few hours, he could quit worrying about Mr. Conahan.

He sauntered into world history class. When he entered and slung the backpack onto his desk, Mr. Mack gave him a jovial smile. Decker remembered he left his history book in the car.

"My book's in the car, Mr. Mack. I'll be right back."

He raced toward the parking lot and grabbed the book off the seat. A single paper floated to the floor and caught his eye. He picked it up and read.

I felt somebody tailing me. I combed the area and found your phone. It has some interesting texts and phone numbers and photographs on it you probably don't want made public. Forget the man in the hospital. Forget the house. This is not your business. If you know what's good for you, you'll stay away. Bad things could happen to you. Or to your family. STAY AWAY.

Sweat beads popped on his upper lip. The letters moved on the paper. He blinked and realized his hand shook. The man knew Decker followed him...knew he was in the house. How did he find his phone? Why did he wait until now to reveal he had it? Was he tracking him? His family?

Was he watching Mr. Conahan? Was he the one who asked the nurse for Conahan's room number? Was he a dangerous criminal? The one who sliced his tire? Who tried to take him out with a baseball?

From pursuer, he'd become the pursued. He had to calm down and decide what to do. Make a plan. He shoved the paper into the glove compartment and locked it. He'd study it later to see what he could glean from it. Stiff-legged, he wrenched himself from the car and headed back to history class.

CHAPTER THIRTY-TWO

QUEASY AND WEAK KNEED, DECKER DROPPED THE HISTORY book on his desk. Mr. Mack stopped talking and squinted at him.

"Are you all right, Decker?"

"I'm okay. Didn't eat much breakfast."

"I see. If you start feeling badly, you can leave. Go see the nurse."

"Yes, sir." He sank into the chair.

"We'll continue with our discussion of settlements in Europe, where people emigrated from, where they settled, and factors that distinguished them into separate regions and countries. Please turn to page 159."

Decker fumbled through the book to the right page and stared at it as the teacher's voice faded to a hum. All he could think of was the note.

The creep knew he'd been in Conahan's house. *Had he seen his face? Is that how he knew who he was? Or did he sense somebody following him, find the phone later, and retrieve information from it?*

He couldn't recall texts or photos he thought were problematic. He didn't care about weird stuff. And he didn't take selfies.

If he called Mom or Dad about Decker, they would have told him. If the creep said he saw Decker in the house, he'd have to explain his own presence there and Mr. Conahan's injury.

He remembered the photo he snapped during the chase. It showed only that Decker followed the man. It didn't further implicate either one of them. He doubted the scumbag knew enough to search for the IMEI code.

The neighbor who caught Decker picking through his shrubs, was most likely to have found the phone. *Did he give it to this creep? Was Mom in danger?* The phone call she mentioned where nobody spoke—was it him? His head spun.

Maybe the lowlife held some old grudge against his parents and followed him to Dad's. After the attacker discovered who Decker was, did he decide to square things for some past grievance against his family? He figured since the smart aleck kid followed him, he'd devise a way to implicate him and his family to get himself off the hook. He might be biding his time, waiting to blackmail them.

He couldn't ask the police for help. He put his head in his hands, then sat up so Mr. Mack wouldn't ask him what was wrong.

What would the man do with his phone? Use it to prove Decker was in the house? If the man was apprehended, would he claim Decker attacked Mr. Conahan instead of him? He couldn't prove otherwise.

He heard a bell ring, sensed movement, and realized people were leaving class. He closed the book, stuffed it into his backpack, and shuffled out of the room with the crowd.

Decker shambled into chemistry class, trudged to his seat, and folded himself into the chair. Hopefully, the teacher would lecture the whole time and not ask him any questions.

Dr. Fortner was drawing a bunch of unintelligible shapes and formulas on the board. When everyone was seated, the professor turned to them with a delighted look on his face and peered over his bifocals.

"Today we're going to study atoms and molecules and how they balance in chemical equations."

Decker closed his eyes.

"Decker. Are you all right?"

Decker jerked up. "Yes, sir. Sorry, sir. Stayed up too late."

Fortner looked disgusted. "That's too bad. All right then, let's begin."

Decker stared at the board to appear interested. Fortner ran his finger around on the board through images of atoms and molecules, and his voice faded into the background.

Decker's mind was a jumble of questions, options, and fears, thoughts too chaotic to seize and mold them into coherent plans. He thought about how the man got his phone, what he was planning, and the dangers he and his family faced. Scenarios raced through his head until it began to throb. His stomach cramped. He wondered how much longer he could sit there without springing out of the room. A century passed before the bell rang.

He knew he needed to eat, bounded to the cafeteria, and got in line. Everything looked disgusting. He grabbed a banana, an apple, and two chocolate milk cartons and took them outside, sucking in fresh air like it was a lifeline. He headed for the big oak in the grassy oasis between buildings. Hungry for solitude, he plopped against the trunk under the tree's protective shadow and tried to collect himself.

He slipped a textbook out of his backpack and laid it to one side. If somebody sauntered his way looking like they wanted to talk, he'd grab the book and hide behind it.

He peeled the banana and chewed it. If the culprit put the note into his car at home, he knew where he and Mom lived.

She was also in danger. Had he involved himself in a scheme that would implicate her in something criminal? He had to know if somebody held an old grudge against one of his parents.

A group of girls emerged from a building and headed in his direction. Ashley Montrose was with them. He raised the book in front of his face. One girl pointed at him. They all looked his way, changed course, and walked on. She obviously told them about their date. They'd tell everybody in school. Some of them had boyfriends on the baseball team. Before he got the assailant's message, he'd might have worried about what she said.

The note must have been in his car before this morning. Maybe the louse was a spectator at ball practice and placed it there. Did he lock it? Was a window down? *Did the scumbag have something to do with baseball?* He crunched the apple.

Did the creep follow him to the hospital? That's probably how he knew where Conahan was. He could have knifed his tire there. He had to assume the weasel would attack again if he had the chance. He would bide his time. When Mr. Conahan was the most vulnerable, he would act.

Decker slurped milk through the straw and replayed the note in his head, trying to remember specifics that would yield clues. Since the man knew who he was and where he lived, his hopes of secretly identifying the attacker were slim.

He heard the bell, scraped himself up off the ground and dragged himself toward Speech class. Walking with his head down, he didn't see Mr. Baker stroll up.

"You look kind of down, Decker. Something I can help with?"

"I don't think so, sir. I'm not sure what to do."

"Churchill often felt that way. There were lots of times when everybody hated him. He said: 'You have enemies?

Good. That means you've stood up for something, sometime in your life.'"

"I guess so, sir."

"Things will get better. They always do. Like the man said: 'Attitude is a little thing that makes a big difference.'"

"I'll try to remember that."

He peeled off toward the science wing. "Good luck, son. I've got a class."

Decker waved an acknowledgment and remembered a Churchill quote that seemed more appropriate. "If you are going through hell, keep going." He tossed his empty cup into a trash bin and headed for speech class.

Miss Hensley's class assignment was to prepare and deliver a five-to-eight-minute speech describing some combination of Christmas break, their return to school or what they expected this semester. Three students gave speeches each class period with breaks between for class discussion about points they made, good or irrelevant.

After the first round of speeches, they were to apply the critiques and textbook information to their second speech. Hopefully, round two would be better.

Fortunately, it wasn't his turn to make a speech. He lagged during date selection and managed to secure a late February date for his first public utterance. Sophomores through seniors took the elective, so students varied widely in their speaking ability. Most of them were terrible.

Sally Thompson stood up, a sophomore who talked about Christmas parties. Bored stiff, Decker decided it was a good time to speculate about the speech he could give.

With my family breaking apart, we had a miserable fall and a wretched Christmas. In January, my dad moved out and my mother prepared to file for divorce. I was so depressed I went to mope at the Broadway Cafe. Soulful songs blasting through the speakers parodied my misery.

A creepy-looking guy sitting in the far booth with his back to me wore a weird hat. His head and neck coiled down into bulky shoulders. Who should enter the dank den but my mother, who hates dark places and never goes to diners. She slid into the booth across from this creep and they talked intently.

When he abruptly jumped up to leave, she looked upset. I found an exit at the back of the diner and followed him. Was this interloper to blame for the destruction of my family? I wasn't far behind when he padded through the adjacent neighborhood and sneaked into a dark house. I hoped to catch him. Instead, I heard him attack the occupant, who is now hospitalized.

The attacker ran out of the house and so did I. If you don't see me again this semester, I'm probably incarcerated. I'll try to send you the rest of my speech from jail.

Everybody would laugh. Nobody would believe the outlandish story, and he'd probably get an A.

CHAPTER THIRTY-THREE

DECKER DIDN'T HAVE BASEBALL PRACTICE ON THURSDAY. HE tossed his backpack on the back seat, swung behind the wheel, and stared at the glove compartment. The note inside smoldered like radio-active coal.

He tore his eyes away from the glove box and looked outside at a line of cars pulling out of the school lot, their drivers going home, to jobs, to a friend's house, to some oasis of a logical existence.

He had to think. The bastard knew his car, knew where he lived and where Conahan was. He could be watching Decker at this moment, ready to follow. The lowlife probably didn't know Conahan had only one more night in the hospital. Decker either had to warn his new friend or make it safe for him to go home. He had no idea how he would do it, only that he had to.

He turned the key and backed out. When he rolled to a stop at the parking lot exit, he checked the rearview mirror. Only two cars were left in the lot, and they weren't moving. He pulled onto Broadway and headed toward Loop 410, passing a couple of service stations, and glancing into the rearview mirror.

He pulled into a third station, parked by the side of the building. and cut the motor. No one pulled in behind him, and he didn't see anyone suspicious. Pulling on his sweatshirt, he yanked the hood up and walked inside the station to use their phone. The cashier pointed him to a pay phone outside.

He closed himself inside the booth and pushed coins into the slot. "Dad. It's me. You doing okay?"

"Yeah. Sure. Don't you have practice?"

"Not today. I told Mom I'd meet her at home between 5:00 and 5:30, but I might be late. I need to see one of my buddies in the hospital. He broke his leg, a compound fracture. He might miss the whole season. He's pretty glum about it. Think you could check on Mom?" Decker waited through the pause.

"Why? Is she having a problem?"

"We check on each other so she doesn't come home to an empty house."

"She does that a lot?"

"Most days. Since you left."

"I see." There was another pause. "I'm not sure she wants me there."

"You could call her. Or go over there and park nearby to make sure she's okay when she goes inside."

Decker thought he heard a glass clink. The wait was interminable. He looked around to see if anyone was watching the booth.

Dad's voice was muted, like he was farther from the phone. "Sorry. I was looking out the window to see if the guy with the Mazda is there."

"Who?"

"I don't know. The windows are tinted. Some strange guy. I'll catch him next time he comes. I'll call Jillian around 5:00."

"Okay, Dad. Thanks."

It was better than nothing. *Was the creep following Dad?* He'd keep an eye out for a Mazda. He checked his watch. Four fifteen. He needed to beat the IH 10 traffic to find out if the doctor planned to discharge Mr. Conahan on Friday.

––––––

WHEN HE KNOCKED ON 627, CONAHAN BELLOWED THROUGH A mouthful. "Come in."

"I didn't mean to interrupt your dinner."

"I'm not very hungry. I've had a few pains. Makes you not want to eat."

Decker's heartbeat quickened. "What are the pains from?"

"They don't know. They'll do some tests in the morning. Doubtful I'll be going home at noon."

Decker felt a weight lift from his shoulders but quashed the emotion before it showed on his face. "Maybe I should let you enjoy your dinner."

Conahan chuckled. "Might be my last one."

"I didn't mean—"

"I know, son. You're better medicine than anything they have around here. Sit down, Corey. I've been doing a lot of thinking and more remembering. Not all of it good. After I finish this, I'll tell you about it. Never want to miss dessert. It's the only edible thing on the tray."

Decker sat in the chair and waited, trying not to watch Conahan hoist every spoonful into his mouth. He looked at the TV. A basketball game.

He looked out the window. A gray, dismal sky hung over the gray asphalt parking lot. He looked at the flowers from

Conahan's daughters. Somebody had changed the water, keeping them fresh. He considered calling his mother to tell her to be observant when she went home and that Dad might call. He nixed the idea. He'd have to explain.

The nurse's aide popped through the door. "All done, Mr. Conahan? Shall I take your tray away?"

"You sure can. Thanks."

Decker remained silent and waited for the door to close behind her and for Conahan to speak.

He leaned back against the pillows and closed his eyes. "I was about to drift off today when I remembered. As soon as I saw him that night, I realized he was someone I knew. We apparently had some kind of recurring argument."

Decker leaned forward, hoping for a name or a description.

"I could make out his form, but his face was fuzzy, indistinguishable. The voice was familiar, yet indiscernible. Maybe a voice I'd heard before." Conahan frowned, bent forward, closed his eyes tight, and shook his head. "I made mistakes in my business and in my marriage. I'm afraid I treated this person shamefully."

"I'm sure you didn't…"

"I did." He nodded, "I did."

Decker couldn't imagine this kind man mistreating anybody. He was understanding and caring, like Granddad Hank. Decker needed Mr. Conahan to be perfect. Somebody had to be perfect.

"I thought we were finished with it, this never-ending argument." His eyes closed. Tears squeezed from the corners. When he opened them, he started nodding, breathing fast. "But now I think he'll be back."

Decker thought he was hyperventilating. He ran to the door and yanked it open. "Nurse! Nurse! We need help."

The nurse whizzed past Decker with another nurse close behind. She looked at Mr. Conahan and grabbed his hand to take his pulse. "Mr. Conahan, can you hear me?"

Eyes closed, he didn't answer. She grabbed a blood pressure cuff, slapped it around his arm, and looked at the heart monitor on the screen. She turned to the other nurse, "Call Rapid Response."

Decker watched Mr. Conahan breathe.

The nurse zoomed into the hall. Seconds later, a voice from the speaker echoed through the hospital. "Rapid Response Team, Room 627. Rapid Response Team, Room 627."

Decker froze, watching his friend struggle to get oxygen into his lungs, unable to speak. His eyes flickered behind the lids, but he seemed unable to open them.

"Time to leave, son," the nurse said.

Decker was glued to the spot.

Two doctors burst into the room wearing green scrub suits with stethoscopes hanging around their necks. More nurses came. A lab-coated technician entered carrying a tray of glass tubes and pulled a syringe from the box. Decker felt queasy.

"History?" the doctor asked the nurse, while looking at Mr. Conahan's face, probing his abdomen and feeling his pulse. She briefed the patient's history while the other doctor read his chart.

"And right before he blacked out?"

The nurse pointed to Decker. "He was here."

"He remembered something. It upset him, and he started hyperventilating."

"Okay, son. We'll take care of him. You have to leave." Decker backed out of the room.

As the door flew open, two people barreled past him

pushing a red cart with labeled drawers down the front, a balloon-like apparatus hanging off one side, and strange looking gear on top with more tubes and a computer screen. Decker stared at it. *What were they going to do to Mr. Conahan?*

Another nurse rolled in a triple-decker stand with another computer on top. Decker stared.

"You must leave, son," the nurse barked. "You can check back later. We'll take good care of him."

Decker nodded and quaked into the hall. Covered in cold sweat, he thought he might throw up. Mr. Conahan was about to remember everything. The man in his room. The attack. It must have been so awful he couldn't face it.

He found the bathroom down the hall, splashed water on his face, took deep breaths and stumbled back to the nurses' station. A new nurse looked up.

"What is the direct line here?" he asked.

She wrote down the number and handed him the paper. Decker scribbled on another piece of paper.

"I need to know about Mr. Conahan. Will you please dial this number and ask for Corey Giles or my friend Decker Savage? I wrote down the names. Please. One of us will be there." He handed it to her, hoping she would call.

He leaned conspiratorially toward her. "I need to tell you something real important. He told me a man visited early without the nurses knowing about it. Whatever the man said, it really upset him." Her eyes grew big.

"The man kept insisting that he remember something he couldn't remember. You should keep any visitors away until you can verify who they are. Check with Mr. Conahan. If he isn't eager to see somebody or doesn't recognize the name, don't let that person into his room. Promise me, you won't let anybody into his room. It might kill him."

The nurse nodded vigorously. "Don't worry," she said dialing the phone. "Security, this is Sixth Floor Cardiology."

Decker maintained eye contact with her, nodded encouragingly, and backed away in the direction of the elevators.

Words flashed across his brain. "Perhaps it is better to be irresponsible and right, than to be responsible and wrong." He hoped Churchill was right.

CHAPTER THIRTY-FOUR

DECKER SAT IN HIS MUSTANG IN METHODIST HOSPITAL'S parking lot and prayed for calm. For the ability to think. For Mr. Conahan to be all right. For some inkling of what to do.

He turned the key, his hand shaking. If Mr. Conahan survived this, he couldn't ask him to remember any more. He couldn't take the chance. If he remembered later, at least he'd be in the hospital with people watching.

Decker drove to the exit and continued to IH 10. It didn't matter how the culprit managed to retrieve his phone. He had Decker pegged, knew he'd been in Conahan's house, and decided to threaten him and his family. He had to protect Conahan, Mom, and Dad until he could expose the assailant.

Since the doctor wouldn't release Conahan on Friday and would probably keep him hospitalized through the weekend, he had time to maneuver. Although the perp might be someone Conahan mistreated who moved from Houston to San Antonio, he lacked the time and expertise to search Conahan's Houston history.

Decker had to assume the assailant was local, an enemy of Mom or Dad taking out revenge on their nosy kid who interrupted his plans, somebody in business or at school with a vindictive connection to Conahan.

He'd go home, check on Mom, set up a meeting with Dad, and figure out a way to search through their associates for possible enemies. He garaged his car next to Mom's and sat for a minute, taking deep breaths to restore himself to normal. When he got out of the car, he had made a decision. Mom was in the kitchen, pouring herself a glass of wine. He pecked her on the check.

"Dad asked me to come for dinner sometime. Since I don't have practice, this might be a good night to go. Did he call you about my coming or anything?"

"No, but he did call to see if I was all right. It was nice. Different." She looked puzzled. "I have a pile of research ahead to gather ideas for new clients tomorrow and dinner with different clients tomorrow night. So, enjoy yourself with Dad. You and I can plan on a lazy weekend."

He called Dad on the kitchen phone. "Dad, why don't I pick up Chinese food and bring it over for dinner? Good. Do you have your school scrapbooks over there? Yeah? Good. It might be fun to look at them."

Mom glanced over and raised an eyebrow.

Decker shrugged. "Something to do. It'll be fun."

He hauled his backpack upstairs, washed his hands and face and called Dad back. "Do you have beer and other stuff there?"

"Yeah. Plenty."

He clomped downstairs. "See you tomorrow after baseball, Mom."

He drove down the Austin Highway to Walzem and crossed under IH-35. The string of strip centers started on the left with plenty of burger joints and liquor stores. He pulled into the first Chinese place he saw and ordered one chicken with snow peas dinner for them to share, a couple of spring rolls, and a serving of rice. An insubstantial meal would be perfect.

After he passed Roosevelt High School, the stream of apartment complexes increased. Lined up like barracks, they were distinguishable only by their entry signs, with names like tree groves to make them sound lush, tropical, and exclusive.

Towering Oaks, Cypress Garden Cove, Paradise Palms. Decker turned right into Tanglegrove Glen, which was tree-less, and drove two rows back until he spotted Dad's white pickup, stark against the faded wood plank structure. He grabbed the bag of Chinese food off the seat, plodded to 237, and rapped on the door.

"Come in, Decker. Glad you came."

"Me too. I'll set the food in the kitchen. How 'bout a beer first?"

"Sure. Let's have one. I'm already one ahead of you." They flopped onto the sofa and stared at the TV.

"Nothing much on except some basketball games I don't care about," Dad said.

"Let's look at your scrapbooks."

"Yeah. Okay." He finished his beer and went to the bedroom. He came back with a 1985 Conroe High School yearbook and one from Texas University. "I haven't looked at these in a long time. Have a look. I'm switching to scotch."

Decker flipped through the Conroe yearbook and found the football team.

Dad came back and plopped on the couch. "That's me, there." He pointed to number 43. "I played running back. Pretty fast dude, if I do say so. We made bi-district that year." He guzzled the scotch and walked back to the kitchen. "This is good stuff. You want some?"

"Maybe later." Dad returned with a full drink, sat, and pointed out various members of his team.

193

Decker listened attentively. None were named Conahan. "Conroe. That's not far from Houston, right? Did you play any Houston teams?"

"We played some 5A teams, but I don't remember much about them. We were more interested in 6A teams from bigger schools that went to state, so we knew who some of those guys were." He downed his drink.

"Did you ever know a guy named Conahan?"

"Conahan." He paused. "I don't think so. There was a guy named Cunningham who graduated a couple years ahead of me. Jack maybe? I knew about him because their baseball team won state. Why? Do you know somebody by that name?"

Decker shrugged. "I met a guy named Cunningham last year from another team whose father and grandfather had played ball. He said he used to live somewhere near Houston."

"Probably not the same guy. You getting hungry?"

"Not yet. Let's look at the UT scrapbook."

"Okay. I'll get a refill."

Decker opened the book and looked for the football team. There was his dad in an orange jersey.

"All the guys at UT wanted to date your mother. Think I'll have a small refill." He wove to the kitchen, sloshed liquid into his glass, stumbled back, and plopped beside Decker.

Dad flipped back through the pages with zigzagging fingers. "See there? This is the sha-ror-ity section." His finger slipped off the page. He leaned back into the couch and closed his eyes. "They were a bunch of gorgeous girls."

Decker nodded. "Looks good, Dad. You guys were huge that year."

"We had to be. Some of those opposing linemen were ginormous. We spent all summer trying to bulk up so we wouldn't get killed." He took a swig. "Two guys on the Oklahoma team were built like refrigerators." He laughed and finished the drink.

He bent over the book, flipped back to his team, and started reading names with slurred speech and pointed to different players.

Decker listened and watched.

"Steely, Newsome, Bergstrom, Chauncey, or was it Chancy, Montrose, Beckendorf..."

"Montrose? Lee Montrose?"

"Yeah. He walked on and did a few practices and a couple games but didn't make the team. I don't know why he's in the photo. Must have been before Coach sacked him. You know him?"

"I met him." He squinted close to the page. It could be the same guy, Ashley's father. "If it's the same man, he recently moved here with his daughter."

Dad gulped the rest of his drink. "He was in San Antonio a few years back. Left after his wife divorced him. I guess he moved back, the jerk. I heard he has a big house. Probably got it from his wife. He wanted to date your mother."

"Mom? When?"

"First time he saw her. She'd never be interested in that Montrose guy." Trent flipped to the sorority picture.

Decker perused the group. His mother was in the front row, smiling and beautiful. He looked at his dad. "Do you want to eat something?"

"Maybe later. You can look at the book first." Dad leaned back into the cushions and started snoring.

Decker left the yearbook open, slid off the couch, slipped quietly into his father's bedroom, and went straight to the desk.

He looked through a Rolodex and recognized neighbors' names and a few of Dad's golf buddies. Names alone weren't very helpful. He flipped through papers on the desk, careful not to make paper-shuffling noise. Nothing interesting.

He considered the free-standing two-drawer metal file cabinet and soundlessly glided open the top drawer. Files hung alphabetically, front to back. He was glad Dad maintained some semblance of order.

Decker fingered through the files, stopping only if he recognized a name or if the file was fat. He found files for Dad's golfing buddies, his insurance company friend Stephen Hall, and his deceased father Austin Hall. A copy of an official-looking document stopped him. The headline read, "State of Texas: Hall versus Savage." It looked like the summary of a legal document. He slipped the paper from the file:

"In a recent filing, Stephen Hall of Hall Insurance Company alleges that Trent Savage, Vice President and COO of Hall Insurance, which operates two insurance companies under the Hall umbrella, stole funds from the companies' reserve funds. Mr. Hall's father, Austin Hall, deceased, was founder of the companies and employed Mr. Savage as the former COO of Hall Insurance. Stephen Hall, Austin Hall's son, is now CEO."

Decker replaced the copy and slid it back into the cabinet. Neither of his parents ever mentioned the lawsuit. He heard his father stir on the sofa and caught his breath. He turned toward the bathroom, ready to barrel toward it if he heard a noise. Dad resumed snoring.

He silently flipped faster through the upper and lower drawers but didn't see another name that rang a bell. As he closed the second drawer, he heard books crash to the floor and jetted to the living room.

His father had slid to a prone position on the couch and knocked the yearbooks off the table. Decker was amazed the noise didn't wake him. He got the blanket off the arm of the sofa and draped it over his dad.

He went into the kitchen, found a pad and pencil, and wrote, "Dad, thanks for a great evening. I loved seeing the scrapbooks. I'm sorry we drank before we ate. I put the food in the refrigerator. I'm fine to drive home and will call you tomorrow. Love, D."

CHAPTER THIRTY-FIVE

FEELING LIKE A TRAITOR, HE DROVE HOME. TO MAKE SURE Mom's car was the only thing in the garage, he shined bright lights into the interior. He put down the garage doors, locked them and used his house key to enter the kitchen, their standard routine when either of them came home late.

Through the kitchen, he saw the long oval dining room covered with furniture catalogs and massive books of fabric samples and wall coverings. Mom must have worn herself out and gone to bed. To appease his rumbling stomach, he made a peanut butter and jelly sandwich, poured a glass of milk, and plopped at the kitchen table.

What was Mom's relationship with Montrose? If Ashley told her dad she was afraid of Decker, the guy would either have punched him or wouldn't have let him in. He was glad he apologized. Maybe her response was an act, and she was still teasing him. Who knew?

He needed to know more about Hall's lawsuit. He might be able to catch Stephen Hall at the club over the weekend, but it was problematic. Since Dad relinquished his membership, Decker wasn't even supposed to be there. He'd rather talk to Hall privately in his office anyway. He could see the man's face and gauge his feelings toward his dad. He didn't want to risk alienating Hall even further.

Churchill's wisdom popped into his head, a short version: "One ought never to turn one's back on a threatened danger and try to run away...If you do that, you will double the danger...If you meet it promptly, you will reduce the danger by half."

Decker didn't know if he could reduce the danger, but he had to face it. He had to flush out Mr. Conahan's attacker before his friend was discharged from the hospital and sent home where he'd be accessible and unprotected.

He would have to catch Mr. Hall on a weekday. Tomorrow was Friday, and Monday might be too late. There was only one way to see Mr. Hall before the weekend. He would run by Mr. Mack's class in the morning, tell him he didn't feel well, ask to be excused third period, and if he'd relay the message to his fourth period teacher.

Mr. Mack would do it. He already thought Decker was ill. They had a scrimmage against Kyle at 5:00 so he'd have to be back for that. He picked up the kitchen phone and dialed the nurses' desk on the sixth floor.

"Hello. This is Corey Giles. I've been visiting Mr. Conahan. When I left earlier today, he was really upset about a visitor who pressed him for information. He was hyperventilating. Is he okay?"

"Hello, Corey. I can't tell you much, hospital rules and all, but we believe he'll be okay."

"Will the doctor keep him there tomorrow and through the weekend?"

"I imagine so. He'll probably order some tests."

"Okay. That's good. He'll be safe there."

"Beg your pardon?"

"You all take such good care of him."

"Yes, we do. Good night, Corey."

Suddenly exhausted, he left his backpack on the chair and trudged upstairs. Mom's door was closed, and a faint light glowed underneath. She probably fell asleep reading.

Inside his room, he doused the lights and crashed on top of the bed. He tried to figure out what to say to Steven Hall and fell asleep with his clothes on.

CHAPTER THIRTY-SIX

TRENT SAVAGE WOKE AT 8:00 A.M. FRIDAY MORNING WITH HIS head full of rocks. He staggered to the bathroom and splashed water on his face until his eyes focused. After downing two aspirin, he minced his way toward the kitchen. When he saw his desk, he paused. Moving his eyes toward it was like forcing his eyeballs through sand grit.

He needed to read up on policies he pulled out and make calls to a few friends. He had really left the papers in a mess. Decker probably didn't notice.

Trent made it to the kitchen, fixed himself a Bloody Mary, and eased down onto the sofa to take a sip. He picked a lousy time to drink so much with Decker there. The kid seemed to enjoy himself, though, looking through pictures of his old dad suited up for football.

He had coached football since Decker was in grade school and always wanted him on the team. After the kid played on his first team, he didn't appear interested. The boy wasn't built like him. Decker was lanky, with a smaller frame like Jillian, but he would grow. With enough practice, who knew?

When they moved to Prospect Heights, Trent intended to

take full advantage of their location: meet prominent people, become affluent like they were, be a star, and have his son be a star—the tough guy, the cool stud everybody admired—like he always wanted to be.

He persuaded Decker to play on a few more teams. His boy could pass and catch, but he didn't like to tackle. He hated football.

When Casey came along, fast, compact, and fearless, Trent thought he might be the one to play ball. If Jillian hadn't been so interested in her damn iPhone at the neighborhood barbecue instead of paying attention to her son, Casey might still be alive. His head throbbed like a bass drum. He still couldn't believe Casey was gone.

After he died, all Jillian wanted to do was buy furniture. Times were hard enough, and she was spending like a banshee. How could he ever get ahead?

Lately, he noticed something different about Decker. He was more serious. He might be wondering about college. Since he was playing great ball, maybe he could get a scholarship. At least they seemed to be re-connecting. Despite all that had happened, they could still be pals.

He thought about the guy he saw parked near the fence in his apartment complex. He walked to the curtain and squinted at the bright day. Nothing appeared unusual. Most people were at work mid-morning.

Why would Hall hire some guy to see where he lived and check his comings and goings? What would be the point?

He didn't think Jillian would bother to hire a private investigator to check on him. He would ask her next time they talked. If he saw the car again, he'd sneak up on the guy and find out who the hell he was.

CHAPTER THIRTY-SEVEN

DECKER WOKE UP ALERT, KNOWING HE HAD A LOT OF PUZZLE pieces to fill in. When he sprang downstairs, Mom was still in her robe sipping coffee. "Morning. I thought you had lots of clients to see today."

She peered dully over the cup rim. "I do. I pored over sample books all day and stayed awake half the night thinking about what to recommend. My first appointment is at ten, so I have time to get it together. How 'bout you? Big day today?"

"No tests or anything." He didn't want to think about the real tests coming up. "We have a scrimmage against Kyle at 5:00."

"Is Dad going?"

"I doubt it. We had a late night."

"He drank too much."

It wasn't a question. "He had a few beers...said he had a lot of work to do today."

"You better go, Deck. If I don't see you between your game and my client dinner, I'll see you in the morning. We'll sleep late."

He pecked her on the forehead. "I bet you knock 'em dead. I love you, Mom."

He started the Mustang and sat in the garage, wanting to stay home, wishing home was like it used to be, and school was just school.

He had to get through English and statistics, get excused from third and fourth period, find Stephen Hall in his office, and try to figure out if he was the jerk making his life miserable.

He had been to Hall's office when Dad worked there. He thought about calling first but decided Hall might not see him. If he appeared without warning, he had a better chance to learn what the man really thought about his dad. He'd catch him mid-morning so he couldn't plead a lunch date. Was he the scoundrel trying to frame Decker for catching him in Conahan's house so he could avenge his father's larceny? He had no idea why Hall would enter Conahan's house, but he had to start somewhere.

The bell ending statistics class finally rang. He marked the chapter in the book about charts, graphs, and probabilities, hoping he could catch up later and fathom the material.

He went to the bathroom and washed his face, wishing he'd snagged a couple bananas to fortify him until lunch. For some reason, he thought about *Don Quixote,* the book they read last year in Spanish class. He read the story in English and remembered thinking that a story about a man chasing a non-existent dream was stupid. With his family crumbling and him chasing a phantom, he understood.

He headed for Mr. Mack's class to feign illness and be excused. Mack was sympathetic. "Maybe you should see a doctor, Decker."

"It's okay, sir. A mild stomach bug. I'll be all right."

He ran to his car and headed north on Broadway toward the building which housed Hall Insurance Companies. The two-story brick structure spread the length of the block and had distinctive sandstone trim on the front. The company name lettered in black steel stretching across the front of the building was substantial, but not ostentatious. Hall Insurance occupied the ground floor and leased the top floor for smaller offices. A low sign on the lawn gave names and office numbers for upstairs tenants.

There were only a few places to park on the Broadway side. What if his dad drove by, saw his car, marched into Stephen Hall's office and made a scene? He drove around the building and parked in the back lot.

He and Dad used the back door entrance, but he didn't want to look like he was sneaking in to cause trouble, so he walked back around to the front and entered the double-wide glass doors. Hall Insurance occupied space on both sides of the center elevators.

The reception desk was on the left side behind a glass wall. The receptionist smiled when he walked in.

"I'd like to see Mr. Hall, please."

"Do you have an appointment?"

"No, but I think he'll see me. I'm Decker Savage."

"Just a minute. I'll see if he's busy."

A flutter riled Decker's stomach.

She returned and gestured for him to follow. "His next appointment isn't for twenty minutes. I'll take you back."

Decker followed her to the office at the end of the hall. He saw his father's office on the right, *Trent Savage, Chief Operating Officer.* The office was dark, and the door was closed.

Stephen Hall smiled at Decker as he entered and extended his hand. After they shook, he stepped behind his desk and indicated for Decker to take the client chair. "What can I do for you, Decker?"

He took a deep breath, unsure of how to start. Might as

well jump in. "I heard you were suing Dad, and I'd like to hear your side of it."

Hall leaned back, put his elbows on the armrests, and clasped his hands together. "Companies selling life insurance are required by state law to keep a certain amount of funds in reserve to pay future claims. If we don't maintain those funds, we're breaking state law. I'm afraid your dad stole money, he says 'borrowed,' from our reserve fund." He watched Decker's face fall. "We can't have that."

Decker hung his head. "I see."

"We're obligated to replenish the money. Your dad paid more than half the funds back before we discovered the loss."

Decker looked up hopefully.

"I told him we would add his buy-in funds to the reserves to reduce the amount he still owes."

"Buy-in funds?"

"Yes. Your dad had no experience in the insurance business when my dad hired him. We took a risk on him; he would have to be trained and might never sell anything. We thought he could sell insurance, and he did, but we had to protect our company and our policy holders."

Stephen paused. "Normally, we don't give out this information, but since you're his son...we had him put up $500,000 against premium income he brought in during his first three years. He would keep what he needed to live on and pay as much as he could against the debt."

"Five hundred..."

"Yes. He borrowed it from the bank and from your mother's father."

"Granddad Hank?" Decker hadn't known Granddad had anywhere close to a half million dollars. He never said a word. Nobody said a word. It explained another reason why Mom and Dad split up. "So, you fired him."

"No. When we discovered the loss, we talked to him. He

wasn't sure when or if he could replace the rest, so we had to sue for it. We couldn't ignore it. We had to report it to the Texas Department of Insurance and assure them we were trying to rectify the problem. We asked them not to publicize our loss or disclose our financial information. Only your dad and I knew how much was missing. And we tried to keep the lawsuit quiet. I'm sorry you found out about it." He threw up his hands, then clasped them.

"It never made the newspapers?"

"No. It was ready to print. A friend showed it to me. But we called people we knew at the paper, and they agreed to keep it out. We told them the lawsuit was a formality. We didn't think it would ever go to court. We made a deal with the newspaper; if the matter went to trial, they would have exclusive coverage."

"Thank you for that." Decker remembered the column he read. "I read about the lawsuit in a news clipping."

"Apparently, somebody from the Texas Department of Insurance leaked the information and a daily business journal picked up the story. When we learned about it, we called the department and the journal, and they put a stop to it. The story didn't go any further."

"That's good news."

Stephen nodded agreement. "Recouping our losses was what we all wanted. Naturally, we were all uncomfortable with the situation. Trent decided on his own it would be better if he left and worked from home. He paid more money back, and if he continues, I might want him to come back to work. Of course, we'd drop the lawsuit. I know how hard it was for all of you to lose Casey."

Decker felt his eyes fill. "Yes, sir. It was...is. It's good that you and Dad—" He couldn't finish.

"I know, son. Is that the reason you came here?"

"The lawsuit, yes. Dad moved out, Mom is overwhelmed

with new clients, and my friend is in the hospital." He swallowed. "And there's some unknown guy following me. I'm not sure what's going on. Do you know a man named Mitchell Conahan?"

"No, I'm afraid I don't. Friend of yours?"

"A new friend. He's the one in the hospital. He's older, sort of like Granddad."

"I see."

He geared up and decided to take a risk. "Can I tell Dad he might be able to come back if he repays the money? That you'll drop the lawsuit?"

"He knows. You can tell him again if you like. The offer is still good."

Decker stood and reached across the desk to shake the man's hand. He knew tears streamed down his face, but he didn't care. "Thank you, Mr. Hall. I'll tell him the offer is still good. I think it will help a lot."

He strode down the hall past Dad's dark door, plodded to the back door of the building, and stepped outside into a howling wind. A cold front had blasted in. Hoodie up, he bent against the wind and pushed toward his car. He got in and sat, wiping his face dry and rubbing his hands together so he could calm down and think.

Hall seemed too decent to hurt Conahan. He didn't think he was the attacker, but what if Hall's company was about to fold? They must already be losing ground.

What if Conahan owed Hall money, maybe over a past business deal that went bad? Hall would know he couldn't recoup losses from the Savage family now, but he would assume Conahan could pay him back. What if Conahan refused? Was Hall desperate enough to threaten or hurt him? He needed to find out if Mr. Conahan had any financial connections with Hall Insurance.

Whatever was true, he needed to encourage Dad to help

him get back on his feet. He'd think through the best way to do it. He wondered if Dad told Mom he borrowed money from Granddad. He sure wasn't going to bring it up.

Decker blew onto his hands. Stephen Hall seemed an unlikely suspect, but you couldn't always tell about people. Decker used to trust everyone until he heard the scumbag attack Mr. Conahan. Now, until he exposed the culprit, he suspected everyone.

Hall said that besides Dad, he and his dad were the only ones who knew how much was missing. Maybe he borrowed from the reserve fund himself when things turned south, information he didn't want revealed.

Decker looked at his watch. He would return to school, suit up for baseball, and head for Olmos Park Field. This was their first scrimmage against another team. The biting cold would revive him.

CHAPTER THIRTY-EIGHT

HE WATCHED THE KID FROM VARIOUS VANTAGE POINTS.

He looked like a walking zombie. The stress of school, baseball, and his hospitalized friend's condition was stressing him out. He must be swimming in confusion. His note apparently had the desired effect.

He started out thinking he might be able to reason with the boy, but the kid was persistent. He didn't follow orders and was apparently strong-willed enough to try to solve problems on his own without involving his family. He had to admit he found it admirable the kid had the strength to forge ahead. He was still going to school, playing baseball, living with his mom, and visiting his dad.

What else was he doing? What if he had the fortitude to press and dig until he discovered the truth?

He couldn't have that. His future was at risk. It was him or the boy.

He looked through an array of paper used by everyone on the planet and grabbed a Bic. It was time to ratchet up the pressure, boost the kid's anxiety. He clicked the pen. What could he write— or do—to stop the boy dead in his tracks?

CHAPTER THIRTY-NINE

DECKER WENT TO THE GYM LOCKER ROOM, SUITED UP, PULLED his letter jacket over his uniform, and drove to Olmos Park Field. The radio announcer said the temperature dropped from sixty to thirty-five and would plummet below freezing overnight. It would be even colder in the Hill Country. He was glad the team from Kyle was scheduled to play here.

Tree branches looked barren and desperate, now, bending wearily from the wind. With everything in his life going downhill, he couldn't imagine ever thinking they looked expectant and optimistic. He was terrified Mr. Conahan's attack might prove fatal.

Dad was on his way to becoming alcoholic. If he didn't get furious about Decker's going there, it might help Dad to tell him what Hall said

Meanwhile, I'm not any closer to finding the creep who hurt my friend and threatened my family. The bastard is plotting to send me to jail.

He pulled up to the field where Prospect and Kyle warmed up. Guys pulled bands through the fence to stretch their arms. They jumped up and down between pulls to stay warm. On the field, they jogged in place between throws. He spotted Coach Branson and loped over to tell him he'd been excused from school but felt better and was eager to play.

"Good, Savage. Make sure you warm up."

His arms and shoulders stiff with cold, he grabbed a J band on his way to the fence and bounced while he pushed the band through an opening. After every five pulls, he did jumping jacks or squats until sweat beaded above his lip. Loosened up, he felt better.

Once he finished arm stretches, he scooped up a ball and ran onto the field. He caught Turtle's eye and drilled the ball at him. Turtle caught it, surprise flooding his face. He probably thought Savage was AWOL, and he was a shoe-in for second base.

Decker glared at him. Did Crush Crocker blast the ball at his head in the parking lot?

After he caught the ball, Turtle collected himself, smirked at Decker and blasted the ball to Sweeney, whose face remained expressionless.

Decker tossed another ball to Paco, and they backed up for long toss. When Coach blew the whistle, they jogged toward home plate. Since Prospect was the home team, Kyle would bat first. Prospect's pitcher was hot, and Kyle didn't score.

The Tigers were up. Decker was seventh in the batting lineup. Doing jumping jacks to say warm, he glanced at the bleachers wondering who cared enough about the team to brave the weather. Diehards Tensel and Baker sat in the stands wearing heavy coats. It was nice to have faculty you liked and could talk to, even about stuff they weren't teaching. He saw Dad wave to him and waved back.

"Go get 'em, Deck!"

Maybe Dad would come to love baseball, and they'd have something in common. Rummaging through Dad's files made him remember what Huck Finn said: "A person does a low-down thing, and then he don't want to take no consequences of it. Thinks as long as he can hide it, it ain't no disgrace." Decker knew better.

Mom might have enemies too. He was glad she wasn't at the game and that her work kept her primarily inside.

Sweeney's parents cuddled in a blanket. He missed his buddy and time with their family. A pang of remorse shot through his chest.

Montrose, in a burly coat and stupid-looking hat, glared at him. On the lower bleacher seats, Ashley sat with four girl-friends, pointedly looking the other way. They huddled in furry jackets, wore ski hats or earmuffs, had blankets spread across their legs, and stomped their feet to stay warm.

Decker managed to stay warm until he got to the batting cage but had trouble watching the ball. He decided the ball was the perp's head, and the seams were his beady eyes, smoldering as he wrote threatening notes. He cracked the next balls hard, sending the slime ball's head spinning down center field.

The Tiger's first six hitters three singles. Kyle's fielders looked sharp and kept their score to zero.

He heard "batter up" and jogged to the plate. Gusts of wind whooshed from the right. He'd have to lean into the ball and hit it harder than usual. Kyle's pitcher was a tall kid with a long face. Decker hoped he knew how to duck.

On the first pitch, he popped up a foul. A Kyle outfielder scrambled for it and caught it outside the lines. For the next pitch, he crouched forward, bat high above his right shoulder, and stared at the ball in the pitcher's hand. It flew at him straight in the zone. He heard the crack of his bat and laced the ball to a gap past the center fielder. He took off, rounded first, and slid into second. The outfielder threw a wild ball that screamed over his head. He barely made it to third.

The next batter was newbie Randy Waller. He connected on a low pitch and sent it flying deep over the wall for a home run. Waller started rounding bases. Decker flew across home plate and waited for Randy. They high-fived and brought the crowd to its feet. Newby Waller might have just earned his place on Prospect's varsity.

The pitcher looked determined. He warmed up and struck out the next three batters. Heights 2, Kyle 0.

Decker was pumped. To stay warm, he jogged in place until Coach pointed him toward second base. He took off.

He cut the noise from his head and concentrated on the ball. As though he willed it, the ball sailed to his glove. He threw the second and third batters out at first. The next batter hit a solid grounder to right field. Decker ran over, bent into position, and snagged the ball just inside the third base line. He heaved it to first base. Out.

The next innings flew by, with Decker thinking only about the ball, where it was going, and how he would field it. With Antonelli's voice in his head telling him what to do, he watched for players trying to steal bases. He was in a baseball dream. Nothing else mattered—not the threats, not the hospital, not Hall insurance.

The game ended at Kyle 2, Prospect Heights 7. He could have played forever.

His Tigers gathered at home plate, slapping backs and shaking hands with Kyle players. Dad was yelling his heart out. Decker broke into a smile. He hoped that despite the cold weather, somebody was scouting his team.

Dad pulled his collar up around his ears, bounced down the bleacher steps, and headed for his car. Decker remembered how he rifled Dad's files and began to deflate. He hoped Dad didn't notice anything different. He didn't know how he'd bring up going to see Hall, but he had to tell him.

Suddenly cold, he curled into his letter jacket and trotted

toward his Mustang, bumping fists with passing teammates. People scurried to cars and climbed onto the bus, eager to warm up. Tensel and Baker, talking and laughing, boarded after the students, heavy coats stretched up around their necks.

He felt like he was being watched, but he looked in every direction and saw no one. He moved around the car, checking the tires. Satisfied that everything looked normal, he slid inside and started the engine.

He thought about calling the hospital when he got home, but doubted they'd tell him anything this soon after Mr. Conahan's attack. He'd call Dad.

Mom probably left for dinner with clients, but she usually left him a note. She would have left her client list at home. Much as it pained him, he planned to rifle her files, too. Someone was making their life miserable, trying to ruin them. He had to find out who it was.

He remembered Widow Douglass telling Huck Finn how "he must help other people...do everything he could for other people...look out for them all the time...never think about himself."

Decker couldn't do the last part, never think of himself. If he didn't find the lowlife stalker, he could wind up out of school, out of baseball, and in jail with his family in tatters. He turned the Mustang toward home.

CHAPTER FORTY

HE ROLLED INTO THE GARAGE ALONGSIDE MOM'S CAR. Someone must have picked her up. When he pushed open his door, a wind gust dislodged a small paper hidden under the seat of the passenger side. Decker stared at it, cold chills wrapping his heart. He made himself pick it up and read the words scratched on the wrinkled sheet of paper.

Nice game, sport. Could be your last. What a shame. Your parents would be real disappointed—if they're still around. Couldn't stay away from the hospital, could you? It was bad enough you broke into his house. Now he might die, thanks to you. Your family is already messed up and financially fragile. Hiring a lawyer to defend you will finish them off.

So, here's the deal. If the old man wakes up, you're going to tell him you broke into his house. You saw him in the neighborhood, elderly and alone. You needed money, hated to ask your struggling mother, and knew your father would not be sympathetic. You were going to take something and leave, but after you got inside, the man called out from upstairs. Without thinking, you ran up to see what happened.

When you reached his bedroom door, he started ranting about

221

his children, how they hurt him and that you were the worst. You stepped toward him to calm him down, explain why you broke into his house, and offer help. He yelled and came closer, and you pushed him back. He lost his balance and crashed to the floor. You heard sirens and thought a vehicle stopped in front of his house. When somebody banged on the front door, you panicked and fled.

You're going to tell your parents the same story. And you're going to convince them. Otherwise, you'll lose everything. School. Baseball. Family. Friends. You'll be in jail with a hopeless future. I'll see to it. If you don't tell them, I will.

CHAPTER FORTY-ONE

HE WAS GLAD MOM WAS GONE. HE DIDN'T HAVE TO TRY TO HIDE the distress on his face about the note, not to mention the guilt for what he was about to do. He'd decide later what to do about the rat's demands. The threat made it more urgent to learn who the bastard was.

He stuck a frozen pizza into the oven. While he waited for it to heat, he drank a half gallon of Coke and crystallized a plan. Mom kept her files on the dining room table. He would leave the sample books where they were and concentrate on the box he thought contained client's names. When the stove buzzer rang, he retrieved the pizza and sat at the kitchen table, tearing off pieces.

If she came in early, he didn't want to be parked at the dining room table rifling through her file box. He'd move it to the other end of the table, out of view from the front door.

If he heard her key in the lock, he'd put the box back where it belonged and race upstairs into his room as fast as he could without making noise. She'd be relaxed, weary, unhurried, and wearing high heels. He thought he could make it to his room without her seeing him.

He finished the pizza and peered into the garage to make sure her car wasn't there. He zipped open his backpack and tore out a sheet of notebook paper to make notes, carried paper and pen to the dining room, and stared at the file box. He had the sensation that touching it would burn his hand. "Sometimes," Churchill said, "It is not enough that we do our best; sometimes we must do what is required."

He sighed. He didn't want to dig through her records. What he was about to do could splinter what little was left of his family. How could he possibly explain the circumstances that led to his actions?

Before he could start, he needed to look around his home and soak it up. He might end up in jail and never see this house again.

He got up to gaze at places he always pictured, the spot where Dad burst through the front door, making a big deal out of bringing home a pizza. Or he'd sit on a stool at the kitchen counter and talk intently with some guy on the phone and doodle on a pad. Dad was Mr. Personality, carrying on about a ball game or hunting or golf, whatever interested the guy.

Decker knew he was laying the groundwork for selling the guy insurance. But first, he took plenty of time to ingratiate himself as a friend.

He smiled, picturing Mom gliding around her Avignon kitchen, fixing dinner among her shiny new appliances.

He peered into the living room at her glass tables. Gleaming wood cabinets and bookshelves stood solidly against walls as if standing guard for the metal-enclosed glass side tables. It was like a joust between fanciful and real. He enjoyed fanciful but was comforted by real.

He never told anybody how he viewed his house. They'd think he was nuts. Most people, he noticed, guys at least, never looked around at much of anything unless it had female parts.

When she and Dad stopped communicating months ago, and Mom re-started her decorating business, it consumed her. If she wasn't perfecting some detail in their house, she was glued to the phone suggesting how somebody could enhance theirs. She searched through furniture catalogues and planned buying trips to the Dallas market.

She was gone a lot, but so was Dad. Over the last months before he moved out, he was frequently absent. Each of them was a closed entity, obsessed with themselves and oblivious to the other. Decker wasn't sure where he fit in. Or if.

He heard them arguing about him—the sports he played, the clothes he wore, the music he liked, his infrequent hair-cuts, how he should study, whether he should go to college, whether his grades would be good enough. He hated being the subject of their disagreements, but he didn't know what to do about it or how to stop it.

He wanted to go back in time and wrap himself inside this room with Mom and Dad and Casey and breathe in love and security. Tears welled behind his eyes.

They were all at the Walden's neighborhood party. Casey grew fussy and needed a nap, so Mom walked the boys home to put Casey down. Decker could stay home watching TV and listen for sounds of Casey waking. The minute he did, Decker was to go to his room and call Mom. She or Dad would come home, check on the boys and determine if there was time to return to the party.

Decker was watching Stargate Infinity when he thought he heard a noise in Casey's bedroom. The cadets were about to discover who the traitor was. As soon as the commercial came on, he went to Casey's room. Casey wasn't there.

He looked under the bed, in the closet, in the nearest bathroom. He charged to his own room, searching places where Casey liked to hide. He sprinted to Mom and Dad's room, peered in closets, flattened himself to check under the bed, scrambled to their bathroom and scanned the tub, the shower, inside the closet. He raced through the house, checking every room—closets, laundry hampers, cabinets. Casey was nowhere.

He raced to the back door and found it open. Thinking Casey was padding toward the Walden's, four houses away, he took off, scanning the yards in route. When he passed by the Talbot's pool, he saw Casey floating face-down, his curly brown hair moving gently on the water.

He tore through the gate Casey somehow managed to open and screamed for Mom and Dad as he dove in to get Casey out. He and Mom got him on the side of the pool and pushed his tiny lungs from the back. He tipped him over, pinched his nose and puffed into his mouth.

Mom was screaming. Dad shouted, "Let me try. Let me try." They tried everything. Casey remained limp. He was gone.

Eyes filling, he remembered reading to Casey before he went to sleep. Every so often, he'd look up at Decker with worshipful baby eyes, and smile. When he got sleepy, he'd lay his head on his brother's shoulder and lap an arm over Decker's chest. Decker was his trusted hero.

He blinked away tears, wiped his eyes and plodded to the dining room while he was still able to go through Mom's clients.

He opened her file box and flipped through A and B cards, not recognizing any names. In the Cs, he stopped at Cunningham and read her notes: Michael Cunningham. Cunningham and Sloan. Business address. Underneath, she listed customers' names and addresses, and made notes of their preferred styles, noting sample books and ID numbers for fabrics or floor samples. Eight homes were listed, all in The Dominion.

Mom had a lot of business coming her way from Michael Cunningham. The list of customers covered four cards with project start dates, occasional notes, and a few doodles. He couldn't make anything of the doodles; they must indicate she was thinking.

A note on the last card caught his attention. "Mike—3rd dinner." After "Mike" and "dinner," she put question marks. He looked at the back of the card for answers. It was blank.

In D through L, he found no familiar names, no mention of dinners, no question marks. In the M's, he found Montrose.

The man knew his mother but said he hadn't seen her since they moved back to San Antonio, yet here he was among her clients. Lee Montrose. No notations for fabric, flooring, or project start dates—only his and Ashley's home address with Montrose's name crossed through.

He made it to the end of the box without recognizing more names. There were no more question marks, no cross-throughs, and only a few doodles.

Easing out of the chair, he slid it under the table and returned the file box to its place. He stuffed the blank paper and pen into his pocket and stopped in the kitchen before going upstairs. He'd leave his backpack there so she'd know he was home.

He felt his pocket. The bastard's note crinkled.

Her key clicked the lock. Bounding for the stairs, he scaled them two at a time and slipped into his room. He closed the door and leaned against it, waiting for her to call his name. He heard her heels click on the kitchen floor and the rush of tap water. He must have made it without being heard.

He stepped into the shower and leaned back to let warm,

cleansing water pour over him. He thought about Cunningham and Montrose. What if he met with the men but mishandled the encounters and made everything worse?

He longed for a life in control, backed by a united family. He always honored his parents, no matter what. He was fracturing what little was left of that bond. No matter how long he stood under the flow, the guilt wouldn't wash off. He was not much better than the man tracking him; the man intent on destroying his family.

Decker got into bed, pulled the covers up to his chin, and turned to the wall, longing for sleep.

Learning their son had entered a stranger's home would split Mom and Dad further apart. His legal defense would bleed them of what little they saved. Dad would sink into alcoholism, unable to sell insurance. Mom would be too distraught to run her business. They would probably lose the house, and he'd be in jail.

Exhaustion finally brought sleep. He was being chased through a tropical forest by Hall, Montrose, Ashley, Cunningham, and a ghost. He ran near a swamp, tripped over a log into a pool of quicksand and started to sink. Casey was sinking beside him. He grabbed his arm.

His pursuers and the ghost slithered to the edge of the swamp, yelling at him and waving clubs. If he inched toward solid ground, they moved in closer and raised their clubs, eager to beat him and his brother deeper into the quagmire.

Mom and Dad were ten feet behind his enemies, chained to trees several feet apart, calling to him and shouting to each other, but unable to help.

A helicopter appeared overhead and hovered above the swamp. Men in the copter shot blanks at the hostile group around him and scattered them into the forest. Mr. Conahan and Coach Branson descended from the copter on ladders and threw ropes.

With one arm gripping Casey's body, he reached for the rope and missed. They sank deeper. The men lowered the ropes farther. With supreme effort, he grasped Casey, stretched his body upward, almost within reach, and strained to grab the ropes.

"Hold on, Decker," his parents shouted.

He woke with one arm clutched against his chest and the other reaching skyward. Sweat drenched his body.

CHAPTER FORTY-TWO

JILLIAN HEARD DECKER CLOMPING DOWNSTAIRS AND LOOKED UP from her Saturday morning coffee. "Good morning to sleep late, huh, Deck? How was the game?"

"Awesome. I was totally in the zone. I knew where the ball would go almost the whole time. We won 7-2."

"That's wonderful! I mixed batter for pancakes. Are you ready?"

"You bet. How was your evening?"

"Lovely. We went to La Paloma. Mike wants me to do more houses in The Dominion and is talking to lot owners to see if they're interested." She smiled before turning toward the stove. "I'm making progress on the others I'm decorating. Everything's going well."

"That's good. Have you ever had a seriously angry client?"

She turned back around, tilted her head, and blinked.

"No. I don't think so. I've had a couple where our design ideas didn't mesh, but nobody got angry. We parted friends. What makes you ask?"

"Just curious. That's good. I'm glad Mr. Cunningham likes your work. Maybe I can meet him sometime."

She looked quizzical. "Sure. He'd like that. I've talked about you a lot."

"Really? Does he know who I am?"

"He's seen your pictures in the house, and I told him you play baseball."

"Does he come to the games?"

"I don't think so. He never mentioned it."

"There's somebody from school who knows you, Lee Montrose."

She turned to the stove, eyes focused on her pancakes.

"I dated his daughter, Ashley. We didn't hit it off too well, but I met Mr. Montrose when I picked her up."

She flipped a pancake.

"He said he knew you but hadn't seen you since they moved back to San Antonio."

"Really. Well, it's probably good our paths don't cross. I knew him in college and didn't much care for him."

"Interesting. I had the same feeling."

"What are you doing today, Deck?"

"Probably hang out with Sweeney." He felt a pang in his chest.

While they devoured pancakes, he described more baseball plays.

"Are you working today, Mom?"

"I'll organize some samples here at home and stay in my pajamas in case I want to read or doze." She grinned. "Builders don't usually work on the weekend, and clients are with their families, so nobody should be calling me."

"Good, Mom. I'm glad you can goof off. Thanks for the awesome pancakes. I'll grab my coat and go see what Sweeney's doing."

———

JILLIAN WATCHED HER SUDDENLY TALL SON BARREL INTO THE garage. The Mustang's engine rumbled.

Deck had developed a sudden interest in her male friends. Interesting. She was glad he didn't like Montrose. She hoped Decker never found out she went out with him. She never intended to see the man again.

She thought about the horrible night Montrose called her at the neighbor's party. If Trent hadn't been so intent on getting another drink at the bar instead of going to check the boys like he was supposed to, Casey would still be here. They would be a whole family. Lee Montrose would never have entered the picture. She took deep breaths and blew out guilt and anger.

She wasn't sure what to do about Mike Cunningham. He was so attractive. She had a physical response every time he got close. Unfortunately, she thought he knew it. Her business-like demeanor displayed signs of crumbling. They dined out with clients, then alone.

Last night was their third evening together. Fortunately, they had dinner with the Handys. Her house was closest to La Paloma, so after dinner, it was logical for him to drop her off first before the rest of them headed west to The Dominion. She would have to decide soon whether to become involved with him or risk losing his business.

She forced herself to switch her thoughts to Decker's happy face telling her about the game. He was settling in.

She was glad she didn't tell him what the school counselor said. With baseball going well, she thought his grades would improve. He was studying regularly so his SAT test scores should be good. Once Decker learned something, he never forgot it.

He did strike her, lately, as being more serious. Maybe it was part of maturing. She hoped his hospitalized friend would improve. Her phone rang.

"Hello. This is Nurse Pearson at Methodist Hospital calling for Corey Giles."

"I'm sorry. There's no one here by that name."

"How about...let's see, Decker Savage?"

"That's my son, but I'm afraid he isn't here right now. He lost his cell phone so I can't contact him. Did you call early one morning a few days ago?

"No."

"Would you like to leave a message for Decker?"

"No, thanks. When he returns, will you have him call the Sixth Floor Nurses' Station at Methodist Hospital?"

"Of course." She dialed Sweeney's house.

"Hi, Sara. This is Jillian Savage. Decker got a call from a nurse at Methodist Hospital. He has a sick friend there. Will you put him on?"

"He's not here. Was he supposed to be here?"

"He said he might hang out with Sweeney. I guess he's running errands. Will you have him call me if he comes in?"

"Sure."

How strange. Where would he go besides Sweeney's? To another ball player's house? Where was he? She wished she had bought him a cheap phone, so she'd know he was okay.

CHAPTER FORTY-THREE

DECKER HAD A PLAN. HE DROVE NORTH ON HIGHWAY 281 AND exited at Bitters. Hobby Lobby was packed but it had a great assortment of items he wanted. He found an inexpensive box he thought would work and a package of alphabet letters.

He waited in the interminable line, paid, hustled to his car, and checked his watch. 11:00 a.m. Didn't people who worked Saturdays try to finish by noon? He pasted letters across the top of the box: "Prospect Heights Baseball Challenge." With his pocketknife, he meticulously cut a two-inch wide slit under the letters.

He drove farther north on 281, took Loop 1604 to IH 10 West, and drove northwest into the Hill Country. When he saw the sign for The Dominion, he exited IH 10, crossed the railroad tracks and pulled up to the imposing gate announcing the subdivision. He rolled to a stop at the guard station.

"Hello. I'm Decker Savage going to see the builder, Michael Cunningham."

The guard checked his watch. "He might still be in the builders' hut up there on the right."

The barrier lifted and Decker cruised inside. He saw signs of construction, bore right, and spotted the builders' hut at one side of a parking lot. The sign in front read, "Build Your Dream Home at The Dominion."

He strode to the hut and opened the door. A man about six foot one stood from behind his desk, smiling. He had black hair, deep blue eyes, and a mouth full of brilliantly white teeth. A secretary perched behind a smaller desk to his right. The man walked to Decker and extended his hand.

"Mike Cunningham. How can we help you?"

"Hello, sir. I'm collecting in various neighborhoods for the Prospect Heights Baseball Team. We have a chance to make State this year, and we have old shabby uniforms. We're hoping to collect enough to buy new ones."

"I see. You play baseball?"

"Yes, sir," he said. "Decker Savage."

"Savage. Are you Jillian's son?" He leaned forward with renewed interest.

"Yes, sir. I know she decorates a lot of homes out here and thought somebody might like to contribute to our team."

Cunningham threw back his head and gave a hearty laugh. "I'll be darned." He pumped Decker's hand. "I know your mom. Now I remember seeing your picture. She's a lovely lady. She's been decorating a lot of my houses. So, she told you I build homes out here?"

"She mentioned your name. I thought The Dominion, with its fine homes and all, might have somebody who would want to help us out."

His laugh boomed. "You're quite the entrepreneur. We should put you on the sales force. I'm happy to contribute, Decker. " He reached for his wallet and put twenty dollars into the slot. "Being Saturday, I'm not sure homeowners want someone ringing their doorbells to collect money."

"I get it, sir. Solicitation and all."

"That's right, son. We don't have much of that around here. Now, I could put a sign on my desk with your box by it and tell whoever I see about your team needing uniforms. Maybe some of them will contribute."

Decker understood why he sold a slew of homes. He was better looking than Dad and a lot smoother. Before Dad started drinking so much, they would have been about equal.

"That's a great idea, Mr. Cunningham. I appreciate that. I'm glad you and Mom get along." He watched Cunningham's expression. "She's a talented decorator."

"We get along fine. Just fine. And you're right. She's very talented."

"Yes, sir. I better go. I'll leave the box with you."

"It's in good hands. I'll see what I can do. You can come back in a couple weeks, or I can give it to Jillian next time I see her."

Decker knew Cunningham would see his mom regardless of what he said. "That would be great, sir. If you'll give it to her whenever you're ready, I'll take it to more neighborhoods." *There weren't any other neighborhoods like this one.*

"Fine, Decker. And good luck. I'll see you again, no doubt. How is your team doing? You think you might have a shot at the state championship?" He smiled again.

"Yes, sir, we have the players. If we can fine tune everything before the season starts, I think we might have a shot. Do you ever come to the games?"

"By the time we get finished around here, it's usually after five. Traffic back to the northeast side of town is grueling. I'm usually ready to go home and collapse. One of these days, though. I'd like to watch you play."

"Yes, sir. I hope so, sir." He shook his hand again before leaving.

Decker got into his Mustang, feeling sleazy. When Cunningham said, "How can I help you," he felt like saying, "I'm a trust fund baby and want to tour the most expensive pad you have in this outrageous display of wealth."

Or even better, "You can help by not pressuring my mom for a relationship while she's still fragile."

He could think of more graphic ways to say it, like "If you hurt my mom, I'll be crawling up your..." He was glad he didn't take that route.

Cunningham didn't appear to be the type to slink down dark streets to break into a house. But what if he was acquainted with the guy Decker followed and learned what happened?

He could decide to fracture their family even further and be there to comfort Mom when she discovered what Decker did. That was a stretch, but the whole sequence of events was bizarre. Anything was possible.

Since it was 12:30 p.m. and he was starving and light in the wallet, he headed home to raid the refrigerator and plan his next move.

He pulled into the garage by Mom's car and bounded though the kitchen door heading for the fridge. "Mom. It's me."

She came in from the den barefoot, wearing jeans and a T-shirt. "I called you at Sweeney's, Decker, but his mom said you weren't there."

"I decided not to go. I felt like driving around so I went out to The Dominion to see your fancy houses. I happened to meet Mike Cunningham."

"Really."

"Yeah. Nice fellow. Our baseball uniforms are getting shabby, so the guys dreamed up a fundraiser for new ones. I thought homeowners in The Dominion were good prospects."

He had to convince the guys and Coach they needed uniforms, or he'd be caught in another lie. "So, what's up?"

"A nurse called from Methodist Hospital and asked for you. She didn't say how your friend is, but..."

He grabbed a hunk of cheese and a banana and scrambled into the garage.

CHAPTER FORTY-FOUR

DECKER DROVE AS FAST AS HE COULD TO METHODIST HOSPITAL. The nurse wouldn't have called unless something was wrong. If the scoundrel went to Conahan's room...he banged his fist on the steering wheel and swerved into the adjacent lane. The driver slammed his horn and Decker jerked back. He should slow down and calm down. Having a wreck wouldn't help anybody.

He parked and raced across the lobby toward the elevators. He pushed the button and stared up at numbers, watching them mark the elevators' incredibly slow descent. When the door finally rolled open, he jumped in and poked the button for six, panting. When the door inched open, he sprinted to the nurses' station in the cardiac wing.

No one manned the desk. He looked up and down the empty hall. Everyone must be busy with patients. He swirled and headed for Room 627, listened at the door and heard nothing.

"Mr. Conahan?" Nothing.

He pushed open the door and walked in. The room was empty. His heart dropped like a stone. The bed's sterile white sheets were tucked in tight. The vase from his daughters was on the windowsill, but the flowers had drooped and died.

Tears formed in his eyes. The nightstand drawers were closed. The moveable bedside tray table was parked and still. The room was cold. Lifeless.

Did he die? Sniffing back tears, he stumbled back to the nurses' station.

A nurse he had never seen before looked up. "Can I help you?"

He swallowed. "Mr. Mitchell Conahan used to be in 627. He's not there."

"When I came on duty at three, the notes said he had an emergency, and they took him to Radiology."

"An emergency." His throat constricted. "Do you know what happened?" He barely managed to get the words out without shouting. He reeled in his emotions. "We're old friends."

She assessed him. "I'll find his chart. Maybe there's something I can tell you."

She reached into a shelf below the counter and thumbed through charts he couldn't see. She pulled one and bent over it. "He had pain." She skipped some words. "His problem was deemed acute." More words skipped. "They took him down to Radiology for tests and evaluation." She looked up.

"Radiology. Is he still there?"

"I'm afraid that's all I can tell you. He's either there or they stabilized him and took him to another area."

"You don't know where?"

"No. I'm afraid not." She slipped the chart back under the counter and folded her hands.

"Do you know if he had any visitors?"

"I'm afraid I don't know. He could have, before I came on duty."

She smiled. She wasn't going to divulge more than

sketchy information. He leaned toward her conspiratorially. "There's something I have to tell you."

She raised her eyebrows expectantly and waited.

"There's a visitor who harassed him, a man who previously caused him to have an attack. I alerted the other nurses. They contacted Security to question anyone who asks to see him. So, if he should be transferred back here…"

"I understand." She reached for the receiver.

"Where is Radiology?" he asked.

"Sub-level Two." She cradled the receiver and pushed a button.

He nodded somberly and gave her a thumbs up sign as she connected with Security. He hurried to the elevator and pressed "SL2." Radiology was underground to protect people on upper-floors from X- rays. The oversized metal enclosure descended two floors beneath ground level like a group casket.

When the door creaked open, he saw a sign that said "Radiology Waiting Room" with a Bluebird stationed at the desk. He conjured up his most appealing smile and approached. Plump with curly hair, she reminded him of Mrs. Sweeney.

"Can you tell me how Mr. Conahan is? Mitchell Conahan?"

"Are you a family member? Name?"

"Corey Giles."

She ran her finger down the page, then down another page. "I'm afraid you're not listed, Mr. Giles."

"I'm really only a close friend. Can you tell me how he is? What kind of tests he's having?"

"I'm afraid not." She smiled.

"Is he still here in Radiology? Or did they take him someplace else?"

"I'm afraid I can't tell you that either." She kept smiling.

"Has he had other visitors?"

She threw her hands up but kept smiling.

"Okay. I see. Thanks, anyway." He turned away from the desk, tears of anger, frustration, and fear welling behind his eyes. The louse could have attacked him. Conahan could have died, and nobody would tell him anything.

He had an idea. He took the elevator to the lobby and went to the Bluebird at the Information Desk. A woman he had never seen before perched behind the counter. "Can you tell me what room Mr. Mitchell Conahan is in?"

"Sure." She looked at her screen, scrolled down, scrolled back through the names, and looked up.

"I'm afraid he's not listed."

"He was here yesterday. Does that mean he was released?" He swallowed back tears. "Or he died?"

She saw the tears. "I'm sorry, son. It could mean one of those things. Or he could be having tests or in surgery and they haven't reassigned him to a room yet. You can check back later."

He wiped his sleeve across his eyes while his insides disintegrated to ash. "All right," he said, his voice gurgling. "I'll do that. Thank you."

He grabbed tissues from the box on her counter and plodded numbly to his car. He crumbled into the front seat and sobbed. His heart ached like it did when Granddad Hank died. He raced to the hospital then too, but he didn't make it. Granddad Hank was gone. Somebody took him away and Decker didn't even get to see him.

Granddad Hank was the family glue, the one who calmed things down, the boulder who held back waves, whose wisdom made sense. In some inexplicable way, Mr. Conahan had filled the empty cavern inside him and renewed his hope. And he was gone.

Grief sucked him back into the bag of fog. He knew it

made no sense, but he felt abandoned by Granddad and by Mr. Conahan.

As far as he knew, he was the only one who cared at all about Mr. Conahan. He couldn't let him fade into oblivion.

He wiped his nose and eyes, opened the window, and leaned his head back against the seat. The bitter wind would dry his face and snap him out of it. When his face went numb, he started the engine.

One bastard would be glad Conahan was gone. He would find that bastard.

Cold wind whipped his face as he drove down the freeway. He shivered and raised the window. The temperature must be thirty-two and dropping. His car lights caught debris flapping across the road. Trees bent with the wind like old men.

He had no place to go except home. He thought Mom would be there. At least, it would be warm. He felt sorry for Dad in his crummy apartment. He was probably watching TV and drinking. Was it drafty? He remembered seeing the blanket on the sofa. He didn't think he'd be cold.

Tomorrow was Sunday. He and Mom had stopped going to church. Neither wanted to answer questions about their situation. If he could concentrate, he ought to try to study.

If he could pull himself together, Sunday might be a good day to catch Lee Montrose. He needed to size him up without Ashley being there. He amazed himself. How cunning and deceptive he had become. He didn't like being this way, but it was the only way he knew to gather information.

When he got inside, Mom was in her pajamas, watching TV in the den. He went in to kiss her. "I love you, Mom."

"I love you too, Decker. I was getting kind of worried. Is your friend okay?'

"I hope so. They took him downstairs for tests." He heard

fear in his own voice. "I'll go back tomorrow and see how he is."

She studied his face and put her hand on his cheek. "I hope he'll be all right, Decker.... Want to watch TV?"

"No, thanks. I'll get something to eat and take it upstairs and try to study. I haven't hit the books much in a couple days. Then I might call Sweeney. Find out what he's doing."

"Okay, Deck. If you're gone several hours, call me so I know you're okay."

He hated lying. "Will do, Mom."

CHAPTER FORTY-FIVE

Mom looked rested and refreshed. "Morning, Decker."

He longed for the days when the four of them went to church on Sunday, then to Jim's Coffee Shop for breakfast. "What are you doing today, Mom?"

"Fine-tuning projects and organizing client presentations. I hope some of them contract for my decorating services this week." Her cheeks were pink with excitement.

"Wow, Mom, big week."

"Yes. How about you?"

"I thought I'd go to the library. Maybe I can study better in a different place. Then I'll go see Mr. Conahan."

"Sounds good, Decker. All of it. Check in occasionally so I know you're okay. I'll be here."

"Sure thing."

———

Decker crouched in his Mustang across the street, three blocks down from Ashley Montrose's house, his car obscured by the trunk of a tree near the road. From his vantage point, he could see if she left.

After an hour, he thought he was going to freeze to death. At three p.m., she backed out of their driveway in her Volkswagen bug convertible, top up, and drove in the opposite direction down the street.

He reached back to pull up the hoodie under his letter jacket and hustled to the front door. Having procured another box and more lettering from Hobby Lobby, he rang the bell. When Lee Montrose opened it, he held the box in front of him, smiling.

"It's nice to see you again, Mr. Montrose. Decker Savage. I was in the neighborhood and thought I'd stop by. Our team is conducting a fundraiser for uniforms."

Montrose looked suspicious. "First, I heard of it, Decker. It's a pretty cold day to be out ringing doorbells. Ashley's not here."

"That's okay, sir, I was hoping to see you. We're just starting to raise funds. We figured we'd get a jump on the other school teams and clubs. Mind if I come in and tell you about it? We depend a lot on our school parents."

Montrose looked resigned. "I guess so. If it doesn't take long. I was watching the Super Bowl."

"I'll make it brief." He stepped toward the door. Montrose reluctantly stepped aside to let him in, his expression sour. He was doubly glad he apologized to Ashley.

Montrose tromped to the den in socks and sweats, his gut popping out between top and bottom. Men went to seed fast without wives around. He plopped onto the sofa and directed Decker to a straight-backed chair.

"Thank you, sir." He proceeded to give him the pitch about their unsightly, fading, practically unusable uniforms and the team's hopes to advance to State.

Montrose half-listened, one eye on the television. When

the commercial came on, Decker made his move. He leaned forward and spoke louder. "So how much would you like to contribute?"

Montrose, looking disgusted, rose to get his wallet off the counter dividing the den from the kitchen. Decker started chattering.

"I already asked Mom to contribute. And some of our neighbors. I thought I should branch out, though, to really help the team. There's a lot of guys on the squad. I guess you still haven't seen Mom. It'll be like old home week when you two meet, since you knew each other in college."

Montrose turned back toward him, a peculiar look on his face. "Like I told you earlier, I haven't seen her."

"You'll probably bump into each other. She'll be glad to see you. You were probably college buds, right?"

Montrose crunched a ten-dollar bill in Decker's hand and slapped his wallet back on the counter. Decker saw him clinch a fist. "No. We were not buds. I wanted to date her, but she met your dad."

"Oh. You knew him, too?"

"We played football together at UT...briefly."

"No kidding. I didn't know that. You guys had a tough team, right?"

"It was okay. Your dad was a better player. The college drafted him. That's why he was in the jock fraternity. I tried to walk on. They kept me for a while, but I didn't make the team. I was more serious about studying anyway—a history major. Your mother liked jocks better."

Decker let that sink in. "I'll have to ask Dad for a donation."

Montrose was suddenly interested. "He's not living at home?"

Decker made his face blank. "It's temporary. Until they get things worked out."

"Uh huh." One corner of his mouth eased up. "That's too bad."

Decker thought the scumbag was enjoying it. When the game came back on, Montrose turned up the volume.

"Guess I better go," he said. He shook Montrose's hand, studying his face, and made his way to the front door. "Thanks for the donation."

"Don't mention it." Montrose shut the door behind him. Decker loped to his car, jumped inside and pulled away.

He needed to tell the guys about these plans for new uniforms—give them a heads up so they could approach Coach together.

He headed to Loop 410 thinking about Montrose. He was grumpy, defensive, sloppy, and creepily interested in his mother. He still carried a grudge because Mom preferred jocks to him. He probably hated Dad. Was that reason enough for him to develop a scheme to hurt the whole family?

What was his connection to Mr. Conahan?

———

HE TURNED NORTHWEST ON IH 10 AND EXITED AT MEDICAL Drive, determined to find out what happened to his friend. He decided to go directly to Room 627. If he had a heart attack and survived, they might have returned him to the same room, or at least to the same floor.

He took the elevator to six and saw another nurse at the desk. If he found Mr. Conahan's room empty, he'd pump her for information.

He knocked on the door and peered in. It was still vacant, and the vase was gone from the windowsill. He went to the nurses' station. He hadn't seen this nurse before, but she seemed pleasant.

"My name is Corey Giles. I'm a friend of Mr. Mitchell Conahan and visited him several times when he was in Room 627. Later, he had some sort of emergency and went to Radiology. I don't know what happened to him after that. Can you please help me find out?"

"I can try. He's not in our wing. I'll call downstairs and see if they have him listed in another room." She clicked buttons on her phone and waited.

Decker's heart leaped to his throat, all the tension he felt about Mr. Conahan rising in a flood.

"Yes, that's correct. Mr. Mitchell Conahan," she said into the receiver. She started writing on a pad. Decker held his breath. She put down the phone and looked up.

"He's in Room 707 in the post-surgical wing." She pointed. "If you take the elevator…"

Decker grinned at her. "I'll find it. Thank you so much."

He bounced from one foot to the other waiting for the elevator, the sound of his heartbeat receding in his ears. His stomach settled back into place. The surgical wing? Heart surgery? No. It must have been something else, or he'd be here on the sixth floor. Or in ICU.

What happened? Could he talk?

CHAPTER FORTY-SIX

DECKER KNOCKED ON THE DOOR TO ROOM 707. THE REPLY WAS a rough grunt. Elated, he stuck his head in. "It's me, Mr. Conahan. I thought I'd never find you."

Conahan grinned. "They've been hauling me all over the damn place. At least they're feeding me, even if it is mush."

Decker looked at his tray and nodded. The food looked terrific. Mr. Conahan, his hair tangled and frowzy, looked fantastic.

"So, sit down. What's going on in the outside world?" The Super Bowl blared on TV. He pointed at the screen. "I'll turn that thing off so we can talk." He clicked the remote.

"Okay. Tell me what happened. When I came, you were gone from your room. They said you had some emergency and went to Radiology, but that's all they would tell me. I went down there, but they wouldn't tell me anything."

"You probably thought I was dead, didn't you, son?" He reached over and squeezed Decker's shoulder. "They can't kill this old geezer that easy. I had some kind of pain, and my stomach was distended. They poked and prodded and took a bunch of X-rays and decided to wheel me to the operating room. I apparently had a pre-existing gastric ulcer. Years of stress plus the trauma of getting my head whacked caused the ulcer to flare up and it ruptured. They took a flap of skin floating around in my abdominal cavity and patched it over the hole. I feel a lot better. They have me eating liquids and mush for a while and taking a bunch of pills. The thing is, my heart didn't even flicker; they said it ticked right along the whole time without skipping a beat."

Decker sank into the chair. "That's fantastic."

"They're keeping a watch on it." He pulled down the top of his hospital gown. "Still have these monitors stuck to my chest, but they say everything looks good. The surgical wound is healing nicely, and they expect me to have a full recovery."

"That's awesome."

"Yes. I can't wait to get out of here. What's happening with you? Pretty cold out there on the baseball field, isn't it?"

"It will be. Last time we played, I felt like I was attached to the ball. We have a day off from practice tomorrow. Then a couple days of hard drills before we start the Fenley Tournament. We were so stoked playing against Kyle, Coach gave us Monday off."

"That's great, Corey. I have some good news too. I remembered exactly what happened. Everything."

Decker's mouth flew open. "Are you sure you want to talk about it? Last time—"

"I know. It's okay. Now that I know what happened, it doesn't upset me anymore. The man who came into my room? The one I thought I should recognize? It was one of my sons. We're estranged, and I haven't seen either of them in years, but I think it was one of them. My intruder had bushy hair and extra pounds, but I'm pretty sure it was one or the other."

"Why would he come see you at night? Why would he hurt you?" Decker couldn't imagine attacking his dad, no matter how angry he was. "No wonder you didn't want to remember. Why did he..."

"Well, son, I think it was an impulsive reaction. He'd been angry for so long, it bubbled up inside until he had to come over. I forgot to lock the kitchen door, which made it easy for him to get in."

"Why was he so angry?"

Conahan leaned back against the pillows and took a deep breath. "Like I said, I was a lousy father. I was so consumed with enjoying what I was doing and making money that I believed my way was the only way. When my kids had other talents, other abilities, I scoffed at them, laughed at them, belittled them. I eventually succeeded in pushing them away."

Conahan's eyes grew wet. He looked at the ceiling and blinked. Decker recognized the pain he felt. It was the kind you couldn't eradicate.

He looked back at Decker with a sad face. "Murray studied petroleum engineering, so I thought he was on the right track. He learned how to recognize geological substrata that might contain oil. He'd identify promising areas to drill. I hoped one day we'd be partners. We would still sell drilling equipment, but we could invest in our own wells. I'd ease him into the business and wouldn't have to rely on high-priced geologists and know-nothing lease hounds like Montrose."

Decker's eyebrows shot up. "Montrose? Lee Montrose?"

"Yep. That's him. He was a history major, but for some reason, he thought he knew everything about finding oil. Can't believe I bought into that. Nothing he ever recommended for lease was even promising. Shoot. He might as well have used a witch's divining rod. I fired him."

"He lives here, right?"

"Right. Teaches at some middle school. So, when Murray said he was quitting the oil business and going back to school to become a teacher, I thought he was a loser like Montrose. I was livid. I called him names, said he'd never amount to anything and told him to get out of my sight."

Decker looked down, grappling with how this man could ridicule and berate his own son. "No wonder he was angry."

"Yeah. I was brutal. I never hear from Patrick either. I told him he was hopeless, then ignored him, so I never learned what he wanted to do. For all I know, he might be teaching too—Lord only knows what. He might still be a hippy in California. At least the girls communicate now and then." He gazed through the window at the barren landscape. Decker thought he was seeing memories.

"It took me a long time to realize why they all left. And to admit I'd been selfish and wrong. By the time I realized what I'd done, it was too late. They were scattered all over, and we barely spoke. The girls were more forgiving. I guess they thought it was a male thing and cut me some slack." Sad resignation settled on his face. "The boys knew better."

"You think it was Murray in the room or Patrick?"

Conahan squinted his eyes closed, trying to remember. "His face was fuzzy, and it was dark. The boys had similar voices, and I haven't seen them in years." He shook his head. "Hard to tell."

"Do you know if Patrick is in San Antonio?"

"He could be anywhere."

"What did the man say that night?"

"He called me every name in the book, told me everything I'd done was wrong, that I was responsible for every bad thing in his life. He said searching for oil was a stupid way to make a life. That all I wanted was money and didn't care one whit about people. I finally had enough, got up, and started yelling back."

"Did he hit you?"

Conahan shut his eyes again, struggling to visualize the moment. "There was shoving and more shouting. I remember being off balance, but I don't think he hit me. I think the shoving made me fall. I must have lost my balance. Maybe I hit the bedside table on the way down."

"Did you black out?"

"For a few seconds. But I remember that his voice changed. It was softer. Then I heard sirens. I must have really blacked out then because I woke up in the hospital." He leaned back and closed his eyes.

Decker watched his breathing become regular.

After an eternity, he slowly opened his eyes. "I'll be all right, son. I'm glad I remembered. It takes the weight off. After I fell, I had the sensation that he was sorry. I know I was."

"I have some things to confess too, sir. First off, I'm not Corey Giles."

Conahan frowned. "Who the hell are you?"

"My name is Decker Savage. I do play baseball, but I had to give the nurses a false name because I'd been in your house."

"In my house?"

"Yes, I followed a guy from the Broadway Cafe because he was sitting with my mother, and she and Dad are getting a divorce. I had to know who he was. But then he sneaked into your house. I followed because I was worried about whoever was in there. I heard yelling and somebody hit the floor and sirens screeched and I had to get out of there." He stopped to take a breath.

"I saw them wheel you to the ambulance, got your name from the mailbox, and followed the ambulance to the hospital to see how you were. I lost my phone, and some guy is threatening me and my family with anonymous notes because I was in there, and my parents will be devastated, and I might never go to college. I could even go to jail."

"Whoa. Whoa. We have a lot to unpack here."

"Decker's eyes were leaking. "I know, sir. I'm sorry for the lies and the whole thing."

"Okay, son. It's okay. Let's take a deep breath, and you can start at the beginning."

Decker told him everything; all the names, lies, fears, and about the notes. Mr. Conahan listened attentively until Decker ran out of gas.

"Feels good to lighten the load, doesn't it, Decker?"

"Yes, sir."

"Well, we know you're not a felon. You entered my house because you were worried about the occupant, and you haven't committed any crime."

"No, sir. If lying doesn't count."

"It doesn't. Not in this instance. I never reported anything to the police, so you don't have to worry about that. This guy threatening you, and I hope it's not one of my sons, has nothing to charge you with. You can quit worrying about going to jail."

Decker felt chains fall from his body.

"And your parents' divorce has nothing to do with you, son. Either they can live together, or they can't. You can't change that."

He hung his head. "No, sir. I guess I can't."

"As for the threatening notes, the guy is apparently trying to scare you away from me for fear I'll tell you who pushed me. He obviously hates me. I'm sorry you got caught in the middle."

"It's okay, Mr. Conahan. You couldn't know he'd do any of this."

"No, I couldn't. And I don't think either of my sons could write those notes. I think the guy who did this is bluffing.

Angry and scared, but bluffing. As we Texans say, I think he's way more hat than cattle."

"I sure hope so, sir."

"So, you keep on trying to find this guy, and I'll think about how to help. You concentrate on studying and baseball without worrying about me. The surgery was Friday. If all goes well, the doc says I might go home Tuesday. I can hardly wait. The housekeeper will have my house ready, and I'm glad Cunningham fixed it."

"Cunningham? Michael Cunningham?"

"Yes. I think I told you before. I knew him from when he played ball in Houston when we were kids. I heard about him because he was an ace player. When I heard he came to San Antonio, I called him. He remodeled my house before I moved in. Fixed my bathrooms for a handicapped person in case I need it later. Since the house has two stories, he made me an elevator. He disguised it with a front like a kitchen pantry so it wouldn't be an eyesore."

"But you're not related to him or anything."

"No."

"Did you ever have a feud with him?"

Conahan furrowed his brow, pondering. "Not really. I thought his charges were kind of high, more like Houston prices, I told him. He got a little miffed, but he got over it. He was kind of touchy back then, trying to build a business, you know. From what I read, he's real successful now."

They sat quietly. Mr. Conahan looked out the window, then closed his eyes. Decker watched his eyeballs moving behind the lids. He must be trying to envision the outline of the man who confronted him or trying to replay the man's voice in his head.

Decker found it inconceivable that the louse who attacked Mr. Conahan was one of his sons. If it was, and Decker found him, then what? "There's one more thing, sir."

259

"What's that?"

"If I find the man who did this, and it is one of your sons, do you want to see him?"

Conahan hesitated, then nodded slowly. "Yes. It's time we bury the past. If he's ready, I'm ready."

CHAPTER FORTY-SEVEN

DECKER DROVE HOME, SORTING OUT THE PIECES. MR. CONAHAN was lucky. The pain could have been his heart. He could have died.

It was natural, carrying his guilt, to think the intruder was his son, but Decker wasn't so sure. What if the attacker did his research, hated Conahan for some past transgression, and knew what to say to him that was believable? He'd throw suspicion on Conahan's sons and Decker and get his revenge. Whoever it was, he had to unearth him.

What about Montrose? Conahan berated him and fired him. And Montrose held an old grudge against Mom for preferring Dad.

Maybe, before he apologized to Ashley, she told her father about their disastrous date. If that were true, Montrose would have thrown him out of the house. Unless he had better plans. If Montrose was the guy Decker followed, he could be scheming to implicate him for a break-in and avenge him, his parents, and Conahan all at once.

There was also the smiling Mr. Cunningham. Was he using him and his mother in a plot to ruin Conahan? He knew it was far-fetched, but he had to consider everybody with connections to Conahan or Mom and Dad.

Maybe Cunningham didn't enjoy being told he over-charged when he was trying to build a business. Had Conahan spread the word in Houston?

Mr. Conahan was aging and retired, but he was still wealthy and probably influential. He undoubtedly had assets a good plaintiff's lawyer could confiscate if he could prove Conahan slandered his client. When people were starting out, and vulnerable like Cunningham, they were more apt to get angry and hold grudges. Old hurts ran deep.

There was also Stephen Hall. He said, "If we don't main-tain enough reserve funds, we're breaking the law." How was Dad going to pay him back? He was depressed, frequently drunk, and not at the club where he could cultivate new prospects. Did Hall also dip into the funds?

Even though Hall reported the loss to the insurance commission and sued Dad for the money, it was hard to imagine how he could make up the loss. If he didn't, his company might go bankrupt.

He and Granddad had lots of conversations about how business worked, but Granddad never told him about the five hundred thousand. If the matter went to trial, Mom would learn Granddad loaned Hall Insurance the buy-in money, money that probably belonged to her by inheritance. Did the money legally belong to Hall Insurance? If Hall saw a way to get Decker in trouble, the Savages would be too busy with their own problems to try to recoup money from Hall Insurance.

He tried to picture each man from the back with a bulky coat and stringy hair. Montrose had the hair; the others didn't. But they could have cut it. They were all about the same height, and a bulky winter coat would work for all of them. He assumed it would also work for Murray and Patrick.

The hat seemed unusual but there were probably several like it around.

If it was Conahan's son, which son was it? How could he flush him out? If he found him, he'd let him know he had no grounds for blackmailing Decker. Then he would press him until he learned his relationship with Mom.

He had a lot to do. Since he came clean, and Mr. Conahan forgave him, thank God, he thought he had the fortitude to forge ahead.

CHAPTER FORTY-EIGHT

When Decker woke Monday morning, it was freezing. He burrowed deeper into bed and pulled the covers to his neck. Then he remembered: Mr. Conahan wasn't going to die. But he only had one day before his friend was discharged and sent home to find the man who might try to kill him again.

He barreled downstairs wearing a flannel shirt and jeans. Mom crouched at the kitchen table in her robe, furry house shoes tucked under her chair, warming her hands around her cup.

"Mornin', Mom." He reached across her shoulders and hugged her.

"Wow. Cold weather really perks you up."

While he toasted bread and slathered it with peanut butter and jelly, he relayed how he lost Mr. Conahan and found him.

"That's wonderful, Deck. He's lucky to have a friend like you."

"He's a great guy. You should meet him. Maybe after work? We don't have practice today."

"Maybe."

"Dad too, if he can come."

"That's what you want?"

"It is." He wrestled into his parka, jerked his beanie off the kitchen peg and stretched it down over his ears. "If I can set it up, I'll call you." He sensed Mom smiling at his back.

———

HE PARKED IN THE SCHOOL LOT. PEOPLE EMERGING FROM CARS enveloped in coats and hats were barely recognizable. They chose all kinds of gear to cover their heads. Girls wore knitted caps with animal ears, ski hats, hijab head wraps, or earmuffs. Boys chose trapper hats, ski hats and masks, jimmy hats, Stetsons, or beanies like his.

He saw Joe Tensel enter the front door, bundled like a bear. Another man, squeezed into a parka with the collar pulled up, called for Tensel to wait up, probably Josh Baker. When Decker reached the door, they'd meandered down the hall and were stuffing hats into pockets and chatting with students. If his homework for the week didn't look too heavy, he might ask Mr. Baker if he could borrow a Churchill book. He also needed to catch Joe Tensel to thank him for letting him leave early on Friday. If he kept playing well and Coach agreed, he might ask the vice-principal to recommend him for a baseball scholarship.

He ambled into English class. He was pleased to learn that instead of *The Crucible,* Mrs. Pritchard had chosen *Atonement* by Ian McEwan for them to read. He wasn't into Salem witchcraft. McEwan's book had to be better. Overwhelmed by other priorities, he hoped he had time to read it.

Mrs. Pritchard was saying why *Atonement,* recently released, was already nominated for the Booker Prize and the National Critics Circle Book Award. When she listed the themes of the book, family, compassion and forgiveness, sex, dreams, plans, and versions of reality, he was intrigued. She read her favorite quotation from McEwan's book:

"It wasn't only wickedness and scheming that made people unhappy, it was confusion and misunderstanding; above all, it was the failure to grasp the simple truth that other people are as real as you."

He was hooked. Next up was statistics. He trod to Miss Folkes' class. Surprisingly, he began to comprehend her explanation of why people in various fields found them so valuable in evaluating the effectiveness of their operations. She should have started the semester with those explanations. Maybe she did, and he didn't absorb it.

It occurred to him that companies or individuals could select whatever statistics they needed to prove whatever point they wanted to make. He was glad when the bell rang.

In European history, Mr. Mack was discussing the twentieth century. Decker's hopes were renewed that he might talk about Churchill, but when the period ended, Mr. Mack hadn't made it to World War II.

By fourth period chemistry, his mind was spinning like a gyroscope. Every few spins, he caught glimpses of three historical periods in Europe, piles of money, and chemical equations, all competing with the pit in his stomach. When the bell finally rang, he hurried for the nearest outside exit to jet across the lawn to the cafeteria.

He saw Mr. Baker and decided to catch him. Instead of heading toward the cafeteria, Baker swerved back toward the building. He probably brought his lunch and planned to eat in his office. Maybe he kept his Churchill books there.

Decker entered the building and headed for the science wing. The hall was empty, but he saw Mr. Baker come out of a room and cross the hall to the men's bathroom. He aimed for Baker's office and stepped inside to wait.

He took in the metal desk strewn with books and papers.

Behind the desk, a groaning desk-wide bookcase had an entire shelf dedicated to Churchill. He'd probably be glad to loan him a book. He started to go behind the desk and peruse titles but decided he should wait for Baker in the lone visitor's chair.

Two photos on Baker's desk caught his eye so he walked over. Baker was with two boys, about six, twins, he thought. They were bundled up, playing in the snow around their snowman, tumbling and laughing. Across the bottom, he read, "Natchez, Mississippi." His wife must have taken the photograph.

He ambled back to the chair, pausing to read Baker's diplomas on the wall. He earned his BA twenty-five years ago. He must be about Mom and Dad's age. The teacher's certificate and MA were recent. He returned to grad school in the last few years. This might be his first teaching job.

In route, he noticed the coat tree where Baker tossed his hat and coat. He'd seen a lot of coats like Baker's. The hat had a stingy brim, not big enough to shield your face in winter. Was that a Fedora? He froze and stared at the hat, his stomach working its way to his chest. He inched toward the coat tree for a closer look. When Baker came in, he whirled around.

Startled, Baker jerked to a halt. "Decker! I didn't expect to see you." His eyes flicked to the desktop and scanned it.

"Uh, is there something I can help you with? Here, have a seat." He started to drag the chair closer to his desk.

"That's okay, Mr. Baker. It's fine." Decker eased the chair back to its original spot and sat on the front edge, parallel to the open door.

Baker made his way around his desk and lowered himself into the chair.

"Great game the other day, Decker. There were several scouts there. Can you believe it? Sitting on those cold bleachers? What can I do for you? As you know, I coach football, so if you need baseball tips, I'm probably not the right guy."

"Thanks. I hope we keep playing well. I thought I might catch you here over lunch to see if I could borrow one of your Churchill books."

"Sure. I have several good ones you might like." He swiveled around to the bookshelf.

Decker studied his back. His neck was short, his shoulders broad and meaty. He pictured him in the diner, crunched down into his coat collar. Or coiling to heave a baseball.

Baker selected a book and turned around. "This one's good, *Churchill: A Study in Greatness* by Geoffrey Best. He's a top biographer in Britain. He dissects Churchill's strengths and weaknesses."

Decker strolled over and picked up the book.

Baker pivoted back to the shelf and picked out a hardback. "This one by Roy Jenkins is another of my favorites. He's good at inserting Churchill's insights and anecdotes. It's very long, though."

Decker picked it up. It was over a thousand pages. "It looks fascinating, sir, but with my course load, I can't take it on right now."

"That's what I figured. Well, maybe in the summer."

"Maybe." Decker sauntered back to the chair with the first book and flipped through pages. *What could happen by summer?*

"Say, Mr. Baker, I noticed the picture on your desk. Is that your family?"

"Yes, those are my six-year-old twin boys. I sure do miss them. I haven't seen them since Christmas." His jaw clenched. "My wife has them."

"Oh, I hope you get to see them real soon."

Baker's face darkened. "She'd like it if I never got to see

them." Brooding anger engulfed him. He looked like he might explode.

"I'm sorry. I guess I'd better go. You probably teach after-noon classes."

Baker pushed down his anger, adopted a pleasant look and leaned back in his chair. "Just one. Since I don't have an advisory period, I'll be back here by two-thirty."

"Thanks, Mr. Baker." He rose and extended his hand. Baker seemed surprised.

"Maybe we can visit more during advisory," Decker said... "talk about Churchill?"

"Sure. Why not?"

"Great. See you then." Decker headed through the door and jogged down the hall.

CHAPTER FORTY-NINE

DECKER WANDERED AIMLESSLY DOWN THE CORRIDOR. COULD Baker be one of Mr. Conahan's sons? He didn't resemble Mr. Conahan. It was hard to believe this science teacher could attack his own father or write threatening notes, even if he did appear kind of jittery.

Joe Tensel was Baker's friend. He might be in his office over lunch, and Decker could learn more. He veered toward the main hall and aimed for the administrative offices.

When he entered, the receptionist at the desk smiled. "Can I help you?"

Behind her desk, "Vice-Principal Joe Tensel" was etched into opaque glass in the top half of a closed door.

"If Mr. Tensel is in, I wonder if I could see him a few minutes. Decker Savage."

"Let me check." When she knocked and peeked in, Decker saw Mr. Tensel look up.

"Come on in, Decker. I just finished lunch." An open wrap with sandwich remains lay on his desk. He rolled it up, tossed it into the trash, and grabbed his soda. "What's going on with you today?"

271

"Well, sir, I wanted to thank you for giving me a pass to leave after third period on Friday."

"Sure. Mr. Mack said you weren't feeling well."

"I think it was a stomach bug. It didn't last long, though. I felt better in time to play ball later. We had a game against Kyle that afternoon."

"I know. You guys played great ball." Mr. Tensel studied his face. "How's everything else going in your life?"

"Better, I think. I can concentrate better to study, and our baseball team is really hot."

"No more bat throwing?" He studied Decker's face.

"Oh, no sir. I'm determined to play the best ball I can. Maybe I can get a college scholarship."

"That's sure something to think about."

"If we play well all season, is it possible you might recommend me for a scholarship?"

"It's definitely possible." He took a sip of his Coke.

"That would be awesome, sir. I'd really appreciate it. It's nice of you and Mr. Baker to come to the games. Have you seen any scouts there?"

He nodded. "Two or three at every game. You guys are getting noticed."

"I hope we can keep it up all season and have a chance at state."

"Sure, could happen." He smiled. "We enjoy watching."

"You guys are good friends? You and Mr. Baker, I mean."

"He's only been here since January, but we hit it off. He came from Mississippi. His wife lives there with his boys. It's tough on him, real tough. But he likes to watch sports and so do I. I admired his hat so he told me where to get one." He slurped his Coke and pointed to the coat rack, a nicer rack than the one in Baker's office. The coat looked warm, and the hat was a Fedora.

Speechless, Decker was ready to leave. "Thanks, Mr. Tensel. Hope to see you at the next game."

He wandered down the hall with his stomach growling. He should eat something. He turned toward the cafeteria. There must be lots of Fedora in San Antonio. He had to think this through.

He passed through the cafeteria line, put an apple, banana, two milks and three cartons of pudding on his plate and slinked to a corner booth to weigh options. *Could either man be vengeful enough to shove his elderly father and leave him lying on the floor?* He fiddled with the straw in his milk.

Whoever wrote the threatening notes was cunning. He had it all worked out—how Decker would confess to get him off the hook. If he hadn't kept the notes, the scoundrel might have pulled it off. They weren't in a deposit box, but it might be a good idea to put them there.

Maybe he should sneak back to Baker's office and leave a note inside his hat. If the door was closed, he could leave it under the door. Even if nobody saw him, Baker would know who wrote it. If he *was* the culprit and Decker had him pegged, he'd probably figure out how to blackmail Decker with his own note.

Were the notes about him and his family empty threats to get him to back off, or were Baker or Tensel dangerous? Of the two men, he viewed Baker more apt to attack Conahan than Tensel. Baker's pent-up anger lay just underneath the surface.

What triggered it? He'd never seen Tensel appear mildly irritated. Could the two be partners? He couldn't imagine a reason why either would harass him and his family. Decker slurped the last of his pudding.

He'd heard Baker was a good teacher. Decker hated to be the one to ruin his career and keep him from his twin boys. If he did attack Mr. Conahan, he'd hate seeing his ugly face every day at school. He needed charges brought against him. If it came to his having to testify about the notes he received to protect himself and his family, he could ruin the man who wrote them.

He had more thinking to do before he saw Baker again. He needed to find out more about both men. He sucked up the last of his milk and hurried into the hall. If Baker showed up to meet him at two-thirty, he needed ammunition.

CHAPTER FIFTY

HE ZOOMED TO THE LIBRARY, SPOTTED A FREE COMPUTER, AND scurried toward the empty chair. He passed Todd Messner staring at a screen. "Hey, Messner. What's up?"

"Research for history class. I'd rather be playing ball." He looked up. "You?"

"No kidding. Just Googling stuff I'm interested in."

He plopped down, turned on the computer, punched the search button and entered Texas Department of Public Safety. Sergeant Thorn told him about DPS's Computerized Criminal History database listing people with criminal histories. DPS shared it with the FBI. Decker had to know who he was dealing with. He clicked in.

Anyone with a Class B Misdemeanor or greater violation of a Texas statute was listed: arrests, prosecutions, and the dispositions of cases. The most recent dates tabulated were 2005-2010, so he searched those years for names: Murray Jackson Conahan, Murray J. Conahan, Murray Joshua Baker, Patrick Conahan, Patrick J. Conahan, Patrick Joshua Baker, Lee Montrose, Stephen Hall, Michael Cunningham, and

Tensel. He couldn't remember the vice-principal's first name, although he must have seen it in print.

He viewed Hall and Cunningham as unlikely suspects but searched anyway. No records surfaced with any of them. So far, so good.

He scrolled down the DPS screen. "If dispositions are absent, either (1) the arrest was not reported or (2) the court didn't report it because the offense had not been disposed of."

According to Sergeant Thorn, Texas reported criminal history records to licensing agencies like medical, law, and education boards. School districts would surely check teachers' licenses before hiring them. The men's employers or colleges would report them if they had a criminal offense.

What if one had ill-defined anger issues? What if his colleagues witnessed his anger, but he convinced them his flare-ups were rare or uniquely justifiable?

Switching to state records, he searched Texas and Mississippi for males aged thirty to fifty but found nothing. Neither state listed people who obtained a License to Carry. You had to have individual license numbers to find licensed gun holders.

Licensed or not, any of them could own a gun. He leaned back in his chair, stymied, and watched a pretty girl swivel out of the library.

He wished he could ask Sergeant Thorn what to do or have him stand by as backup. He'd have to tell him everything. Thorn would start an investigation or arrest the guy. Baker would lose his job and visitation rights with his kids.

If the culprit was Tensel or Montrose, they'd be fired. If the suspect was one of Mr. Conahan's sons, his friend would want to be consulted before anybody filed charges. Before making accusations, he had to be sure he had the right man.

The databases didn't show employment records, only criminal records. He knew Tensel had been at Prospect High for several years. In the three and a half years he'd been there, he never saw Tensel lose his temper. Of course, people's private actions could be very different from what they displayed publicly. He had an idea.

He shut off the computer and strolled over to Messner's desk. They'd played ball together since grade school.

"I've got a problem. I lost my phone and really need one the next couple hours. Can I borrow yours if I get it back by four?"

"Yeah, I guess so. Do you leave from the front doors?"

"Yeah. I'll be there when school's out and give it back."

"That works." Messner handed him the phone and looked back at the screen.

Decker trekked toward speech class, his thoughts revolving in circles. He was glad he didn't have to learn anything complicated. He'd use the hour to think through his next move. Today's orator stood to perform. He smiled at her encouragingly, then tuned out.

Although Baker and Tensel had Fedoras, the only ones he'd ever seen, he didn't think Tensel was the man he followed. If either was the culprit, he was one mixed-up guy. His actions were inexcusable. If either had the courage to talk reasonably with his father, adult to adult, all this could have been avoided. Decker knew how hard that was.

Maybe Mr. Conahan wouldn't listen. He was probably gruffer when he was young.

If Josh Baker wrote the notes, his hurt was so deep he'd lost the ability to reason. How could he revere Winston Churchill without some of Churchill's wisdom penetrating his skull?

Decker used to think academic intelligence and emotional intelligence were intertwined. Now he knew they weren't connected. They were two separate realms operating in the same brain.

Class members laughed at something the speaker said, so Decker did his best to look pleased. She smiled appreciatively, wrapped up her speech and sat down. Everybody applauded. Decker was clapping and thinking about the photo of Baker's boys playing in the snow when it hit him. It rarely snowed in Natchez, Mississippi, especially not enough to build a snowman.

Baker lied to Tensel and the school about where he was before he got this job. He was living someplace where it snowed. His boys were five or six years old in the photograph, and he said they were six now. He didn't think teachers had the means to travel to snow country for Christmas.

After Baker and his wife separated, did he flip out, convinced he'd been wronged? *Did he fly into a rage?* Maybe he had to change his name and location to try to change his life.

He obviously loved his boys. Humans were such a hodgepodge of good and evil, reason and emotion, love and hate, courage and cowardice. No wonder he was floundering around in limbo land.

If Josh Baker was the scoundrel, he should be punished. Even if the injury to his father was accidental, he could have killed him. He just left him there. Plus, he threatened Decker and his family. In a court of law, his sinister notes would doom him, even if he was bluffing. *How should he deal with this man making his life so miserable—a man whose father was his friend?*

He looked at his watch. Baker might flee and not return to his office at two-thirty. No, he'd be there. If he was the culprit, he'd have to determine if Decker knew what he'd done and whether he'd report him to police and the school. He could never get a teaching job on the run. He'd lose access to his boys permanently. He was glad Baker had time to think about that.

By accusing Baker, he'd have to own up to breaking and entering and lying. Each parent would view what he did differently—one more reason for his family to fracture.

As everyone filed out of class, he fumbled with his backpack trying to figure out what to do. There was still the matter of a gun: whether Baker had one and whether he'd use it.

He had an idea and raced to his car. Grabbing the European history book, he stuck it inside the backpack. It might be dense enough to deflect the bullet from a handgun. He checked his watch. Two o'clock. He had enough time to check.

He sped back to the library and raced to the chair. Messner was gone. After logging in, he typed, "Do security guards at San Antonio's Methodist Hospitals carry guns?"

He learned security guards had to have additional training and obtain licenses to carry firearms. With the crazy shootings going on, he thought hospitals would make sure their guards were well-trained and licensed to carry. He hoped so.

CHAPTER FIFTY-ONE

DECKER PLODDED TOWARD THE SCIENCE WING, STEELING himself. He could message Dad with Messner's phone that he was meeting with an angry teacher at two-thirty and might need backup.

He fingered the phone in his pocket, cold sweat tingling on the back of his neck. Backup would be nice. He slipped his hand off the phone and wiped his hand on his pants. He got himself into this mess. He should get himself out.

He hoped he was all wrong, that Baker didn't have a gun in that desk. At the entry to the science wing, he took a deep breath and surveyed the hall. He was glad to see a few people milling around, and the door to Baker's office open. Baker must be inside.

He slipped off the backpack and put an arm through the straps, ready to yank it in front of his chest. Approaching Baker's door, wary of his surroundings, he peered in. The teacher sat at his desk, deep in thought, his face taut, his hands on top of the desk.

Decker took a step inside and positioned himself where

he could keep an eye on the men's bathroom across the hall. The man might have an accomplice.

Baker looked up and started talking. "I see you decided to come back. Good. We can talk more about Churchill."

Decker watched his face and hands and didn't move. "I want to talk about something else."

He shrugged and clasped his hands on top of the desk. "Okay. Not long, though. I only came back to work on some papers."

Decker stood in front of the door, making sure it stayed open. Cold crept into the room.

Baker swept a hand over his desk. "Sorry for the mess. It's usually a little better than this."

When his hand slipped inside the top drawer, Decker's heart skipped a beat. Baker set a tin of almonds on the desk but didn't close the drawer. "They keep me going between meals. Want some?"

"No, thanks."

Decker eased down on the chair near the door. He scanned the diplomas and the photo of Baker's twin boys in the snow. His eyes flipped to the hat. Time was running out. He decided to gamble.

"I recognize the hat you wore in the Broadway Cafe."

With an almond almost to his mouth, Baker stopped and stared back.

"After you left there, I saw you sneak into the side door of Mitchell Conahan's house."

Baker produced a crooked smile, popped the almond into his mouth and started crunching.

"Where are you getting this stuff from, son?"

"Mr. Mitchell J. Conahan lives at 303 Terrell Road. I followed you inside and heard you upstairs. You argued with him and shouted at him. You attacked him. They had to take him to the hospital."

Silence hung heavy in the room. Cold encircled them until Decker's hands and feet grew numb.

Baker leaned forward and put his elbows on the desk. He folded his hands, covering the lower half of his face, squinted, and looked at Decker a long time.

"How do I know you didn't do all that? Why are you trying to pin some nonsense on me?" His eyes shifted briefly to the open door.

Decker's stomach lurched. The door was wide open. What was Baker thinking? They both knew Decker could get to the door first.

If Baker was the attacker, he was cunning enough to compose threatening notes. What else was he capable of?

Baker looked back at him, sighed, and leaned back in his chair. He dropped one hand behind the desk, his eyes glued on Decker. "Have you told anybody this tall tale?"

Decker's heart beat a staccato rhythm. *How dangerous was this man? Was he being courageous or stupid to accuse him with no one else present?* Maybe having courage included being a little stupid. He took a deep breath and kept his eyes on Baker. "You'd like to know that, wouldn't you? Do you even know where Mitchell Conahan is?"

"If he was attacked, I guess he's in a hospital."

"Yes. He could have died. He didn't, but he could have."

The man across from him exhaled, swallowed, lifted his hand above the drawer, swiped it over his mouth, stared at him and put his hands back on the desk.

Decker exhaled. At least he wasn't going for the gun. Not yet.

"He had a heart attack," Decker said. Baker maintained a blank expression, but Decker thought his face lost color. "He's okay for now, thank God. No thanks to you."

He decided to take the leap. He leaned forward in his chair.

"You're Conahan's son, aren't you?" Murray J. Conahan. Is the J for Jackson, like your dad? Or maybe you simply decided to be Josh. Josh Baker. When was that?"

Murray Conahan exhaled, and his lips thinned. "My father and I have been estranged for a long time. I studied petroleum engineering and used to be in the oil field equipment business. When I decided to become a teacher, he thought it was a waste of time. He felt betrayed, and I was angry. I knew he moved here, but I'd learned to suppress my anger. When this job came up, I thought it was simpler to change my name." He was calm now, telling a folksy story, as if what happened to his dad had nothing to do with him.

Decker stared at this man sitting behind his faculty desk. "Murray J. Conahan. Like the drilling company MJC Drill. Maybe you wanted to inherit some of that—you didn't want him in your life, just in your pocketbook."

Murray shook his head. "No. No. It was nothing like that." He paused a few beats before he decided to continue. "I knew Jillian lived here, too."

At the sound of his mother's name, Decker tensed. Adrenalin pumped blood through his body as his anger rose. He leaned further forward. "How do you know my mother? What is she to you?"

"I met her in college, briefly, and fell in love with her. She never knew that. She preferred your dad."

"Why did you meet her at the diner?"

"I guess I just wanted to see her again...see if she was the same."

There it was. This was the guy.

"I knew about your dad, that he played football in high school and college. I heard their marriage was in trouble and decided to call her. When she agreed to meet me and said your dad moved out, I was sorry for her and for you. Talking with her, I felt abandoned again. My old feelings welled up. When she talked about how your father left, it sounded like he practically abandoned you and she had to support both of you. The pain of being emotionally ignored by my dad welled up, and I blasted out of there."

Decker glared at him. "What do you want with Mom?"

"I thought I could help her with you. I knew you were a good kid, an athlete, a good student. I knew what you were going through. I'd been through it myself. If I hung around you too much, you'd get suspicious. Tensel knows you, and when we started going to games together, I told him my concerns."

Tensel knew all about Decker's family. Great. He knew all along. Decker should have realized it before now. He leaned back in the chair and crossed his arms. Joe Tensel might have helped him secure a baseball scholarship. But if Decker exposed his friend Baker and cost him his job....

"You were going to help my mother deal with me. The thoughtful friend. And in case she and my dad divorced, you'd be there to pick up the pieces."

He hung his head. "I guess so. I hadn't thought through everything. I went a little nuts after my wife and I split. She says I'm too adamant and start yelling. But she's the one with the temper. She limits my visits with my own boys."

His face took on a purple hue and his jaw clenched. "The court upheld her claim, but I'd never hurt any of them." He looked at the photos of the twins and sighed. "I love Jesse and Jake."

"So, you decided to come here, break up a marriage, and attack your father?"

"No. It wasn't like that. After I got my Master's degree, I had the opportunity to come here. If I do well, I have a chance for regular visits with my boys. As part of the decree, the judge made my wife and me enroll in anger management.

He reached into the tin. Hand shaking, he popped an almond into his mouth.

Decker stared at him. *Why were his visits limited? Did his wife convince the judge he had uncontrolled anger issues?*

Decker lowered his voice. "I followed you to Conahan's house. I heard you shouting at him upstairs. I was there when you attacked him. I heard him fall."

"I don't know who you followed, Decker, but it wasn't me."

Decker sat still for a long time, soaking it in, evaluating the man sitting across from him, watching him fumble for almonds and try to ratchet down his emotions.

"He regrets putting business over his family," Decker said. "He knows he was wrong." He stopped talking and watched Baker's face. "He could have died, you know."

Murray leaned his forehead against his hands and shook his head from side to side. "I could never do that do him."

"The notes you sent threatening me and my parents. What was that about?"

"When I was walking around in the dark to calm down, I caught a glimpse of somebody following me. After I got through wandering and returned to my car, I heard the ambulance. I drove back to Dad's and saw you talking to the driver. I was afraid you'd think I was the one who hurt him and accuse me." He was breathless. "If you did, I'd lose my job, my career, and never see my kids. I could even go to jail." He rolled an almond between his fingers.

"I know exactly how that feels."

Murray stared ahead. Moments passed. Decker watched his hands on the desk and waited, watching him try to slow his breathing, grinding one almond, then another, then another. Decker tensed, ready to spring in any direction.

"Did you throw a ball at my head after the game?"

Murray looked up at him. "Yeah. And I missed on purpose."

"You could have killed me."

"No way. I've thrown a lot of footballs. Baseballs, too. I know how to aim. I just wanted to scare you." He looked down. "I shouldn't have done that."

"No kidding," Decker said.

Silence followed. "Did you cut the tire on my car?"

His head jerked up. "What? No. I wouldn't do that."

Decker studied his face. Okay. Maybe he ran over sharp glass or metal. The silence lasted for so long, Murray began to squirm. He reached for the tin. Decker watched and waited.

Murray felt for an almond and stopped. "Are you going to turn me in?"

Decker studied him. He thought about Murray's weakness, Dad's weakness, Mr. Conahan's weakness, his own weakness. "I'm going to think about it."

He got up, his eyes still on Baker, and backed into the hall. He walked a few steps, turned back toward Baker's office and stopped. He pulled Messner's phone from his pocket and punched numbers. He waited. The sound was faint, but he heard the familiar ring of his own telephone.

He strode back to Baker's office and slipped into the doorway, still watching Murray's hands.

"While I think about it, give me back my phone." Murray reached for the desk drawer.

Decker went on alert, ready to dive for the hall. Murray brought out the phone, held it up for Decker to see, walked toward Decker and handed it to him.

Decker stared back at him and stuck the phone in his pocket. "Where did you find it? How did you know it was mine?"

"After the ambulance pulled away, I drove back toward

the diner and got out to walk and think. I stumbled onto something, saw a reflection from the glass and picked up the phone. My charger fits it. When I scrolled through photos, you were there. And Trent. And Jillian. And the photo of a man in the dark caught by house lights. That was me."

Decker nodded. He would put a pass code on the phone a.s.a.p.

"I'm leaving now, but I'll be back," Decker said. I need time to think about what I'm going to do." He backed into the hall.

Murray looked crestfallen.

"We'll meet and we'll talk," Decker said, "the two of us. Inside the front doors of the school at four."

Kids would be milling around, the school cop would be scrutinizing everybody, and a faculty member would be there smiling at kids as they left. He wanted Murray in that place to contemplate all he'd lose if he didn't cooperate.

Murray went back to his desk. Decker saw the muscles in his neck twitch as he lowered his hand behind the desk. Decker froze, ready to jump in any direction.

Decker cleared his throat. "By the way," he said, making his voice louder. "I kept the notes you wrote me. They're in a safety deposit box with instructions to arrest you if anything happens to me, my family, or Mr. Conahan." A necessary lie.

"Another thing," he said in his normal voice. "Looks like you have the wrong name on those diplomas," Decker said. "That could be a problem. I'll see you by the front doors at four."

CHAPTER FIFTY-TWO

AFTER DECKER LEFT, MURRAY CONAHAN SAT RIVETED TO THE chair, stunned. His career and his kids were on the line. He'd be ruined. He had to figure out what to do. He shook his head trying to clear it so he could think.

Maybe Decker was lying about keeping the notes. He thought the kid was lying. He apparently didn't have much practice. If the kid wasn't lying, he had to derail him before he told his parents, and they called the authorities. Jillian's face flashed across his brain.

He tried to relive the conversation. Every time he opened his desk drawer, the kid focused on it. He probably thought he had a gun in there. After his last threatening note, he could understand why the kid wondered. He did have one at home.

The kid gave him the idea of slicing his tire. Not a bad idea. If he did it during school hours, he thought he could slash it in the parking lot without being seen. But what was the point? The kid might get injured and be more determined, have the police start investigating. He looked at his watch: 3:10. He jumped up and bolted for the lot.

When he slid behind the wheel of the Mazda, his hands were shaking. He took Basse Road to Highway 281, hoping to get home quickly without side-swiping anybody. He managed to make it to the last exit before Loop 1604, took the turn-around to the southbound access road and turned right by Oak Gallery Center. He passed beside the stores and slowed entering his neighborhood. He pulled up in front of his house, the unkempt one, and looked around. Fortunately, it was too cold for anybody to be outside.

He decided to pull into his garage, put down the door and enter through the kitchen. The garage door squeaked, par for this crummy rental, but at least he'd been able to find one. If somebody stopped him on the way out, he'd say he had to get a book for his last class. He checked his watch. He had twenty-five minutes to get back. He'd have to make it fast to return before school ended.

He'd piled dishes in the sink, and the garbage smelled. If he could get this disruptive business over with, he'd have time to clean up this dump.

He went to the bedroom and pulled open the bottom drawer of the nightstand. There it was, the nine-millimeter "baby" Glock he bought his wife. If she ever needed protection when the boys were babies, she could grasp it with her smaller hand.

When the boys were toddlers, she developed a very short fuse. Every time he suggested she do something, she started yelling she was tired of him losing his temper and bossing her around. She got so angry, he decided to hide the Glock in his tool bucket in the garage. When he moved out, he took it with him. He was glad to see the box with the bullets still inside. He took those, too.

What if the kid brought cops with him to the front of the school at four? The quilted vest in his closet had a pocket in it that would hide the gun under his coat. He found it and stuck his arms through the sleeves.

He went to the bed and sat on the edge, his head in his hands. What was he thinking? Did he want a shootout at school? He'd already let one confrontation get out of hand. The kid was probably bluffing anyway.

He stood, eased the gun into his vest pocket and the bullets into his pants. In the garage, he raised the door, sprang into the car, and headed back to school.

CHAPTER FIFTY-THREE

LIKE A ZOMBIE, DECKER PADDED TO HIS LAST CLASS. *Was Murray's denial sincere or a ruse so Decker wouldn't turn him in?* He seemed remorseful to learn how badly his dad was hurt. *Was that enough to erase what he did?*

If he didn't show up at four, Decker would call the cops. If he did show up, he had to convince Murray to follow the plan he concocted and hoped nobody got hurt.

Murray knew his job and family were on the line. Decker thought he was more pathetic than dangerous. He didn't expect to receive any more notes. He doubted Murray would attack him or his family.

But he couldn't be sure.

CHAPTER FIFTY-FOUR

DECKER ARRIVED AT THE FRONT ENTRANCE BEFORE FOUR AND stood to one side of big double doors closed against the weather. When the bell rang, a teacher arrived to open the doors. Kids poured into the hall and swarmed toward the exit.

Todd Messner showed up, and Decker slipped the phone from his pocket.

"Thanks, man. I really needed it."

"Sure. See you at practice." Messner loped down the front steps. Decker envied him for all he didn't know.

Murray arrived a couple minutes later looking like he'd aged ten years in an hour.

Decker maneuvered him to the right of the doors with Murray slightly behind the edge. If Murray went for a gun, Decker would try to kick him down and shove him behind the door.

Murray started talking. "I didn't tell you everything about my family," he blurted.

Decker glanced at the pockets of his bulky coat and watched his hands.

"There's more. I think my father hid assets from my mother. Mom was several years younger. Dad was always worried she'd leave him."

Decker didn't really care. He waited. "So he wasn't the perfect father."

"Far from it."

"Okay. I get it." He stepped closer to Murray and spoke in low tones. "I did some research. You changed your name to secure your diplomas. No school would hire you if they learned your wife kept you away from your kids. But you don't have a criminal record under either name. To reunite with your boys, you have to maintain a clean record. So, here's what's going to happen." He checked his watch: 4:15.

"Plan to arrive at the main entrance to Methodist Hospital by 5:45. Don't stop anywhere on the way. The traffic's terrible and you won't make it on time. A police officer will keep an eye on you from the minute you approach the hospital."

He raised his phone and snapped a photo of Murray. "I'll show him your picture and tell him you're a member of an angry, estranged family meeting after many contentious years."

He paused and fixated on Murray's face before he continued. "He'll check to see if you're armed, so don't pack any weapons." Murray's expression didn't change.

"Go to the seventh floor. I'll meet you at the elevator and take you to see my parents."

Baker's shrug was between bored and defiant.

"I'll have told them what you did and what I did. When you arrive, you will tell them everything that happened that night and answer their questions."

His eyes darted from Murray's face to his hands. When Murray reached inside his coat, Decker tensed and scanned for the school cop but didn't see him.

"You might as well tell the truth. I still have your notes."

Murray dug inside a front pocket, brought out loose almonds and crunched them around in a tight jaw.

Decker cleared his throat. "After that," he said, "if your dad agrees to see you, you will go to his room and apologize." Murray stopped chewing. Decker saw him work to control his anger.

"You can tell him how you felt all these years. He'll probably tell you how he felt. I'll be listening outside the door. My phone's on speed dial to the police. If you so much as raise your voice, I'm coming in with cops. I'll press charges against you for trespassing, assault with intent to cause bodily injury, and felonious threat charges that will cost you this job and send you to jail."

He saw a question pass over Murray's face.

"By the way," he held up a finger, "I made copies of your notes with instructions to mail them to the principal and school board as well as the police if any harm comes to me, my family, or your dad."

He leaned toward Murray and stared deep into his eyes. "One more thing. If you're not at the seventh floor by 5:45, I'll call the police."

Murray's mouth hung open.

"Where's your car?" Decker asked.

"In the side lot."

"Get into your car and stay there. I'll drive over there to watch you leave. Don't even think about going anyplace except the hospital."

He slung his backpack to normal position and followed Murray down the steps, hoping he didn't throw up before he made it to his car.

Murray hooked a right and plodded to the lot. Decker checked the Mustang's tires and eased in. He drove to the side lot, idled the car where Murray could see him and sat there until Murray drove the Mazda out of the lot. He couldn't believe he was telling a teacher what to do. This guy had it coming.

CHAPTER FIFTY-FIVE

REVIVED BY FRIGID AIR, HE FELT HIS STOMACH SLIDE BACK INTO place as he drove the speed limit to Methodist Hospital. He made up the part about a policeman checking Murray at the hospital, but it wasn't a bad idea. He'd arrive before 5:00 to set it up.

At Methodist, he parked, entered the lobby, and looked around for a security guard. Not seeing one, he went to the information desk. "Do you know where the security guard is? I'd like to speak to him."

She looked around. "I guess he's on break. Can I help you?"

"No, but thanks. If you see him, will you ask him to come to the seventh floor? On second thought, do you have paper so I can write him a note?"

She looked directly at him and furrowed her brows. "Is there a problem?"

"Not really. We have a family member here and we expect more family to come visit. Some of them have been estranged for years, so they might be sort of testy. The guard's presence might lend calm to the situation, that's all."

"I see. Here's some paper."

He scanned the room for a chair with a table alongside and went to write. The note had to be perfect. On the back of the paper, he listed points he needed to make before writing. He had to compel the guard to come to the 7th floor and make his presence known but not call the militia. He wrote his cell number and said when the guard called, he'd send him a photo of the family troublemaker.

When he finished, he walked back to the information desk. "The guard's name is...?"

"Sergeant Miller is on duty today."

Decker folded the note and wrote Sergeant Miller on top. "Is he a San Antonio policeman?"

"He used to be."

Decker's insides dropped. He hoped the guard wasn't 8000 years old. He handed her the note.

"Please be sure he gets it as soon as he comes back. It's important."

"I'll tell him."

"Thanks. And if anyone asks for Mr. Conahan's room number, will you please tell them we'll meet them at the elevator on seven?"

He walked to the elevators, pressed seven, leaned on the wall and sent up a silent prayer that the guard read the note and nobody got hurt.

When the door opened, he walked straight to the nurse's station.

"There's a man coming to see Mr. Conahan. Please don't tell him the patient's room number. Tell him Decker Savage will meet him here, okay?"

"Sure."

He leaned down conspiratorially. "Mr. Conahan is his father. They haven't seen each other for a long time, so it might be kind of a shock. You might say something about Mr. Conahan looking forward to seeing him."

"I understand. I'll tell the other nurses."

"Thanks. My parents are coming to visit, too, Mr. and Mrs. Savage. Will you direct them to the visitors' lounge?"

"Of course."

Decker went to Room 707, glad it wasn't visible from the nurses' station, and knocked.

"Mr. Conahan?"

"Hey, Corey...uh, Decker. Come on in."

Decker entered and crossed the room, smiling at Conahan's ruddy face and the sparkle in his eyes. "How are you?"

"Great. Mostly hungry. I'm getting used to your new name." He looked at his watch. "They should be wheeling in dinner soon, such as it is. I'll eat every morsel."

"I found him."

Conahan stared at him intently, raised one eyebrow, and waited.

"You were right. It's Murray. He was in your house. He changed his name to Josh Baker to teach science at my high school this semester. His diplomas say M. J. Baker. He goes by Josh."

Mr. Conahan nodded, resigned. "His middle name is Joshua. His mother picked it from The Bible. Murray Joshua Conahan." He expelled a big sigh. "Deep down, I thought it was him. I just didn't want to believe it."

"Well, he denies it was him, but I knew exactly where he was before he entered your house and what happened inside, so I know it's him. He sent me the threatening notes, so I have samples of his handwriting. He told me about conflicts you had and how you worked all the time."

Conahan closed his eyes and nodded.

"He was afraid I'd seen him and would reveal who attacked you." Decker stepped to the door and looked down the hall. It was empty. He turned back to Mr. Conahan. "Has he ever been violent?"

"No. Never. That's one reason I kept telling myself it couldn't be him."

Decker exhaled. "All right, then. If you're ready to see him, he'll come in later to apologize."

When he looked up, the twinkle was back.

"How did you manage that?"

"I told him if he didn't, I'd press charges, and he'd lose his job and go to jail."

He threw his head back and guffawed. "That got his attention. Way to go, son."

"Are you ready to see him?"

"Sure." He blew out air. "This estrangement business takes it out of you. It's time we got re-acquainted. He's teaching at your school, huh?"

"Yes, sir. I hear he's a good teacher. He loves Winston Churchill, like I do. We talked about Churchill a few times before I knew who he really was. He also coaches football. He loves what he does."

"Well, that's important. I've thought more about that."

"Yes, sir. He's divorced, and his wife has custody of his twin boys. If he chalks up a good record at this school, he can be with them again."

"Hmm. I'll be damned. I'm a grandfather to twins. When is he coming?"

"Around six-fifteen."

"You don't waste any time, do you?"

"I try not to, sir. You're sure you're ready to see him? It won't upset you?"

"No. It's about damn time we had a good talk."

"I think both my parents are coming about five. I want them to meet you."

"You don't say? This is turning out to be an interesting day."

Decker hoped that's all it was.

What if Baker showed up with cops and an arrest warrant? Or he showed up planning a bloody rampage of revenge? Why hadn't the guard showed up?

He left the room and walked the opposite way from the nurses' station. He saw an exit door at the end of the hall and pushed it open. Fire stairs led down.

He smiled at the nurse as he went back past the station and walked toward the visitor's lounge, hoping to locate another exit door. If everyone stayed calm, they wouldn't need it. He saw a door marked "Staff Only"— it might do in a pinch.

Past the lounge, there was another door at the end of the hall marked "Fire Exit." He went to it, pushed it open and peered in. More stairs. If things got unruly, he'd direct his parents' there. If there was time.

CHAPTER FIFTY-SIX

HE FOUND MOM AND DAD AT THE NURSES' STATION. "THANKS for coming. I really want you to meet this guy. I'll tell you why later." He led them to Mr. Conahan's room and introduced them.

"So, you're Decker's parents. We've struck up quite a friendship. We're both baseball fans. I used to play, so I gave him a few tips." He turned to Dad. "I hear you had some practice sessions over the holidays. It apparently made a huge difference in his game."

Dad beamed. "I like to think so. I've been watching his team play. Wouldn't be surprised if they made it to state."

"When I get out of this place, I'd like to watch." He looked at Mom and Dad. "You have a fine boy, here."

Mom smiled, nodding.

"I couldn't agree more," Dad said.

Decker's heart finally stopped racing. He broke into a grin. "When can you go home, Mr. Conahan?"

"They say tomorrow, son, if everything looks like it does today."

"Awesome."

"You bet it is. My housekeeper is cooking up a storm to bring food so I won't starve."

"Perhaps you'll have dinner with us sometime?" Mom said.

Decker smiled. "She's an amazing cook."

"I'd like that."

An orderly came in with a tray. "Dinner time."

"Thanks." He waited until the orderly left. "This may be my last dried-out meal." He grinned.

"We'll let you eat," Decker said. "I need to talk with Mom and Dad. I'll be back later."

He steered them down the hall into the empty visitors' lounge, glancing around for the security officer. "See why I wanted you to meet him?"

"He seems like a super guy," Dad said.

Mom nodded. "I understand why you like him. He reminds me of Granddad Hank."

"There's another reason I wanted you to meet him," Decker said. He took a deep breath and spilled the story—seeing Mom at the diner, following the mystery man, entering Conahan's house, hearing the shouting and the thud, following the ambulance, and getting anonymous threatening notes. He played down the threat level of the notes.

"And you kept all this inside?" Mom asked.

"I didn't know who the guy was. With you and Dad planning to divorce, he could have been a P. I. ...or anybody."

Dad looked bewildered.

Mom nodded. "I see."

Decker heard the elevator ding. "I told somebody I'd meet him at the elevator. I'll be back in a few minutes."

He returned to the elevators. The security guard stepped off and looked around. Decker walked to the guard, extended his hand, and spoke to him in a low voice.

"Decker Savage, sir. I'm the one with the contentious family. Will you hang around outside the visitors' lounge so everyone in there is aware of your presence?"

"What do you think might happen?"

"One member of the family who's coming to visit gets pretty angry sometime...shouts, you know."

"We can't have that in a hospital."

"Right, I know. I think that will be the worst thing to happen, but you might come closer and check out the people in the room, maybe with your hand on your holster?" He looked down at the man's belt. "You have a pistol?"

"There's usually no need to carry. We keep them with ammo on the eighth floor in lockers. Do you think I might need it?"

Decker's hands started to sweat. He tried to appear casual and shook his head. "No, sir, I doubt it. I think your presence will have a calming effect. If he sees your gun holstered, he might be less apt to start anything, that's all."

He was eager to cut off more questions. "Thanks for hanging around. I'll go visit my parents." He wanted them to know the truth before whatever was about to happen.

He looked back over his shoulder. "The man who might cause trouble is supposed to arrive soon. I'll hear the elevator and come get him. After we talk with my parents in the visitors' room, I'll take him to room 707. We'll pass right by you. If you'll stick around outside the room for a while that would be perfect." The guard frowned.

He's not happy about it, Decker thought, but he's here. He walked back to the lounge. Fortunately, the lounge had two entries.

"Thanks for coming. Let's sit over there." He maneuvered his parents to chairs near the entry closest to the fire exit. They sat, and Decker resumed the story.

"So, you followed the man into the house?" Dad said.

"Yes. I heard two men arguing and heard one of them fall. I hid and saw a man run out of the house. I didn't know how badly Mr. Conahan was hurt or who hurt him. I saw you sitting with that man who escaped, Mom. I had to know who he was. I found out today. He's Mr. Conahan's estranged son. He's on his way here to apologize to his dad." He turned to Dad. "You know him."

"I do?"

"You met him in college. Murray Conahan."

The man Decker knew as Josh Baker, who was Murray Conahan, appeared at the door to the lounge. He must have heard their voices and followed the sound.

"Hello, Trent. Jillian."

She looked at him and didn't smile.

Decker looked at his hands and pockets. His hands hung at the sides. No pockets bulged. He realized he forgot to show Murray's picture to the guard.

Dad puffed up and walked toward Murray. "This is the man you followed? What were you doing with my wife?" he said in a loud voice.

The guard appeared in the hall, gun holstered.

Decker turned toward him. "Hello, Sergeant." Sergeant Miller tipped his hat to the gathering, looked at each person a long moment, then walked on.

Mom shook her head and folded her arms. Decker knew the look. She was angry, disgusted, or both. "He said he knew Decker at school and wanted to discuss him with me because he was worried about him." She glared at Murray as they approached.

"You hung around Jillian in college," Dad said suspiciously, getting in Murray's face.

Murray glared back. "Yeah. But she preferred you."

"Yes," Mom said, looking pointedly at Dad as she touched his arm. "I always did."

Decker stepped closer to Murray. "Tell them what happened the night I followed you," Decker said, "every detail."

"Sit down," Dad directed Murray. "Looks like we're going to be here awhile."

Murray started out like he was going to reveal events the way they happened. He admitted he'd gone into his dad's house but didn't confess to anything more than yelling at him. He said that Decker didn't hurt Mr. Conahan or disturb anything in the house.

Mom and Dad quizzed him at every point. Decker studied Murray's jacket and tensed every time he moved his hands.

"One more thing," Dad said. "Do you drive a Mazda 3?"

"Yes."

"You followed me home and sat on your ass behind tinted windows? Why?" Dad stood and got in his face, clinched fists pinned to his side.

Murray stood, then looked down and shrugged. "I wanted to see where you lived. I did some crazy things."

"You sure did," Dad said, moving closer to Murray. "You're lucky I didn't catch you." He stepped close to Murray's face. "You won't contact my wife or send my son any more notes."

"No," Murray said. "That was...stupid."

"Dad," Decker said, sliding between him and Murray so Murray had to back up.

"He needs to see his father... And Dad, I stopped by to see Mr. Hall. He said he'd like to have you back once you straighten things out." Decker looked at his mom. "Can you two wait here a few minutes?"

CHAPTER FIFTY-SEVEN

HE WALKED MURRAY TOWARD ROOM 707. THE GUARD STOOD down the hall, feet planted, arms crossed and looked at them from under the bill of his hat. Nobody else was around. Decker gave Murray plenty of time to see the cop.

"So far, so good, Murray. Don't screw it up." He glanced at the guard, wishing he'd come closer. Murray started to push open the door to Mr. Conahan's room. Decker had one foot ready to trip him if he reached inside his coat.

Murray stepped back and looked steadily at Decker. "I'm sorry about the notes. I can't believe I threatened you like that...and your family....I wasn't thinking clearly."

Decker locked eyes with him. After seconds passed, he nodded slowly.

Murray cracked the door and peered in. "Dad?"

Conahan stretched out his arms. "Come in, son. We have a lot of catching up to do."

Decker stood outside listening to them talk in low voices with occasional laughter. He made out a few words and concentrated on Mr. Conahan's voice. He sounded happy.

Relaxed. The guard sauntered up. Decker put a finger to his lips to indicate he should listen.

They heard Mr. Conahan.

"I must have blacked out. It's a good thing that ambulance came," he said.

"Who do you think punched the button on that medical alert gadget, Dad?"

"You?"

"Yes."

Decker stuck his hands in his pockets and exhaled. After they listened a few minutes longer, he gestured for the guard to come to the elevator. "Looks like everybody might be okay. I'm glad you're here. If you can wait a few more minutes, I think it will be safe for you to leave."

"Put my call number in your phone. Dial "O" for operator and punch 28 if you need me. I'll stroll around the floor and be here fast. Carrying."

"Thank you, sir. You're great."

"Sure, son."

Decker went back to the door to listen. More talk. More laughter. When Sergeant Miller came back into view, Decker gave him a thumbs up and watched him step into the elevator.

He walked back to the visitor's lounge. Mom and Dad stopped talking and looked up. "I think they'll work it out."

"That's terrific, Decker," Mom said.

"You sure about this guy?" Dad said. " I can't believe you didn't tell us about those threatening notes. I would have clocked him."

"I know, Dad. I had to find out who he was. I didn't want to involve you or the police until I found out."

"Maybe we should stick around, Deck, to be sure everything's all right," Mom said.

"It's okay. I heard Murray tell his father that after he fell, he punched his medical gadget to call 911."

"Uh huh. Interesting," Dad said.

"Well, then," Mom said, "we should celebrate. You'll be nineteen tomorrow."

Decker smiled and shook his head. "I think I've had enough excitement. Let's celebrate later."

Jillian checked her watch. "It *is* getting late."

"You must be tired. I want to stay here awhile. If you guys agree, and Mr. Conahan says it's okay, I'll let Murray know he's off the hook."

"Looks like Murray has the picture, son." Trent looked over at Jillian. "Shall I follow you home?"

She smiled. "You don't need to. I'll call you when I get inside."

Decker walked them to the elevator, then strolled to a picture window overlooking the parking lot. Clouds were sharp against the clear sky, each one distinct, imperfect, moving in a unique pattern.

Dad walked Mom to her car. Before she slid completely behind the wheel, she reached up and put her hand on Dad's cheek and he nodded.

Decker walked back to Mr. Conahan's room just as Murray came out. He had taken off his coat and held it over his arm. He wore a quilted vest hanging open over his shirt.

"Why don't you wait for me over there," Decker said. "I'll be out in a few minutes."

He stepped inside the hospital room and let the door close.

"Decker. You still here?"

"Yes, sir. How did everything go?"

"Better than I imagined. I think I have a son again. And grandsons. He'll take me home after school tomorrow."

"Are you sure it's okay? That you'll be okay?"

"I'm sure, Decker. It's amazing what mutual apologies can do."

Decker felt like a hundred-pound sack lifted from his shoulders. "Should I tell him we won't press charges?"

"Yes. You can tell him that. He knows he made a terrible mistake. We don't want to ruin his career. It means a lot to him."

Decker nodded and grabbed a pad and pen from the nightstand. "Here's my cell phone number, sir. It's the real one." He looked at the paper. "Guess I better put 'Decker Savage' on here." He scratched his name. "Call me anytime." He took a deep breath. The air in the room smelled fresh.

Conahan took the paper and grabbed his hand. "I'll do that, son. You can count on it. Thank you."

"Yes, sir. I was glad I..." his eyes filled.

"I know, son. I'll see you soon."

Decker walked out of the room, swiped his eyes, and walked toward the nurses' station. Murray waited off to one side, shuffling his feet. He had put on his coat, which hung open over his vest. Decker watched Murray walk toward him. A memory popped into his head about the man who sprang up from the table and barreled his way out of the diner. He recognized the gait. How did he not notice it before? This man seemed content.

"Sounds like we're good, Mr. Baker, uh, Murray. You don't intend to write more threatening notes to me, my parents, or your dad?

"No." He dropped his head and shook it side to side, eyes closed. "I was wrong. It's not going to happen again."

"In that case, we're not filing charges, me or my parents or your father."

Murray Conahan closed his eyes. As he opened them, his facial muscles relaxed. "You don't have to worry about my having a gun, Decker. I never had it at school. I kept one at my house."

He looked at the floor. "After you left my office, I charged to the parking lot to blast home and retrieve it." He shook his head like he couldn't believe he'd done it. "It's in the glove compartment. I don't ever plan to use it. I'll drop it by a police sub-station. That's not the way I want to live my life. I'm sorry about the notes. I'm glad you persisted despite the pressure I created."

Decker studied his face. "That's good to hear. You have a lot to look forward to. We both do." He thought he might keep the notes awhile, for security. "Are you going back in to see your dad?"

Murray nodded, and they shook hands. Murray straightened and walked with anticipation into room 707. Decker stood outside. The low buzz of chatter and laughter drifted through the door like a salve.

He waited until Murray came out.

"I never thought I'd be glad to see him," Murray said. Dried tears lined his face.

The elevator door opened. A family got off, and the security guard followed. Murray walked over to him. "Glad to see you here, looking after everyone in the hospital."

Sergeant Miller stood his ground. "Happy to do it." He spread his feet and waited.

Decker watched Miller's face.

Murray walked over to Decker. "You don't have to worry about me. I'll see you at school."

After Murray stepped into the elevator, Decker walked over to Sergeant Miller. "He's got a gun in his car, but says he'll drop it by a sub-station. I think he's okay. Is that how you read him?"

"Hard to tell. I'll go down and follow him when he leaves

the parking lot...see if he gets the gun out. Any problems, I'll call backup and let you know." He stepped into the elevator.

Decker waited a few minutes, took the next elevator, and cruised down, balancing everything he knew.

For the first time in weeks, he felt weightless. Clear-headed. He didn't expect Sergeant Miller to call, but he waited twenty minutes in the lobby. Then he dialed Sweeney.

"It's me. Decker. Are you busy? I thought maybe I'd come over."

There was a pause. He heard the kids playing. The little ones were squealing in the background. Todd and Mr. Sweeney were laughing.

"Sure, Deck," Sweeney said. "That'll be great. See you in a few."

The End

ACKNOWLEDGMENTS

This is a novel I really wanted to write. I couldn't have done it without help and support from:

Publisher Nancy Schumacher, editor Sybelle Maloney, and formatter/cover designer Caroline Andrus, who are talented, industrious, and patient.

Baseball players Ryan Bader, Tim O'Gorman, Matt Belisle, and Don West who love the game and know the lingo.

Authors/reviewers Alan Orloff, James Ziskin, Diana Hockley, Linda Lovely, and Debbie Shrack.

Reader/reviewers Lisa Swann, Joseph and Mary Lambert, Susan and Gilard Kargl, Kathleen Danysh, Kathy Schlosberg, and Elizabeth Cauthorn.

THANK YOU

Don't miss your next favorite book!

Join the Fire & Ice mailing list
www.fireandiceya.com/mail.html

———

THANK YOU FOR READING

Did you enjoy this book?

We invite you to leave a review at the website of your choice, such as Goodreads, Amazon, Barnes & Noble, etc.

DID YOU KNOW THAT LEAVING A REVIEW...

- Helps other readers find books they may enjoy.
- Gives you a chance to let your voice be heard.
- Gives authors recognition for their hard work.
- Doesn't have to be long. A sentence or two about why you liked the book will do.

ABOUT THE AUTHOR

Nancy West is a recovering business major who discovered that creating stories is a lot more fun than accounting. Her novel of psychological suspense, *Nine Days to Evil*, won the Clue Award, and *The Plunge*, a mystery/suspense novella, was a June 2019 selection for ALA's book club and is Book 1 of the spinoff series, Aggie Mundeen Lake Mysteries. Her Aggie Mundeen Rom-Com Mysteries included a Lefty Award Finalist, Chanticleer Awards, and a Raven Award from Uncaged Book Reviews. She loves "writing stories about ordinary teens and adults thrown into dangerous, suspenseful situations...a literary thriller, like *Risky Pursuit*.

nancygwest.com

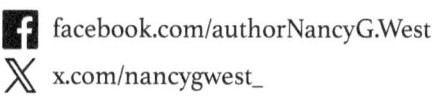

facebook.com/authorNancyG.West
x.com/nancygwest_